The Lilac Bowl

Melanie Wyllie

ISBN 978-0-9956431-2-3

Book design by Barbara Wyllie

Contents

Snare

She sat — her short hair black and straight, long and skinny in the oversize faded denim shirt and jeans.
He could not see her expression behind the dark glasses.
Perhaps she was not even looking at him.

The dark green Perrier bottle stood between them on the table — the breeze gently ruffling the fringes of the sun umbrella.

A small bar had been erected outside the rear entrance of the Festival Hall — there were drinks and snacks — tightly vacuum-packed biscuits and cheese — rigidly boxed sandwiches of Chicken Tandoori, Ham and Coleslaw, Salmon and Cucumber.
She picked the ham out, hiding it under the paper table napkin.
There were dark patches in her mind — shiny sucking mud.

He longed to reach across, to touch the long fingers, the bony wrist, to feel the pulse.

'You could invite me to tea,' he said.

Jeanne fished the lemon slice out of her drink, sucking at its bitterness. She shouldn't have come. She would never have agreed to meet him if she had known he was going to talk such drivel.

'I'm crazy about you,' he said.

She thought him a contemptible worm — she ground him into the mud with her heel.

'I belong to Piers,' she said, (and I wish you would shut up).

Oliver banged the table with the flat of his hand. 'Oh God Jeanne,' he said, 'Give me a chance!'

The tide was out. The shallow waters acrid in the heat, dirtily frothing the pebbles, the exposed mud dark and greasy, imbedded with rusty fingers of metal, wood, and bits of scarecrow cloth.

She recoiled, stiffening her back against the hard posts of the chair.

'Nobody can OWN you,' he said.
'I like it. It suits me' (and it's none of your business).

Jealousy fought desire. He longed to smash her cold indifference. Despite her relaxed pose, he could feel the inner tension — a coiled spring. He wanted to release it. She might shoot like a rocket into the sky, tracking stars. He imagined her saying 'I belong to Oliver.' Humbled, compliant. He wished she would remove her dark glasses.
'There's no harm in tea,' he said. 'Piers is away.'
She finished her drink. 'I must go.'
'Please,' he begged. 'I love you.'
'Nonsense,' she said — the mud was moving fast, pouring from the corners.
She got up and walked away. He was a pathetic fool. What did he know about her — or love — or anything...?

Piers provided her with her wonderful house, surrounded with trees. The floating linens and scrubbed pine. The one long room coloured with cushions. Tall windows filled with leaves.

Piers was in Los Angeles.

She entered the peace of the hall — red roses spilling from the pottery bowl on the curly legged table.

She went through to the kitchen, taking a bottle of Evian from the fridge, and pouring herself a glass of water.

Outside the kitchen door the laburnum dangled yellow papery flowers. Soon the poisonous black-seeded pods would fall. She could put some in the tea.

She saw Piers clutch the edge of the table, slumping to one side...

She dismissed the image. Pity there had been no laburnum tree on the farm. She could have laced Mrs Turner's tea.

Mrs Turner had regarded her with cold dislike. The feeling was mutual, but it was still better than when her mother was there.

Her mother hit her often. Hard stinging slaps — on bare arms, legs, face — leaving angry imprints on her pale skin.

Swearing round the kitchen — the perpetual cigarette twisting her mouth — the wild uncombed hair.

Her rage an inarticulate stifling misery — vented on her surroundings. The soured milk on the bare wooden draining board.

The bitter cold and the mud — mud and mud and more mud.

The cracked concrete floor of the chill wash house. The smell of washing boiling in the copper — stirring it with a long wooden oar-shaped piece of wood. Turning the handle of the ringer. Bringing it in from the line in the yard stiffly frozen.

Her mother's oilskins split and muddy.
The iron bath spotted with rust which chilled the water before there was enough to wash in — a weekly misery — the hard yellow soap refusing to lather.

There was always a shotgun leaning against the dresser in the kitchen.

It was her job to pluck the dead birds. Chickens, pigeons, ducks, the rare pheasant. Suffocating feathers — the popping, grating sound as she pulled them away — leaving minute holes.
Mashing the steaming buckets of old potatoes — sliding in the mud to feed the pigs — standing in the cowshed in her filthy gumboots, shovelling out the mess of straw and dirt — and mud — the floor slippery with rain, hating it all with a cold white hate.

The ill-fitting window of her bedroom, icily patterned with frost. She slept with her underwear under her pyjamas, her toes swollen with chilblains, itchy and throbbing.

At least the mud was frozen, its hard ridges cutting at her feet through the rubber soles of her boots as she struggled with the heavy buckets of pig swill, before slipping and sliding down the lane to take the bus to school.

Bread and margarine and strong stewed tea for breakfast.
Bread and margarine and strong stewed tea for tea.

Her mother hardly ever cooked.
As she got older she got her own food — porridge — frying an egg in the rancid fat from the bowl by the sink.

Her mother had gone, leaving the breakfast dishes haphazard on the table. Gone with the 'grain man' — sly, quiet moving, gypsy skinned, whose black transit van was more and more frequently parked in the yard.
As she turned, her arms heavy with the bucket of potatoes, he was there behind her in the dark shed, blocking the doorway.
She thought he was smiling, the cunning smile.
Fear punched her stomach. She stood completely still as he stepped towards her.
He put out his hand and ran a finger down the side of her face, down her neck.
She moved backwards, but there was nowhere to go, just the heap of old potatoes.
He laughed softly, a chilling sound.
'Don't worry', he said, and moved her chin between his fingers.
'You're a bit too young for me,' and he stood aside to let her pass with a mocking bow. She went as slowly as she could, not looking at him.
He must not see that she was afraid.

Her father's heavy sobbing filled her with disgust.

Mrs Turner came, wobbling up the rutted lane on her high-wheeled bicycle, an old brown bag in the basket containing her indoor shoes. The house was clean. There was hot food, and she was able to do her homework in peace. Mrs Turner, ungenerous of spirit, stern and ignorant, thought all school work to be some sort of punishment, and would allow her to do nothing else until it was all finished. Complaining that she was dirty and lazy, she surely didn't want to turn out like her mother. Fancy leaving the house like a pigsty, worse than a pigsty...

Jeanne shot her between the eyes as she turned from the sink, her arms lathered with suds.
She felt her cold loathing as she put on her coat and hat and changed into her outdoor shoes to cycle home.
'Pride comes before a fall,' she said. 'Just you wait and see...'
But it was still better than when her mother was there.

She went upstairs. It was too hot for jeans.
Donald, Piers' accountant, and Caitlin were having a barbeque tonight, and Earl was going to pick her up at about 7.30. There was plenty of time.

She took off her jeans, and put on a cooler shirt. The room was peach-gold in the afternoon sunlight.
Whatever happened with Piers, she would keep this house. She had to have this house — the trees filling the windows with leaves in the summer and clean brown branches in the winter.
They had come in the winter.

Lying under Piers as he humped and groaned, she walked knee deep in wet bronze bracken — her boots sinking in the soft earth — in the mud. She opened her eyes quickly, seeing Piers' tanned shoulder and the side of his blonde head.

Perhaps he would soon tire of her. She wondered if Polly knew about her. She really didn't care. If she didn't know her husband was keeping a mistress she must be pretty stupid.
Adelaide had said 'She's rich of course! "Daddy" is loaded...'

As personal assistant to Adelaide Cromer her job was very interesting and varied. The Agency was doing very well. Adelaide was extremely successful. Ultra smart, ultra efficient. She whirled in and out, laughing a lot, never looking at her watch.
They got on well. Adelaide liked her unobtrusive way of getting things done. Her well-groomed understated appearance. Nothing out of place, and she didn't flirt with the clients.

Jeanne was in charge of arranging meetings, shoots, locations. Travel, hotel bookings, expenses, taxis — setting up lunches, drinks, tea — booking restaurants, theatre tickets, meeting clients.

They got the account for a new French perfume — 'La Reve du Printemps'. It was to be shot in a studio in Maddox Street.
The French client, small and dapper with a red spotted tie spoke little English. He made up for this with elaborate gestures and facial expressions.
He had brought a case of champagne.
His assistant, a willowy slip of black trouser suit, carried a number of folders and tapes of 'Romantic' music to be played in the background. She handed out sample bottles of perfume to everybody.
They had persuaded Piers at great expense, to direct.

He arrived with Adelaide. Thick white-blonde hair, steady grey eyes. Tall — stooping slightly, followed by a twittering retinue — of whom Oliver was one.

The unreally beautiful model, Vanessa, had her hair blown around by a wind machine as she lay on a bed of flowers, her glistening lips slightly parted, waiting for the embrace of the unreally handsome young man bending adoringly over her.

Apart from Vanessa getting pins and needles, and having to hop round the studio clutching her foot, all went very well.

The client was delighted. He embraced everybody warmly, particularly the girls, and the champagne flowed. The music waltzed and sang, blending with the smoke. They danced and drank and laughed, and suddenly Piers materialised, whirling her around. He was a very bad dancer. And then when the music finished he refused to let her go.

That's how it started. Almost a year ago now.
That night the mud stayed away, and her head was full of bubbles, thousands and thousands of bubbles.
At about 4 o'clock in the morning she was very sick in the bathroom of his suite at Grosvenor House. He didn't wake.

He was her first lover. Exuberantly passionate, floating on champagne and laughter, falling into immediate slumber.

She did not expect a continuation of the liaison in the cold light of morning, but when he opened his eyes he had smiled at her, and pulled her towards him.
He phoned Adelaide to say she wouldn't be coming to work that day.
He phoned Polly to say he would not be coming home.
It was a magical day.

The house had belonged to a friend of his who had gone to work in New York. He needed to sell the house and everything in it as soon as possible.

Piers called her at work about it. 'I've found us a house', he said.

Adelaide was completely taken aback. 'Well darling!' she said. 'You've certainly hit a golden seam!' and then added, 'You do know he's married don't you? Of course you do, everybody does. Two kids.'

Jeanne turned her back, bending over her desk, rearranging papers. She levelled the shotgun, pointing at Adelaide's chest. She fell backward in astonishment, lying in a pool of blood on the ridged rubber mat by the sink, next to the congealed stiffened body of Mrs Turner.

The house was perfect.

*   *   *

Earl allowed the automatic doors to slide silently open.
There were palm trees in the foyer, and a small waterfall slurping
onto a pool of polished stones.
He moved soundlessly across the thick-piled sage green carpet,
past the exposed glass box where the uniformed porter watched
television and brewed tea.
The mirrored lift smelt of air freshener.

Melvyn was making a salad. He shook the carefully measured
ingredients in a bottle, the tight ringlets of his Shirley Temple perm
bobbing foolishly.
Earl was not sure that he liked Melvyn taking over the kitchen. He
didn't really want him to stay. He preferred to be alone. He had a lot
of photographs to develop. The third box-like bedroom had been
turned into a dark room.

The coarse-woven clotted cream curtains at the full length windows
overlooking the Park swished together at the touch of a button. Earl
closed one side to shut out the brilliance of the morning. There was
a group of riders trotting sedately in Rotten Row. The horses were
the colour of mixed toffees.
The satin ribbon of the Serpentine slotted among the trees, widening
into a glossy lozenge towards the Hilton Hotel.
The room was expensively, tastefully furnished. Sofas and chairs of
soft leather. Deliberately positioned objects. A piece of slate, a china
egg painted with a black serpent, a thick amoeba-shaped glass bowl,
a carving of an African warrior with spear and shield. A large print
of Picasso's 'Still Life with Blue Guitar', and a smaller woman's head
by Modigliani.

Melvyn had used a variety of lettuce, radicchio, frissée, Batavia,
a little raw spinach, a bunch of water cress. They verged towards
vegetarianism. He had bought Dolcelatte, smoked Austrian cheese,
and Red Cheshire from the cheese counter at Harrods where he had
struck up a friendship with one of the assistants.
He always got the best pieces of cheese — Crispin cutting little

squares for him to sample.
He arranged the tray, using a large white serviette as a tray cloth, breaking off bits of parsley in a cut glass tumbler to decorate the plate. The bread was brown and grained.

Earl lay back in one of the capacious armchairs, his eyes closed, totally still.
He did not really want cheese. He did not really want Melvyn to be here. He did not want to talk to anyone.
He said it was too hot to eat, and unfolding his long legs, went to the kitchen to get orange juice.

*   *   *

Oliver lived in Battersea with his girlfriend Becky, a pale and freckled redhead, an opinionated feminist, expecting automatic orgasms and the equal sharing of household duties.
She was flabby despite the weekly aerobics class, smelling of toothpaste and Valderma, sweaty despite the deodorant sprays.

She was annoyed that Oliver had not got home in time to help with the weekend shopping. She loaded her Peugeot 205 with the groceries.

He said he had to meet a publicity agent. With Piers away he was expected to take more responsibility.

He had been a bit strange recently. She had found him looking at her with distaste. Perhaps this was to be another foundered relationship. He was always making excuses when they went to bed — too tired — too hot — not in the mood — headaches!

She wondered about that dark girl — Piers' girl.
He had started behaving oddly soon after that drinks party at Adelaide's after the first screening of the perfume ad.
The day they made the ad he had come home very late and very drunk. Perhaps it was after that he had started behaving oddly?

Polly and the girl had practically stood next to each other at the party. Pretty cool!

Oliver had talked to her most of the evening, and hadn't wanted to leave, which was strange as he didn't usually like drinks parties, and he didn't like Adelaide — she was too assertive.

She sneezed — the pollen count was high.
Becky suffered with hay fever.

They were buying the house together, in Balfern Street, not far from Battersea Park — not that they ever went there. It was a small street of terraced workmens' cottages, 'refurbished' with pine doors and jolly brass knobs and letter boxes — windows artfully draped with bloomer blinds and ethnic bamboo.
Outside the painted wooden fences and boxed potted trees stood the BMWs, Audis and Volkswagen Golfs of the up and coming — the young elite — heating mugs of coffee in the microwave and pretending to read *The Independent*.

She put the groceries away — muesli and sea salt, recycled loo paper, natural yogurt, wholemeal pasta and free-range eggs.

Oliver came in, miserable, edgy and hot. He took a can of beer and went into the living room.
He could think of nothing but Jeanne.
It was continuous longing.
He should have insisted on going with her — or he could have followed her — or could just turn up at her house. He knew where it was.
He sat down on the stiffly upholstered sofa. It had wooden legs.

Becky stood in the doorway. She wore a skinny ribbed top.
He had once desired her heavy breasts and gingery armpits. Now all he wanted was Jeanne.
Piers was married. Piers would dump her. The thought of her with Piers made him physically ill.
'Do you want anything to eat?'

'No thanks,' he said and got up to put on the television. There should be some cricket.

They were going to dinner with friends of Becky's, Hilary and Desmond.
They lived in a plate glass apartment in Docklands, a tortuous metal staircase leading from the lounge to the bedroom.
Not a very suitable home for heavy drinkers.

He wished Hilary would get ready prepared food from Marks and Spencer's, or get a take-away — or anything!
She would spend hours preparing a really disgusting meal. Halibut with apricot sauce and curried swedes.
They would discuss environmental damage, and global warming, and whether unleaded petrol would make a significant difference to acid rain.

They could have gone to Donald's barbeque. He didn't like Donald. He didn't trust him much either. He had noticed him eyeing up Jeanne. Hardly surprising with that bag of a wife. Perhaps he could make excuses — go to the barbeque on his own. He couldn't very well pursue Jeanne if Becky was there. Why not? His passion for Jeanne was such that he really didn't care.

He wanted to go upstairs and rest, but was afraid Becky might follow him. He tried to make himself more comfortable and drank his beer.

*   *   *

'You should be thinking about going to university', Miss Plant had said, studying the papers on her desk, lifting the cold appraising eyes.
Jeanne studied the blood red veins in the dark carpet. She was silent, thinking of the gun.

Her mother had resented her obvious intelligence, her success at school. Setting her tasks to delay her, so that she had to run to catch the bus.

Later she acquired a rickety old bike, and cycled to the main road leaving it in the hedge.

Her mother thought school a waste of time — 'What good is all that book rubbish going to be to you?' — complaining about the expense of the uniform. She never had anything new. Once a term there was a sale of second-hand uniforms. Her mother would grudgingly hand out a few pounds to buy necessities. She had to have a blazer, regulation skirt, and shorts for gym.

She was top in everything. She enjoyed the work.
She knew that good academic results were the only way to escape her oppressive environment.
She kept aloof from the other girls, making few friends, despising their comfortable homes and caring parents who fetched them in cars, and came to end of term plays and concerts. Unimpressed by their birthday presents and parties, their foreign holidays. She was regarded as a strange loner, snooty and superior, unpopularly clever and hardworking.

In her years as headmistress Miss Plant had developed a non-committal neutrality in the face of parental ambition, aggression and guilty indifference.
The girl sitting opposite her now was of high intellectual calibre, her school record exemplary, but she had never seen her parents.
She understood that the mother had left home, that she lived with her father on one of the remoter hill farms, straggled with dirty sheep.
She had never joined in after-school activities. Buses to those isolated places were not exactly frequent.
Internally she sighed. All the eager and self-important parents with their average and under-achieving children, destined for the shoe shops and factories, the banks and building societies.
This girl whose O level results were expected to be outstanding hadn't even put herself down for the sixth form. No A level subjects had been discussed. Surely she wasn't going to leave?
She noticed she had taken Business Studies — perhaps she *was* going to leave. She felt deadened.

The girl was very self-possessed, good looking, serious.
She didn't look up.
The reports from the teachers had said she was coldly self-contained and difficult to approach, but that her work was always first class.
Was she going to have to let this academic promise go to waste?
Without a degree the girl would never get a job worthy of her abilities. She would probably end up as someone's PA.
She shuddered.

The girl, immobile, studied the carpet.

Her father expected her to take her mother's place on the farm when she finished school that summer.
He would no longer have to pay Mrs Turner to do the household chores.
She stared at the blood-veined carpet, and knew that she couldn't explain all this to the cold-eyed Miss Plant.
There was no possibility of university. None at all.

*   *   *

Earl, a deep shade of caramel, had the bones of a prince.
He wore fine gold chains and silk shirts.
Tonight he was wearing a red silk shirt and white trousers.

He was late. The traffic in Hyde Park was unexpectedly heavy, and Melvyn had thrown a tantrum. He had wanted to come with him.

Earl shut himself in the marble-floored shower.
When he came out Melvyn was on the phone, arranging to meet some people at the Glass House in Chelsea.
He was still huffy.

Earl was weary of Melvyn, the pouting and posturing.
He wished he would go off for good.

Earl did a lot of work for Adelaide.

His photographs were of a very high standard — artistic and imaginative.
He and Jeanne had got on immediately. Together they were completely at ease.

Adelaide said 'I'm afraid he's gay darling, so not much doing there!'
Jeanne reloaded the gun.

Tall, bonelessly loose-limbed, Earl was a wonderful dancer.
They went to jazz clubs, eating first at the Golden Cob Vegetarian Restaurant in Romilly Street.
He often came to the house. They would drink mixed fruit juices, and listen to music — Wynton Marsalis — a new young pianist, Julian Joseph, on his way to the top — Miles Davis — Charlie Parker.

The back seat of his black Jaguar XJS was piled high with photographic equipment.

*   *   *

Donald always organised the barbeque.
Caitlin had gone to Sainsbury's the day before with the detailed list, the important items underlined. The boot was loaded with chicken drumsticks and various sorts of sausage, herbs and spices, special oils for the marinade. The recipe was a closely guarded secret.

Caitlin had little to do with the preparations. Donald was fiddling and swearing in the kitchen.
She poured herself a large gin, and put stuffed olives, nuts and crisps in small blue Chinese bowls.
Nobody ever ate the stuffed olives.

That morning she had received a curt note from Melissa's headmistress saying that if Melissa was caught smoking again *anywhere* on the premises she would be suspended, and that pink plimsolls were not regulation wear for PT.

She supposed she would have to speak to Melissa — she wouldn't do it now before the party.

Melissa was being strangely quiet up in her room. Perhaps she wasn't there? Better not investigate.

She poured herself another large gin and went upstairs to change. She was particularly pleased with her hair. Andre had said she looked so young and beautiful. She had overheard him saying the same thing to the yellow-skinned woman with the steely grey waves. He was probably just being polite!

Donald had done the invitations.
The luscious Earl would be there. Donald said he was a poof — but she wasn't at all sure — he probably just needed a sympathetic woman. And Piers' new girl — dark and spiky. Donald called her The Ice Maiden, making coarse remarks about how he would like to have a go at melting her, which Caitlin ignored.

The house in Barnes was double-fronted, semi-detached.
The neighbour's dogs barked. The top half of the front door panes of coloured glass.
The dusty-bushed driveway was full of cars.
Earl parked the Jaguar further down the street.

Caitlin wore a white embroidered peasant blouse with elasticated neckline, and a long skirt of roughly sewn ragbag patches. Her designer-tangled hair hanging frizzed on her pink marshmallow shoulders.
Melissa, sullen in designer-holed jeans, torn bespattered olive green T-shirt and black fingernails, wandered around with a bottle, sloppily filling people's glasses. She chewed gum, and didn't speak.

Outside on the urned patio, sausages and chicken sizzled on the grid of the barbeque.

Donald, his shirt sleeves rolled up, his soft belly gently swollen over his tightly belted jeans and striped 'Chef's' apron, wielded the pronged forks and skewers, stirring the jug of marinade with which

he basted the meat.
Bellicose, belligerent and boring, as Earl called him.

'I hear Piers is having a wonderful time in Los Angeles,' said Caitlin,
carefully placing the drink-unsteady words, staring meaningfully
at Jeanne. 'All those beautiful girls! I don't know how poor Polly
stands it!'

'No,' said Jeanne. 'I don't know how she does.'
Ignorant cow! She didn't care how many wonderful girls Piers slept
with.
She asked the sulky-faced Melissa for a soft drink, and went outside.

'Let's have a quickie!' Donald had followed her down the patio steps
and caught her arm. The bushes were high there, obscuring the
house.
The ice tinkled against the side of his glass.
'Caitlin is busy with your sunshine boy!'

She aimed the gun. There was blood mixed with the mud.
'Let go,' she said.

'O come on luvvie.' He swayed pressing against her, pulling her
shirt. 'I know you are hungry for it and your coloured friend is no
use to you!' He stank of drink.

The mud spread creeping pink sludge.

She kicked him very hard on the shin, he fell backwards awkwardly
onto the grass, the whisky spilling down the front of his shirt. She
turned away stiffly, the mud dripping — sticky, clinging — and
went back to the house.
Earl and Caitlin were sitting on the floral dented sofa.
Caitlin was crying, sniffing feebly into a handkerchief.
She was quite drunk.
The room was pungent with smoke and garlic fumes.
There were a lot of people lying about on the floor and the furniture.
Revulsion choked her. She went to find the bathroom, climbing over

masticating people spread on the stairs.
The bathroom was a mess of dirty clothes and smeary bottles.

She washed her hands several times, picking the hairs from the soap
with a piece of toilet paper. She closed her eyes trying to dislodge
the mud.

Earl drove her home. He played a new tape of Wynton Marsalis.
Outside her house he asked what was wrong.
She didn't answer for a moment — and then — 'Filthy Donald made
a pass.'
Earl chortled quietly, 'He's a fool,' he said. 'She is a fool. They are
both fools.'
He turned up the volume, the flying notes of 'Stardust' soared into
the night.

Piers came back. He came briefly to the house, dumping his Vuitton
cases in the hall, filling the house with his restless presence —
holding her by the arms as he kissed her — leading her to the kitchen
whilst he got a drink — selecting music for the hi fi — dropping the
linen jacket on the floor — buttering a hunk of bread — eating it
hungrily as he talked on the phone — pulling her down beside him
on the bright spilling cushions to kiss her again.

*   *   *

It was a wet summer. The hillside ran with muddy rivulets.

Mrs Turner had cycled down the lane for the last time.
She had given Jeanne a tin of fruit drops, grudgingly wishing her
well, and left a blackberry and apple pie for supper, acknowledging
Jeanne's aversion to meat. It was the best she could do. They shook
hands, relieved that their acquaintanceship was over.

Evenings her father sat staring at the flickering images on the black
and white television, sometimes he drank and wept, and drank and
wept.

She despised him for his weakness.

She was supposed to cook — sometimes she forced herself to do him a chop or some bacon. She never touched meat It was forever tainted, muddy, vile. The thought of eating cooked animals filled her with unspeakable horror.

Pushing her bike up the lane, laden with groceries, her feet sodden in the muddy cart tracks.

Mr Caradon cantered past on his chestnut hunter — it's hooves throwing up knots of mud, spattering her clothes. He reined to a stop, and waited for her to draw level. Muscular in his tweed hacking jacket, quietly menacing. He asked her how her father was.

She didn't like the way he eyed her up and down, his eyes cold, lingering.

'I could find you some work if you like,' he said. 'I pay well.'

His 500 acres of arable land stretched behind, the crops flattened by the rain.

She thanked him, staring him straight in the eyes.

After that he often rode past the farm, stopping at the gate, coming into the yard leading his horse.

She watched him from an upstairs window, the gun levelled at his heart.

She got 9 A O-levels, it should have been 10, but there had been a bus strike the day of the Chemistry exam, and she had missed it.

She met the postman in the lane.

Her things were all packed.

Somehow she managed, piling her bike, the bags balanced on seat and handlebars, abandoning it in the usual hedge at the main road.

She took the bus to Hereford.

It was easy enough to get the job in the bookshop.

Mr Bernard was kindly and vague, his too-long hair bedraggled on his collar, his glasses on a string.

The floor was thick with books, in loose piles and unpacked parcels.

The order book an illegible mess.
Jeanne took pleasure in putting everything in order. Arranging displays of the more interesting and best-selling books in the window, sorting the shelves in alphabetical order.

In the evening she worked at the Kings Arms, a beamed country pub on the outskirts of the town.
She worked with two other girls, Carmel and Sandra, in the restaurant.
The dining room had brown Formica-topped tables and paper mats printed with cocktail recipes.
They served conventional food. Grapefruit, prawn cocktail, chicken in a basket, steak, jacket potatoes, Black Forest gateau.
Carmel and Sandra wore tight skirts and skimpy tops, their eyes heavily blackened, their lips pale and moist.

They chatted and flirted, playfully provocative.
Leaning closely to point things out on the menu — just brushing bodies and arms — a gentle pressure a sexual fencing match.
They talked about men all the time. 'You got better tips if you were *nice* to them.'

They were quite nice to Jeanne in a pitying way.
They thought her innocent and naive.

She kept her distance from the straying hands, efficient and polite.

The owners, a tough cockney couple, who had had a sandwich bar in Billingsgate, treated them fairly, but didn't stand any nonsense.
They were expected to work hard — no slacking or short hours.
They gave them a meal every evening, which meant Jeanne didn't have to eat at lunchtime.

She had a room in a bed and breakfast place. Mrs Bonner gave special rates to permanent guests, less for Jeanne who only had 'Continental' breakfast.
The room was sparse, only the bare necessities, but it was like a palace after her room at home.

The sheets were pink nylon, 'pilled' and snagged. A basin — the water was always tepid — a thin towel and pink plastic tooth mug.

When she had saved enough money, she came to London.

After two routine dull secretarial jobs, she got the job with Adelaide. She had been very lucky.

*   *   *

Piers parked the pine green Bentley on a bus stop in the heavily congested Edgware Road, where it choked its way under the Westway to Maida Vale, the gutter a muddle of garbage. He swung his long legs over the pavement railings, and went into the fish and chip shop to get them rock and chips for supper.

They spread it on the kitchen table, liberally dolloping the blood-red ketchup.
Piers ate with his fingers, drinking beer down in one long pull from the can.
He joked, leaning forward to touch her serious face.

Throwing open the window — pulling his shirt over his head.

The mud was full of roots that caught at her feet, making her stumble.

She heard his voice — felt his weight.

The pools of mud hissed and bubbled.

Evening darkened the room, and Piers slept, one arm thrown across her, his blonde head against her shoulder.

*   *   *

They stood in front of the Francis Bacons.

The Tate was Piers' idea.
He wanted to introduce his children to Great Art.
He wanted her to get to know his children.
She hadn't wanted to come.
She didn't think it was a good idea.
What was the point of getting to know them?

She had met Polly at a party at Adelaide's.
They had stood side by side, unintroduced.
Polly, lanky with blonde dyed hair limply drooping round her face, the boring blue two-piece with the little peplum sticking out over her skinny hips. The bony knees under the too short skirt. The cultured drawl.

That was the evening Oliver had started to be objectionable.
Jeanne was not sure how Piers would react to his assistant's determined efforts to seduce her.

She had met the two children briefly at a film premiere.
Piers had got her tickets. She was with Earl.
They had shaken hands, smiling politely, before taking their places in different parts of the cinema.
Polly was wearing silver, the décolleté loose on her flat chest, a long silvery wrap, a dazzling necklace.
The children were nice kids, with their father's white-blonde hair and steady grey eyes. Sophie, teeth caged in wire, had a flounced red tartan dress with velvet ribbons, Justin serious in miniature dinner jacket, a small version of Piers.

They went to boarding school — this was the beginning of their summer holidays.
Polly had come up from their place near Chipping Norton, to go to the dentist and do some shopping.
Piers was to have the children for the day.

She tried to protest — it really wasn't a good idea. After all at ten and twelve, they were quite old enough to wonder what was going on.

She didn't say that their affair would probably soon be over, that he would tire of her and find someone else, that in any case he would always stay married to Polly.

What was the point of involving the children in an adult game?

She was quite satisfied with things as they were. The unstructured casual relationship. No commitment. And when it was all over, all she wanted was the house.

Somehow she must have the house.

So why bring the children into it?

Piers was adamant. He wanted them all together. He wanted to see them together. They wouldn't think anything. Why should they? He wasn't going to embrace her passionately. He wouldn't even hold her hand! She was just a friend — a colleague.

So they stood in front of the Francis Bacons.

The strange twisted, raw-sinewed bodies — inside-out faces.

Jeanne felt a strange sense of exhilaration — of recognition.

This man's mind had surely had its own haunting.

Sophie and Justin, awkward, unsmiling, listened to their father's eager dissertation.

Sophie said they were queer, and she didn't like them.

Justin stood silent beside Jeanne.

They moved on to the green slimy Freuds.

They didn't like them either, but were kindly indulgent towards their father's enthusiasm.

He relented, and took them to see the Turners, only stopping briefly to extol the wonders of William Blake.

He forgot not to hold her hand.

They had tea at the Ritz.

Piers did most of the talking.

Expounding his theories on painting — its connection with film — the comparative value of photography.

He asked them whether they wanted to go to Italy during the holidays.

'Your mother is talking of the Adriatic,' he said.
He ordered extra sandwiches — ice cream for Justin.
Sophie sat primly avoiding her eyes.
Justin looked her full in the face with his candid grey eyes before carrying on with his tea.

After tea they walked in Green Park. The grass scruffy and scuffed in the afternoon sun.

They shook hands politely mumbling platitudes, and Piers took them in a taxi to Grosvenor House to meet their mother.
They were going to see Starlight Express that evening.

'Do you suppose he's in love with her?' Justin asked Sophie later when they were alone.
'Don't be silly,' said Sophie, 'he's in love with Mummy.'
'I don't think he is,' said Justin, 'he's never like that with her.'
'Like what?' asked Sophie tartly.
'Oh, I don't know — sort of happy, I suppose.'
'Don't be silly,' said Sophie.

He phoned at one o'clock in the morning.
'I miss you,' he said.

Jeanne, unable to sleep, went downstairs and made herself some tea.
The flowers of the laburnum luminous white in the sable darkness.

*   *   *

Caitlin had quarrelled with Melissa.
She had refused to come for a 'Bloody boring weekend in the country.'
They had also quarrelled about Melissa having her nose pierced.
She already had five earrings in her right ear.
Caitlin had felt weak and hungover. She had gone upstairs to the bedroom, wishing she had never chosen the striped duvet cover. It gave her a headache.

Polly gave them a primrose yellow room with matching en suite bathroom. Polly had a lot of money. She paid people to choose her decorations, everything blandly tasteful, with a few obvious eccentricities.

Donald had driven down very fast, overtaking, flashing cars in front of them in the fast lane. Wagner's 'Rheingold' filled the car with obsessive noise, Donald occasionally burping stale wine.

They had had a letter from France that morning, from Mr Senteur, it had a bill enclosed for work now completed.

They had bought the house in France on the spur of the moment. A few days in the wine-soaked Loire Valley — many tastings — the Range Rover stacked with prettily labelled bottles.

They had had a particularly good lunch at an auberge on the banks of the river — ending with cognac and chocolate-sauced profiteroles.

It was uninhabitable really.
The walls and uncertain beams blackened by smoke. The floor tiles brokenly covering the earth beneath.
A wooden step ladder with missing treads leading to the cobwebbed loft showing recent signs of mice and birds. Light seeped through the gapped roof.
The garden deep in grass and weeds — split sagging apple trees — the fruit spotted and deformed.

In the tipsy sunlight it was like a fairy tale. Hansel and Gretel, Red Riding Hood, Snow White and the Seven Dwarfs.
They shook the Estate Agent warmly by the hand, effusive with gratitude, sealing the deal with several glasses of Pastis.

Later they were not sure.

At the autumn half term it was chillingly cold and damp.
The workmen had not finished the floor or the roof. There was no electricity, the water an unconvincing trickle.

The fire belched choking smoke.
They crouched over their camping stove, thankful for the paraffin lamps.

Melissa had brought a friend, Hannah. They were dramatically bored. The only entertainment a foray to the local supermarket — to sift through plastic hair ornaments — sitting lengthily in a cafe filled with leery coughing locals in identical caps and overalls, putting off returning to the cold dark house and the sleeping bags on the hard damp floor, unable even to read for long in the dim light. The girls resisted all entreaties to go for a 'walk in the village' — a huddle of firmly shuttered dwellings — bales of hay covered with sheets of flapping black plastic, and an occasional black-scarfed old woman clutching a loaf of bread.

Caitlin found, and confiscated after a considerable tussle, Melissa's overworked copy of *Lace*. This did not go down well.
Later on she discovered Donald reading it.
Melissa called her a stuffy undersexed old bag. 'I'm sorry for you,' she shouted. 'Really sorry! Poor frustrated cow!'
She and Donald drank a great deal of wine.

Drink made Donald amorous. Gratification was not a very practical possibility with the two girls cocooned beside them in one poky room. She did not flatter herself that she had suddenly become irresistible — anybody would do.

Increasingly black-tempered Donald drank himself into insensibility, to be woken by Melissa screaming that there was a rat running over them. 'A rat!' she screamed. 'I'm getting out of here!'
Hurriedly struggling from the sleeping bag, he trod heavily on one of the rustic terracotta candlesticks that Caitlin had bought from The French Way in Putney High Street — badly bruising his foot.

They left the house, a bedraggled nerve-shattered group, after a long session and several bottles of wine with Mr Senteur, who drew swift plans, seeming to assure them that the house would be transformed by the time they came again.

Donald's French was minimal, he was one of those that think if you talk loud enough everyone will understand you.

Caitlin carried a dictionary and could manage basic school-type phrases.

The girls remained stonily silent, despite their privileged education and extra French coaching with Madame Clou.

The crossing was very rough.

The girls shared a large bar of Toblerone and went to the cafeteria and ate sausage and chips.

Hannah was sick.

After they got home Melissa had half her hair shaved off.

Caitlin was aghast. Why had they sent her to that expensive school?

The girls were all decadent.

Hannah had thanked her politely. Shaking hands and mumbling about having had a super time, and thanks very much Mrs Rogers.

Caitlin felt vaguely uneasy about what she would tell her mother. After all, it hadn't been *that* bad! Had it? Oh dear!

*   *   *

Jeanne had tried not to come.

Piers, pulling on his clothes had gone to get the champagne from the fridge.

She hurriedly put on her shirt — she felt at a disadvantage naked.

He stood by the open window, looking out into the dense branches of the sycamore tree.

She tried to persuade him that it was not a good idea. 'Besides, I detest the countryside,' she said.

'It will be fun,' he said. 'Just a few friends — we can swim and play tennis, and picnic!'

'I don't like swimming or tennis and I hate picnics,' she said.
'Well, you can just sit and look beautiful,' he said, and started kissing her again.
'What about Polly?' she said.
'What about Polly?' he said.

*   *   *

A buffet lunch had been laid out on the long verandah, which stretched the length of the rambling grey stone house, its ornamental trellis burdened with wisteria and hanging baskets of geraniums and lobelia — the comfortably cushioned chairs and loungers warm from the sun.

A vase of blue and pinkish delphiniums stood tall on the white-clothed table, the ice buckets of champagne, twined with vine leaves. Little parcels of hot crab, prawns in aspic, salmon mousse, a ham glazed with pineapple, strawberries and cream.

Oliver was enraged. Jeanne was here! Cool and distant in a light blue cotton frock and espadrilles. How could she be here? He hadn't considered it.

He had let Becky drive. He chain-smoked, thinking about Jeanne, while Becky wittered on about God knows what.

They had a chintzy bedroom, with mahogany fitted bathroom.
He lay on the bed.
Becky said maybe she should have brought a dress for the evening. She thought it was going to be casual.
Oliver shutting his eyes to shut her out, refused to listen — refused to answer — and then — descending to the verandah — there was Jeanne, sitting next to the nut brown golden Vanessa, completely at ease! She shouldn't be here, in Piers' house.

Polly was wearing a floppy sun hat and strappy dress with daisies, talking to Karl, a young German actor — square-faced, square shouldered, teutonically fair — tanned nearly as dark as Earl's natural colour. He wore pale blue seersucker and a wide-linked gold bracelet.

Piers was exuberant. He poured frothing liquid into the sparkling glasses, turning up the music so that the comforting sound of Ella Fitzgerald's easy, swinging voice urged them to 'Take a Chance on Love', making her way through 'A Foggy Day in London Town' to the streets of 'Manhattan'.
They lounged by the pool.
Jeanne had put on a wide straw hat — inscrutable behind her dark glasses — watching the others cavort in and out of the water.

Polly's scrawny blue-veined legs, her body slack in the blue bikini.
Vanessa's amazing beauty — her lips and toenails frosty orange.
Karl self-consciously posing as he eyed the languid Earl floating with his eyes closed.

Donald did an untidy crawl churning up the water, and covering Becky, who was rubbing suntan oil on her blistering shoulders, her substantial curves barely covered by her scarlet bikini, with spray.

Oliver tense — the bony ribcage taut, stood in the shallow end trying not to look at Jeanne.

Caitlin uncomfortable in her bathing costume, which seemed to have suddenly become too small, dangled her feet in the water.
She decided she must diet. Her full skirts successfully hid her spreading hips and thickening thighs, a bathing costume was a different matter.
Here she was surrounded by thin people — apart from Donald, and he didn't count, and the full-figured Becky — Vanessa thin thin — Polly was scraggy thin — Earl was elegantly thin, Karl athletic thin, and Piers tall handsome thin!
They all seemed to eat a great deal, except for Jeanne, cracking their way through the langoustines, scooping the salmon mousse, pouring cream on their strawberries.

The initial shock of finding the girl here had been blunted into a dizzy surprise by the amount of wine she had drunk.

She certainly had a nerve. Perhaps this was one of those situations she had read about in *Cosmopolitan*! That weedy Oliver couldn't keep his eyes off her either. She couldn't understand the fascination. If it had been Vanessa, golden perfect Vanessa, she could have understood. She made her feel uneasy.
Had something happened the night of the barbeque? She tried to remember if they had been alone together, not that the girl took the slightest notice of Donald. She didn't seem to take the slightest notice of anybody.

She slid cautiously into the water.

Piers was showing Sophie how to prepare properly for a dive. Justin swam under water.

As the shadows lengthened, one of the Spanish maids in long black sleeves and frilled white apron carried out jugs of fresh lemonade and trays of tea.

They played tennis. Piers and Vanessa against Donald and Karl. Donald was a strong player, and Karl unflinchingly serious, turned out to be very good indeed. He kept a wary eye on Earl, who was stretched out on the grass, whilst he fetched balls for his service. They won easily.
Donald was in good humour. He liked winning.
Pretty blatant of Piers bringing the girl down here. Perhaps he could have another go at her later. She wouldn't have got off so easily that night if he hadn't had too much to drink.
Bitch! He must find out which was her room.
He would tell Caitlin he was going for a walk.
He shook hands with Piers. 'Great game old man!' he said. She wouldn't believe it. He never went for walks. He'd think of something...

Earl had been pleased to drive down with Jeanne.
Their relationship was mutually undemanding.

It was an unusual situation.
He did not care much for Polly, she was a snob.
Pampered by money, indulged by her husband and father —
disinterested in her children. The smooth running of her life taken
for granted.
All the same!
He had no idea what Jeanne felt. Sometimes cracks appeared on the
ice-smooth surface, and he glimpsed the turbulence beneath.
He was glad to get away.
Melvyn had finally gone. There was a last pathetic quarrel.
Melvyn was jealous of Jeanne. He thought they were sleeping
together. 'You love her,' he kept saying. 'You love her more than me.'
He sat heaped on the sofa, his face crumpled with tears.

Earl stood at the window. The summer evening had finally dwindled
into night. The red and white dots of car lights wound through the
Park. Dim figures walking, becoming briefly illuminated as they
passed under the round old-fashioned street lights. The Hilton a
lighted beacon above the dark trees.

His mother lived in a tower block.
Sitting squat in the ugly flat — slow moving now, her feet misshapen
in her woollen slippers.

Once when he had lived with Edwin they had gone to a performance
of Bach's St Matthew Passion at the Albert Hall. 'Practically in our
back room,' as Edwin used to say.

It had been a revelation.

When they reached the agony of 'Golgotha', he was quite overcome.
He did not see Jesus splayed on the cross on the hill of Death. He saw
the blackened tower blocks rising from mounds of rotting rubbish
— discarded drunken hands reaching for money. The walls swirled
with graffiti — the stinking lifts, stained with urine and dried
vomit. Empty-eyed young, crouched by cardboard fires, sniffing
glue, stealing purses, jeering at the well-dressed, the disabled, the
old, spraying the concrete walls with obscenities.

From his mother's flat on the eleventh floor you could see across the river to the solid balconied buildings, red brick mansions, tree-lined squares, and shops with jewels on velvet necks, Hermes scarves, inlaid antique desks, the price tags turned discreetly inwards. Greengrocers piled with Muscat grapes, pomegranates, prickly-skinned lychees, Italian sun-dried tomatoes.

Down below the young fought and spat, the foul language of despair fogging the air.

His mother didn't want to move. She had been there too long. She was not frightened, safe behind the double-locked doors. He gave her money and bought her things to make her life more comfortable. A huge TV, a microwave, a new washer-dryer, a reclining armchair. He paid some lads he knew to bring them up and do the fitting. No respectable store would deliver to such a God-forsaken place. Even the postman didn't come alone.

He always came on foot, or in a borrowed, beaten up Ford van. He had seen a bright red mohair cardigan in one of the shops across the river. It had large red glass buttons. She would like that. One day, perhaps he would be able to persuade her to move.

Melvyn was whimpering about how badly he had been treated. Earl felt ill — violated.

It was perhaps true that *if* things had been different, he might have loved Jeanne — but things were not different. He shrank from the bold-eyed women who sought to 'convert' him to normality. Jeanne accepted him as he was. They had an easy familiarity, a mutual liking, which was not motivated in any way by sex.

In the end Melvyn, his eyes swollen from weeping, left to share a flat with two dancers from the Royal Ballet. Clutching his lizard skin holdall, his long tan suede coat and the new salad spinner he had bought at the Conran Shop. He would have to come back later for the rest of his things.

Earl lay on the springy grass, content in the warm sunshine and the scent of flowers — the murmur of voices — clinking ice. He saw Karl's eyelids flicker as he dropped his gaze. It would be amusing perhaps — a titillating diversion. He didn't know if he could be bothered.

Jeanne had moved into the shade of the willow tree, the umbrella-tendrils gracefully sweeping the lawn.
She didn't like the water.
She didn't like the sun.
Piers had raced his children up and down the pool — they were all good swimmers — long arms slicing the water, pretending to lose, ducking Justin — throwing water over each other — laughing.

Oliver managed a feeble breast stroke. He held the rail by her feet.
'Why don't you come in? he said. 'It's wonderfully cooling.'
'I don't swim,' she said.
'Didn't expect to see you here,' he said. 'Under the circumstances…'

Jeanne didn't answer.
She shot him through the head — his thin sensual mouth open in protest as he sank under the water, a crimson shadow spreading on the surface.

She could swim — at school they were herded into a bus once a week, and taken to the local pool.
Miss Seymour, 'The Toad' as the girls called her because she squatted grossly at the side of the pool, a whistle hung round her neck on a length of black tape, shouting 'Come on now! All in there. No messing about', and the girls grouped, shivering and muttering, flopped one by one into the choking chlorine.

Jeanne had hated it. Hated the water. Angrily self-conscious in her bathing costume, trying not to swallow the polluted water.

Polly and Caitlin lay side by side on padded loungers — pale, sandy-bristled sows, basted with oil — roasting in the sun.

She smelt the pork cooking... her father slicing it with the horn-handled knife, the fork with its two sharp points, her mother shouting 'Eat!... Eat your food! Eat it, eat it!'

She had cold lead in her stomach, weighting her down.
She couldn't move.

They were discussing the lack of leg-room on aeroplanes.
'Anyone would think we were all about four foot six,' said Caitlin, turning over to cook her back, 'and had no arms either, for that matter!'
She couldn't hear Polly's reply.

The crackling still sprouted hairs.

She was glad when they decided to play tennis.

Piers had insisted on candles, curled silver candelabra, branches of melting light, the crystal chandeliers ghostly in their reflected glow. The long burnished table, brilliant with glass, gold-edged plates — overflowing bowls of fragrant stocks and Love in the Mist, fat cabbage roses and soft pale ferns.

Piers and Polly sat at opposite ends.
Jeanne was on Piers' left next to Earl, Vanessa on his right next to Karl.
Polly with Donald and Oliver on either side — Becky and Caitlin faced each other, Sophie and Justin squeezed between.

There was smoked salmon and goose pâté — poussins, braised chicory, pommes Dauphinoise.
The poussins on a large oval white platter, split in half, the charred skin liberally sprinkled with tarragon, gave off a pungent aroma, smothering the smell of grilled birds...

Limp feathered necks — sharp bloody beaks — stiff yellow scaled feet... frenzied squawking...

She asked for mineral water, refusing the chicken, taking a few potatoes.

The two Spanish maids moved slowly and silently about on black soft soles — black spider arms serving the food — clearing the dishes — filling the glasses.

Adelaide had warned Polly about Jeanne.
'I think Piers has a bit of a "thing" about her,' she'd said.
She was flying off to Geneva, so couldn't come for the weekend.
'Desolated darling!' she said. 'But work comes before pleasure as they say!'

She wondered whether she should have told Polly.
They had all met at Art School. Piers had been brilliant.
She was adequate — Polly useless, no talent whatsoever.
Just filling in time until she found someone to marry.
Of course Piers had married her for her money.
She had flattered his ego, with her constant adulation, but Adelaide was sure he had never been in love with her.
Carried away by dinners at the Savoy, holidays on the Riviera, butlered houseparties.
Perhaps she shouldn't have said anything — better not to interfere really.
She found she had mislaid her diary!
Oh God! She was going to miss the plane.

Polly took no notice of Adelaide's warning.
She couldn't really believe that this thin cold creature with her straight black hair could possibly pose a threat to her marriage.
In black silk shirt, and long skirt — no jewellery.
She ate little, drank little, spoke little.
Certainly enigmatic… No, just dull!
Complacently assured in her role of hostess, she turned to speak to Oliver. Glancing down the table she saw Piers put his hand on the girl's arm — an intimate caressing gesture. She felt a sharp feeling of unease.
He bent his head close to hers.

'I will give you a "Pocketful of Dreams" my love,' he said, his lips brushing her hair.

Jeanne felt Polly watching them.
'That would be a bit difficult!' she said — too late to draw away.

There was champagne, white wine, rosé, Beaujolais, Bordeaux for the cheese.
Raspberry tart, raspberry mouse, a large white bowl of fresh raspberries. A sweet dessert wine.
Caitlin, hung about with beads, could hardly see across the table.
Karl was openly flirting with Earl — lapsing into German.
Vanessa's golden hair had come unwound, curling softly down her back. She had the hiccups.
Donald and Becky, who had been arguing all through the meal, were now shouting at each other.
Donald became more offensive as he became more drunk.
'Women are only good for one thing,' he said, beckoning for a refill.
'On their backs — and some of them aren't much good at that!'
Becky was furious. 'You are disgusting!' she yelled. 'Drunk and disgusting.'
Donald made an obscene gesture and lit a cigar.

Earl, in white frilled dress shirt smiled impassively, ignoring the increasing mayhem. He fingered the diamond on his index finger...
Donald was a complete oaf!
He decided that any liaison with Karl was definitely out of the question. Much too heavy going. He was too German!

Drink had made Piers dangerously indiscreet, he was openly holding Jeanne's hand.

Justin and Sophie, in her Alice in Wonderland white dress with wide blue sash, had left the table, and gone to watch TV.

'How long have you known Piers?' Polly handed her the gold-rimmed coffee cup. 'Do you want milk? I am afraid I don't remember him mentioning you.'

She was aware that her speech was drunkenly slurred, and tried to overcome it.

'No', said Jeanne. 'I work for Adelaide.'

'Yes,' said Polly. 'She told me.'

They stood face to face. Jeanne cold, long-limbed, gracefully self-possessed. Polly disdainfully upper class, her ill-chosen blue strapless taffeta accentuating the prominent shoulder blades, the long neck.

Jeanne sipped her coffee, it tasted of mud. She dropped her eyes and studied the Afghan rug in front of the marble fireplace, guarded by a huge ugly china dog, with snarled gold nostrils.

'Well,' said Polly. 'I hope you enjoy your stay.'

She moved away to hand coffee to Earl, who was standing studying a bewhiskered bemedalled portrait of an elderly gentleman holding a plumed hat.

Jeanne set the dog on her — watching her dragged away — a broken rag doll.

Oliver was beside her. 'Having a good time?' he said. He too was drunk, his voice unsteady. 'You really are a cool one!'

Jeanne didn't reply. He was already dead… a bloated corpse at the bottom of the swimming pool — blotched purple…

He tried to touch her.

'You are neglecting Becky,' she said.

'To Hell with Becky!' he said. 'I want you.'

'Oh do go away!' she said, and went out onto the terrace.

It was not yet dark. The sky blue-grey dusted with stars.

The air was warm and full of garden scents.

She sat on the low stone wall, looking into the shadows, keeping her hands very still, holding herself very still…

This time it was Justin who was beside her.

They sat in silence, and then Justin said 'You aren't drunk are you?'
'No,' she said.
'All the others are drunk — even Mummy...'
'Yes,' she said.
'Don't you like drinking?'
'No,' she said.
'Have you ever been drunk?'
'Yes,' she said. 'Once...'
'What was it like?'
'Well it was nice at the time — but horrible afterwards... I was sick.'
They sat quietly together until Piers came to find them, sweeping
them into his arms... leading them into the house.

Polly saw them come in. She was shocked. Piers exuded warmth...
love... surely not... surely not!
'It's time you were in bed,' she said to Justin.
'Oh come off it Pol,' said Piers. 'Let the boy enjoy himself!'

Later he came into the room.
She lay under the starched white sheet in her short cotton nightdress.
The night was hot.
He sat on the bed and bent to kiss her.
She turned her head away, avoiding his lips.
'No,' she said.
He buried his head in her neck, murmuring.
She felt the steady beating of his heart.
'No,' she said. 'Not here.'
The scream unravelled inside her, forcing its way up — hovering
desperate in her throat.
'I can't,' she said. 'Not here.'

*　　*　　*

They were to picnic on the top of the hill behind the house.
Struggling through the close undergrowth of the wood — brambles
tearing at their legs — slipping on slimy toadstools and wormed
branches — each laden with 'something' for the picnic.

Piers had delegated the provisions — dividing them into carrier bags.

Justin and Sophie were in front — clambering expertly — their bags full of cheese and hardboiled eggs — boxes of prepared salad.
Becky clambered behind them, her feet sliding on the sandy slopes between the tufted stringy grass.
Her bag contained cold chicken and tubs of potato salad.
Her arms sore red from the sun, she wore white tracksuit bottoms and white sleeveless top.
She sensed Oliver's dissatisfaction with her, and his obvious infatuation for Jeanne. She was thoroughly fed up with the whole thing. She had a headache and would rather have stayed by the pool.

Oliver reluctantly behind her, carried bottles of wine and a corkscrew.
He had caught his foot in a root and twisted his knee.
It wasn't his idea of fun lugging bags up a hillside in this heat.

He had spent a miserable night.
Thankful for the single beds, so he had no need to make excuses for not availing himself of Becky's curves.
Obsessed with thoughts of Jeanne in Piers' arms he became agitated with rage and desire.
He had tried unsuccessfully to lag behind so that he could be with her.
He was hot and disgruntled.
The sky was beginning to cloud over. There was going to be a storm. He was sure of it.

Vanessa, her wonderful hair cascading round her shoulders, wore tight pink and white striped pants and pink silk top.
Somehow managing to smoke a cigarette as she searched for a foothold and balanced her bag of bread.

Polly was with Piers — both in old tennis shoes and long khaki shorts. He carried a cool bag with champagne and ice. They were talking.

Jeanne had managed to drop behind — she disliked being followed.

Donald was in front of Caitlin, hotly uncomfortable in her too-tight jeans — complaining at the weight of her bag, filled with ham and pâté and more bread.
Donald strode on without looking back. He had a hangover, and an acid stomach — he was not very fit, despite the weekly squash and sporadic bouts of jogging.
He had fallen into a snoring slumber before being able to investigate Jeanne's whereabouts.
Maybe for the best!
Piers might have been there already!
He would have liked to have had a go at them both... the skinny bitch and the opinionated busty one. All in the same bed taking turns.
As it was he had a tongue like the inside of a parrot's cage and pains in his chest.
And this damned picnic. It was too hot. And this damned bag. He had plastic glasses and more wine.

Earl moved forward with graceful ease, swinging the bag of fruit — a tartan rug draped over his shoulders.
Karl walked beside him, matching his strides, brushing against him as they negotiated the uneven path.
There was no harm in a bit of suggestive banter.
They would be back in London tonight.

Jeanne had paper plates — crisps and serviettes. Her hair stuck to her neck, the pale blue shirt damp on her back.

Polly and Caitlin laid out the cloth on the bumpy ground, and they all subsided gratefully, dropping their bags in a heap.

Justin and Sophie took bread, ham and crisps and ran away back down the hill to the wood, calling to each other. Sophie, the eldest, shouting orders.

Donald lay on his back eating a chicken drumstick.

He rolled over to put the bone in the rubbish bag, and then on his hands and knees approached Jeanne, stretching out with his head on her lap.

The heavy sweaty head pinned her legs. She tried ineffectually to dislodge him.

Oliver opposite, propped on an elbow, jerked upright. 'Get off her you slob!' he said.

Donald didn't even open his eyes.

Piers was opening another bottle of wine.
He turned and looked directly at Jeanne.
'Move your carcass Don,' he said, icily amiable.

Donald laughed. 'You shouldn't leave your belongings lying around old man,' he said.
Oliver was on his feet — dragging Donald by the arms.
They tussled together — rolling — hitting — swearing across the tablecloth.

Piers didn't take his eyes from Jeanne's face.
'So what games have *we* been playing?' he said, his voice harsh with pain.
'Hey man!' interrupted Earl. 'Cool it, man! There haven't been any games. No games, man!'

Jeanne stood up, her arms loose at her sides.
She looked at their faces — Piers hurt and angry — Polly shocked — Caitlin weepy — Becky flushed, staring at the ground — Vanessa trying not to laugh…
The two men locked together, punching — grappling.

The muddy jaws of the vermin trap closed on her heart.

She started wildly down the hill — slipping and sliding.

A few large drops of rain spat on the grass — the small stones rattling before her.

She reached the dark wood — blinded by the muddy torrents pouring through her head.

She forced her way through the stinging branches — whipping her legs — her arms — her face.

It was raining harder — hissing on the leaves.

Through her distress she heard an urgent cry for help.

It was Sophie.

She met her head on — dishevelled, torn and muddy, breathlessly sobbing, 'Justin... Justin!'

Creepers hung in shaggy ropes, trailing in the murky waters of the stagnant pond — the rain now falling heavily, scabbing the putrid surface.

Justin was in the middle, the evil smelling waters almost reaching his waist.

He had swung on the branch — hand over hand along its cracking length. Snapping abruptly, it had brought him down with it as it sank into the water.

Sophie had tried to find something to help pull him out. Frantically digging in the compost leaves — crumbling logs, brittle twigs, finding nothing — nothing!

The boy was white under his tan, coated with mud.
He tried to smile — fear in the clear grey eyes.
'I can't move', he said, his voice unsteady. 'I'm sinking...'

Jeanne told Sophie to go and get her father.

'As quickly as you can — go on — hurry!'

She tucked her skirt into her pants and took off her shoes.

She stepped into the cold horror of the sucking mud — moving towards Justin — pulling her feet behind her.
She had to get near enough for him to hold on to her and pull himself out.
She swallowed hard to dislodge the mucous blocking her throat.
'Almost there,' she said — surprised to hear her voice — normal... cheerful!
She had to keep moving otherwise she would sink too.

She held her hands out to him — the small fingers, thick with mud, clutched hers.
'Pull one leg out at a time,' she said. 'And then move towards me — try to keep moving.'

Slowly, carefully, he freed one leg and stepped towards her, pulling the other one out of the clinging mud.
She felt her terrified way backwards, slithering in the unseen awfulness — holding Justin's hands firmly — hearing her disembodied voice reassuring...

It seemed an impossible distance to the bank.

They came crashing through the undergrowth, a tangle of arms and legs and voices.

She was dimly aware of Piers and Earl — Oliver's swollen face and Karl shirtless and bronzed.

Piers lifted Justin — carrying him on his back.

Jeanne couldn't move. She clung to the roots protruding from the broken sides of the pond, engulfed with nausea. The mud was drowning her — she could taste it.

Earl prised her hands away, and pulled her up the side.
She couldn't hear what he was saying for the noise of the rushing mud.

Her teeth chattered uncontrollably. She was rigid with cold.

Earl spoke calmly, slowly, helping her walk — comforting her with careful words.

The others were ahead of them. Karl and Oliver and the three white-blonde heads — laboriously making their way back up the side of the hill, slippery now from the rain, which had ceased as quickly as it had begun.

Polly, anxious, had come to meet them.
Donald sat sullen — his shirt torn.
Caitlin was packing up the bits and pieces.
Becky glumly folding the cloth.

Sophie was glowing with relief, the blonde hair, escaping from the thick plait, hung wispily round her pretty face. 'She was wonderful,' she was saying. 'She was wonderful!'

Piers turned towards them. He shook Earl by the hand.
'Thanks, man,' he said, and then hugged Jeanne quickly, fiercely.

Jeanne felt his warmth against her numb fear, unable to dispel it.

Justin hugged her too.
'Thanks Jeanne,' he said. 'Wow that was awful! Really scary — just like a film!'

Sophie kissed her. 'Thank goodness you were there!' she said.

She couldn't speak.

Earl took her home.

She had bathed twice and thrown away her clothes, but the mud still clung.

She went straight to bed — curled tightly beneath spotless covers — staring into the soothing darkness.

Piers phoned in the early hours of the morning.

'Are you OK?' he said, and then, after a pause, 'I should have come with you... Sorry.'

*   *   *

'I don't want to lose you,' he said, holding her so closely she thought her bones might crack. 'I can't lose you!'

He was going to Los Angeles for at least six months, maybe longer. He wanted her to go with him.

He had told Polly.
He had had to after that dreadful Sunday.
She had laughed in disbelief, and then had sprung cat-like, tearing at his face with her nails...

'I want you with me,' he said. 'I want you with me all the time.'

He stood with his back to her — at the window, where the yellow leaves of autumn still clung.

A small voice inside her urged her to say 'Yes'. To go! This would be the nearest she would ever get to love... But the voice of mud and blood and nightmares said 'No'.

He said she was sure to change her mind... that he would be back... of course she would change her mind.

*　　　*　　　*

It was winter.
The trees a bare fretwork of branches bending against the wind —
scratching at the windows.

Polly had joined Piers in Hollywood. Hoping for a reconciliation,
Earl said.

Oliver had gone as well.

She had been promoted. She had her own department — Art and
Design.

The tide of mud came and went, its waves forever lapping the
shore — sometimes hardly visible — a distant rim. Sometimes a
thundering flood.

She kept the laburnum seeds in a jar in the kitchen cupboard, on
the shelf with the herb teas — camomile and jasmine — the rosehip
jelly and quince jam.

She read the letter from Justin again.

'Dad says it will be fine for you to come down and take me out one
Sunday — but better not tell Mum! I will say you are my Aunt.
Please do come. Love, Justin.'

A cautious pleasure caught her unawares. She smiled, touched by
unaccustomed warmth.

Holding the letter in her hand, she went into the living room to
answer it.

But for the Grace of God

'You can't stay here luv.'
The younger of the two policemen leant towards her, holding his breath against the stench.

The white-gloved ushers were fastening back the high glass doors of the Opera House.
The performance was over. The audience began to leave — silk scarves and shiny boots — black merino coats, floor-length furs — warm air gusting.

She had worn jade green silk, draped and flowing, long matching gloves, silk shoes, a necklace of crystal and pearls…
Was it Tosca or La Bohème? Or Les Sylphides or the Sleeping Beauty? They had sat in the stalls…

She thought she had been sick, but she couldn't remember.

'Do you think she's ill or just drunk?' the young policeman asked his companion.
They stood uncertainly.
'We'd better take her to the Station,' he said.

It had been five years — well almost five years.

The evening of the Board meeting. Tania, Roland's secretary had already gone home.
She was left clearing up the papers, putting away the Waterford glasses in the mahogany cabinet.

He came in behind her, standing in the doorway. 'Ah Olivia!' he said, 'Still here! Why not come and have a drink — you deserve it.'

And then… and then.

It was so easy. Blissful dangerous subterfuge.

That first night they had gone to a discreetly expensive hotel.
He folded his clothes neatly on a chair, and told her he mustn't miss the 11.45.

Frail-boned, her childishly blonde hair wispy and fine, giving her a misleading appearance of fragility which men found irresistible, women merely irritating.

She enjoyed her position as the Managing Director's mistress. It gave her a sense of power, a superiority over the other women in the office — even Tania, the super chic PA, was only his PA.

They dined at Rules and Chez Solange, lunched at Veeraswamy's and the Savoy Grill.
They went to the Opera and the Ballet.
He gave her money for clothes — the jade green silk — a black sheath of jet embroidered crêpe...

He rented her a small furnished flat in an exclusive block in Ovington Street. Bedroom, living room, gleamingly fitted kitchen, luxurious bathroom... a lift... a porter.

Furnished with William Morris prints and heavy plum-coloured velvet curtains with fringed pelmets and tasselled cords.

Filled with flowers — long stemmed roses, sheaves of cream and red gladioli, waxen lilies, musty carnations wrapped in spidery fern.

She went to Harrods and bought linen, flounced and frilled. Goose-down quilts and pillows, deep-piled towels.

Roland bought her Nina Ricci bath oils and soaps, a full length pink towelling robe with her initials on the pocket.

They had made love everywhere, whenever they could.

Roland was masterful and adoring.
Olivia was pretty sure this was not the first time he had had an affair.

He handled everything with such expertise…

He lived in Hertfordshire. He had a wife, Rosamund, and two sons at prep school. They had never discussed his home, marriage or children.

How many Christmases was it? Two… or three?

They tearfully agreed on a trial separation… It wasn't fair to Rosamund…

Olivia was fed up with the restrictions of their relationship. She was tired of being 'fitted in' possessively between legitimate domestic arrangements.

The unaccompanied holidays… the bleakness of New Year's Eve.

She had spent a particularly tiresome Christmas with Felicity and Gordon in their underheated house in Wimbledon.
Gordon was very careful with the central heating, continuously adjusting the thermostat.
Gordon didn't approve of Olivia. Somehow she posed a threat. Unmarried, wayward, she made him feel uncomfortable.
Gordon's mother was there, her powder blue twinset creased with fat, sucking peppermints for digestion.
The boys were tidy and well behaved as usual, preoccupied with their new toys.
Felicity hot and bothered, red-faced from basting the turkey.

Boxing Day they held an incredibly boring drinks party.
Among the guests, however, a wonderfully tall — Roland was not tall — handsome Captain in the Life Guards. She flirted with him, which was fun, he had his wife with him, a noisy young woman in an aged Aran sweater.

During her brief separation from Roland, she visited him a few times in his rooms at the Wellington Barracks. It was a diversion.

They came together again with renewed intensity, increasingly daring, barely attempting to conceal their affair in the office. Tania was coldly disapproving. Olivia blithely satisfied.

They even managed a few weekends… at elaborately comfortable Country House Hotels, with log fires in the bedrooms, home-made bread, and fresh caught trout.

And then… and then. Somebody told Rosamund.

It was over.

White-faced — white knuckled — he told her it was over. That was that.

At first she didn't believe it. He was bound to change his mind. She went into work, waited for him to phone, wrote unanswered letters — waited for him to come.

Surely he would be back, begging her forgiveness — surely. It didn't happen.

She went sick. She spent a week lying in the suffocatingly sensual bedroom, weeping and drinking.

She drank everything in the flat. Gin, whisky, brandy, sherry — a whole litre bottle of Grand Marnier. She lived on rich tea biscuits and was very sick.

She returned to work, but it was impossible.

She started going to the Wine Bar at lunch time, washing down a toasted sandwich with half a bottle of wine, swaying her way round the office, her work full of errors.

Tania said, 'He's dumped you, hasn't he?' and abruptly, 'I'm sorry.'

She had to leave.

She went to the DSS.

The Indian lady had a cold. She blew her nose on an apricot Kleenex, her gold trimmed sari draped over a thick royal blue sweater.

She was not entitled to unemployment benefit because she had left her job of her own accord.
Personal reasons were not sufficient.
She couldn't afford the rent for the flat. Roland had paid it. She got notice to leave.

She was sure she had been sick.
The young policeman was trying to lift her — her legs, plasticine-pliable, would not hold her up. The other policeman helped, half carrying her awkwardly to the Squad car.

Olivia found a cheap bed-sitting room, dim and dirty, with grimy net curtains and a rod in the corner for hanging clothes. There was only a small chest of drawers — the mattress was disgusting.

She put all her stuff in bags and took a taxi to Wimbledon to leave them with Felicity.
Her sister was not very pleased, especially as she had to pay for the taxi.
Why on earth had she given up her flat? What had happened with her job? What *was* going on?
She grudgingly agreed to put the stuff in the loft, and grudgingly got her coffee and a sandwich, muttering about Gordon not liking irresponsible people.

Olivia was drinking.
She lay on the dreadful bed in the dreadful room, frayed hessian matting on the floor, and drank.
At first she only drank when it started to get dark, and then earlier, and earlier.

She was very short of money. Her small amount of savings shrinking away.

She hadn't gone back to the DSS. She didn't want anybody prying into her life.
She tried begging at Piccadilly Circus, approaching obvious out-of-town shoppers. There was not enough to pay the rent.

The Greek landlady heavily climbed the stairs and told her she had to pay or go. She owed six weeks' rent.

She phoned her mother in Jersey, reversing the charges. A vain, selfish woman, living with her third husband, in a vulgar bungalow in the sunny tax haven.

She said Olivia was old enough to see to her own life, and why didn't she get another job? Better still, why didn't she find a nice man like Felicity and settle down?

Violet put the phone down and crossed the shaggy wool rugs to the terrace. Monty was lying on the sun lounger in his summer trousers and short-sleeved striped shirt.

They were having cocktails before going up to the Yacht Club for dinner.

Violet had a new pink-blonde rinse. She had used a lot of mascara and a new lipstick — Orange Sun. She wore a white sundress and high-heeled white sandals.

She was irritated — and annoyed at allowing Olivia to irritate her. Why couldn't she find a husband? She was pretty enough and clever.

She had always been evasive and manipulative as a child, not like Felicity, always obedient and helpful.
What did she mean she was being thrown out? Theatrical exaggeration! And what about her job? Why hadn't she got a job?

The lawn sloped down to the road. There was a small pond with a few reeds and floating plants, with a stone cherub bubbling the water. There were geraniums and lobelia, and some carefully pruned, perfectly bloomed rosebushes. A low red brick wall bordered the road.

She drank the gin and tonic quickly and went indoors to fetch her white handbag and put on some jewellery. She felt naked without it.

Olivia and Felicity were children of her first marriage. Poor Bernard, such a dashing young man — completely feckless. He now lived in a Council Flat in Braintree, shuffling about in bedroom slippers, eating out of tins.

She preened herself in the hall mirror — seeing the glint and glimmer of her many necklaces, the long earrings, the wide bracelets and rings.

She was still very attractive. She smiled at herself — seeing a youthful, vivacious Violet in the elaborately gilt-edged mirror, adjusting her neckline to make sure her bra straps didn't show.
She clicked her way back to the terrace.

*   *   *

Olivia shoved as many of her remaining things as possible into a nylon holdall, and went out into the streets.

She had no idea what she was going to do.

The first night she slept rough was simply because she had nowhere else to go.
She had sat in a café in Tottenham Court Road until it had closed at one o'clock in the morning, and then wandered down to Leicester Square, and sat huddled on a bench until daylight.

It was summer then.

She began sleeping in doorways.
She avoided the more popular crowded places, the 'Cardboard City' at Waterloo, and the murky shadows of the Embankment.

She found them claustrophobic, with a threatening undercurrent of violence.
Some were very young. There were drunks, junkies, the mentally ill.
Some into prostitution — the boys more successful than the girls, who were too unwholesome even for the most avid perverts.

Mostly she kept to the doorways in the Strand, and sometimes round Covent Garden, scrounging scraps from the healthy sandwich bars, the rolls shiny with caraway seeds.
Sometimes on the steps of the Opera House.

During the days she would walk in St James's Park — sit on the wide steps leading to Lower Regent Street, holding out her hands to the people who passed — 'Any change to spare?' She usually got enough to buy tea and a sandwich from one of the stalls in the Park.

Some lunchtimes she would go into the restaurant at the National Gallery and collect leftovers. It was too crowded for anyone to take much notice, and there were a lot of foreigners which made it easier.

She could pile a plate with bits of bread and chocolate gateau, red kidney beans and sweetcorn, morsels of spinach quiche, discarded fat, cheesecake, the occasional roast potato.

Her clothes became filthy from the pavements — the flowered cotton skirt, the fine cambric shirt streaky with stains.
She lost her bravado, and spent her collected pence on cheap wine.

She got to know a few of the others.
There were Marcia and Sadie, their ears multi-pierced, ringed and studded. Short tight skirts, their bare legs mottled and splattered, their anoraks coated with muck.
Tough and abusive, lurching at brisk business-suited men on their way to Charing Cross. 'Want a good time, mister?' Want a good f***?', and then laughing, shouting obscenities at their embarrassment.
They were inseparable.
There was Hannah, but she was crazy.
There was old Dolly who had a permanent pitch outside the Waldorf,

and had been on the streets so long she would never be able to live anywhere else.

There was Victor who played the saxophone on Tottenham Court Road Underground, wearing an embroidered skull cap and black leather biker's jacket.

And Eric. Nobody talked about their background, how they came to be there, except Eric. Eric loved to talk.

When he shared her doorway they would talk and smoke the long night hours away.

Eric had six O levels. His once cropped hair was now a ragged pony tail, secured with a broken shoe lace.

Eric knew where to go for everything — soup, socks, shelter, advice, medicine, drugs.

He was pimp and prostitute, thief and beggar.

They got on well.

Eric had left home, the double-glazed detached house in Cedar Drive — where there were no cedars — after his mother had got a new boyfriend.

There had been an acrimonious divorce.

His father had gone off with a young girl.

'Not much older than me,' said Eric, 'and stupid! She'll probably give him a heart attack.'

His mother had several boyfriends. A motley selection of wimps and blusterers, and then Miles, an idiot, with his three-quarter length brown leather jacket and yellow socks. He read the *Daily Telegraph*, and had appalling opinions.

'Actually we couldn't stand one another.'

Miles planted a selection of mini shrubs and had the cherry tree cut down.

Eric would retire to his room, papered with teenage idols and football pennants, travel posters — vibrating with rock music — and Miles would thump on the door and shout.

Eric was supposed to be taking A levels but he packed his bag and came to London. He wanted to get into television. he couldn't get a job — he had no money, nowhere to live — without a fixed

address there is no dole money — without an address it is virtually impossible to get a job. So here he was on the streets, with the others. Sometimes he would bring a loaf of bread. Once he had some Kentucky Fried Chicken — it was almost painful to eat it, it smelt so appetising.
His body a brittle frame.
The bones of his neck moving as he swallowed.

The policewoman — busty without her uniform jacket — her fair hair trim and short — asked her name.
They had given her a mug of tea.
She sipped it tentatively in case her stomach refused to accept it. She wanted to lie down.
It was warm in the Police Station.

The young policewoman leaned forward and asked again for her name. 'Do you have any family?' she asked.

As the autumn turned to winter, and the nights got colder, she went to Wimbledon to fetch some warmer clothes.

Felicity was horrified!
What was going on? Why was she in such a state?
Nervously glancing behind her, as if Gordon might appear.

Felicity had always resented Olivia. Built on the stocky side with sandy hair and freckles, she could never compete with Olivia's appealing frailty.

She let her in reluctantly — shocked by her dishevelled and filthy appearance — and she smelt terrible.
Felicity stood aside as Olivia moved past her, deposited her battered reeking holdall on the Wilton carpet, and said she had come for some clean clothes.

What on earth was going on? Felicity had long been jealously suspicious that Olivia was having an affair — probably a married man. How come the expensive flat, the expensive clothes? And now

the full cotton skirt, torn down the seam, the hem unstitched and dirty! Well, everything was dirty! The blue T-shirt was disgusting, and the Jaeger blazer faded and misshapen from the rain.
Shocked, Felicity suggested she should have a bath.

Olivia mounted the stairs slowly, her ankles reddened and swollen in the broken shoes.
She bathed and washed her hair, and collected clothes from her suitcases in the loft. A jogging outfit, underwear, a couple of sweaters, a towel, a short raincoat and a pair of trainers. She had no socks.

She asked Felicity for socks.
'Socks!' said Felicity. 'Socks! Olivia what is going on?'
Olivia emptied the dirty clothes out of the holdall, put them on the floor by the washing machine and sat down.
She said Felicity must have some socks. Gordon must have socks, he played squash and badminton — he must have socks. She needed socks to wear with her trainers.

Felicity protesting, found her two pairs.
She made some tea and a cheese and tomato sandwich.
Olivia was very hungry, but the hunger defeated her. She seemed unable to eat. Her throat closed up. She sipped the tea, and wrapped the sandwich in a paper serviette to take with her...

The policewoman stared at the blank form in front of her, and then looked at Olivia slumped on the bench clutching the mug of tea. the fine blonde hair matted and dull, the thin blue-white face, pinched and sickly. The smeared black joggings.
She was well-spoken — in her mid twenties... late twenties? She was shivering — and the smell...
She tried again. 'What's your name? Have you any family?'

Olivia put the mug down very carefully on the bench beside her and slid to the floor.

*   *   *

Lydia coiled her thick wiry hair into a bun on the back of her head, securing it firmly with hairpins.

It was penetratingly cold in the tiny cramped office. Despite the two heavy hand-knitted sweaters, and the thick socks in her black laced boots, she felt its chill. Heavily built, neat featured, her intelligent face pallid in the bad light, she squeezed herself round the desk, snagging her sweaters on the splintered corners. It was a mess of files and folders — a clumsy old black typewriter, telephone, jars of pens and pencils, paper clips, notepads. There were cardboard boxes stuffed with old clothes, a few chairs stacked in a corner, a broken reclining chair, stuck at an angle, several dirty damp cushions.

They had paraffin heaters to augment the tepid radiators. Lydia thought them a fire hazard, especially in the dormitory with the doped, drunk and dotty.

It was her week on night duty.

The shelter had been a warehouse, creaking, perilously lit, minimally warm.
There were twelve beds in the long high room, its barred windows uncurtained. The smell of the paraffin mingling with the sour smell of unwashed bodies.
They had four toilets now, wash basins and one shower cubicle in a thin side room with small square windows high against the ceiling.

She told the WPC they were full up — and then reluctantly agreed to fit in a camp bed.
'Alright, alright,' she said. 'I'll do my best.'

She went to find Cecil in the stone-floored draughty kitchen. He was plugged into his Walkman, washing up a tray of thick white cups and plates — British Rail throw-outs — in the old fashioned sink. The sleeves of his check shirt rolled up his sandy-haired arms, his baggy cords held up with a ragged scarf.

The chipped formica table was cluttered with the remains of bread, a big bowl of butter, a brick-like piece of cheese, a catering jar of Branston pickle. Spilt sugar melted in a pool of tea.

Cecil was a medical student from Barts — undernourished, overworked, he spent the long nights studying. Lydia was a science graduate, who had not been able to bear the burden of her privileged existence. At least now she was doing something useful.

They went together to drag one of the camp beds from the cupboard in the unwelcoming hallway — up the few steps to the dormitory. There wasn't much room.

They had had a Committee meeting about renewing the lease.

'Fancy paying rent for that dump!' she had said to Meg when they met for lunch in the Crypt of St Catherine's.
Meg, tackling a wholewheat lasagne, said it was a disgrace.
Lydia picked gloomily at her aubergine and cheese stuffed baked potato.
'Sometimes I think I'll never get rid of the smell,' she said. 'It permeates everything!'
She swabbed the floors with disinfectant, wiped the beds and chairs, everything she could — as for the toilets!...
'Some of them are only kids,' she said.
Meg said it was a disgrace. She worked at the Bank of England.
It was a good thing they had plenty of Army Surplus blankets.

She asked Cecil if he could prepare the porridge for the morning. Porridge was the most filling, nutritious and cheap thing they could supply — and lots of sweet tea.
They made it in huge pans on the aged gas cooker.

Lydia knew the young policeman, but not the WPC.
They supported Olivia on either side. The WPC gingerly carrying the nylon holdall.
They had tried to clean her up, washing her face and hands, sponging the sleeves of her raincoat.

The doctor had said too much drink, too little food, needed some warmth.
Eric said she shouldn't drink. It was stupid. It was a waste of money.
He had had a successful night, and had brought plastic-lidded mugs of tea and hamburgers from the Wimpy bar at Charing Cross.

She tried to eat.
She kept mostly to her position, in a doorway opposite the Savoy, where she could watch the nightly arrival of the beautiful people to dine and dance — the Rollses, the Daimlers, the fleet of taxis.
The stout, sober-suited going to Simpsons to eat roast beef and cabinet pudding.

She felt no self pity, remembering she was once one of them, pampered and perfumed, picking at the creamy lobster mayonnaise with the heavy silver cutlery.

Apathy, insidiously invasive, spread its infection among them all.

Lydia asked if she was alright. If the woman was ill she shouldn't have been brought here.
The young policeman said the doctor had seen her. She just needed to sleep it off really. The cells at the Station were full up.
'We've cleaned her up,' said the WPC.

Lydia, feeling her stomach heave, called Cecil. He was better at this sort of thing.
They got her onto the camp bed, covering her with the coarse blankets. The street lights cast orange circles on the concrete floor.

Father Brady came at 7.30. He had already taken Mass. Just the two old ladies and the tall thin man with glasses, smoothly shaven in his long gabardine raincoat.

Father Brady had the uncomfortable feeling that the man was Evil. He felt he should refuse to give him the Holy bread and wine. What dreadful sins had he committed? He was definitely not right.

His youth had ill prepared him. He prayed for guidance, dispiritedly aware that it did not come.

He stirred the porridge in the big pot, his bony hands, raw with cold, protruding from the sleeves of his frayed cassock, its loose folds discoloured, thick with incense, stale food and morning fog. He looked half-starved himself.

Cecil had fallen asleep with his head on his books, his sandy hair greasy and thin.

Lydia looked very tired. She had managed a few hours' sleep on the broken recliner, and her neck was stiff and painful.

She was worried about the young boy who said he was fifteen, but looked twelve.

One never asked questions. The shelter was there to provide a bed and a meal, not to ask questions, or offer solutions.

Olivia was one of the last to leave.

Lydia suggested a shower, and found her a clean pair of briefs and a vest from one of the cardboard boxes. She washed her hair with the carbolic soap, had a bowl of porridge with a lot of sugar, and felt somewhat better.

Lydia would have liked to tell her to come back, but there was never any room. They had to turn so many away.

*   *   *

The dark shroud of winter hung over the city.
Uneasy sunshine, hesitant, fragmentary.

They foraged cardboard boxes from behind the Regent Palace Hotel, tearing them apart to spread beneath them on the unyielding chill pavements, among the piles of crushed windblown rubbish.

The tinselled shop windows filled with spangled gifts. Stuffed snowmen draped in ties and scarves. Sprigs of holly, shiny red ribbons, boxes striped and starred. Expensive clothes and belts sprinkled with silver dust among frosted fir cones. The meaningless repetition of 'Silent Night' from the smart-booted shoe shop. The sombre Christmas tree, a shadow of war, in Trafalgar Square.

The sophisticated tree, sparkling white, which could be glimpsed in the foyer of the Savoy.

Eric came less often. he found Green Park and St James's more lucrative.
He brought fish and chips in greasy white paper — tantalisingly crisp and hot.
He had developed a harsh rasping cough.

The tearing sound jolting Olivia momentarily out of her lethargy, to say he should go to Casualty at St Thomas's or University College. She could hear him breathing. A painful sound.

Then one night she saw Roland, sleek in his cashmere coat, paying off a taxi.
He was with a girl — definitely not Rosamund — tall and dark, the collar of her long black coat turned up against the bitter wind, standing slightly to one side — the folds of her dress glimmering in the light from the flower shop on the corner, its windows massed with forced narcissi, golden daffodils, satin-petalled yellow tulips.

He took her arm, whispering in her ear, and the green-coated gold-braided doorman swung the doors open for them to enter the soft warmth.
The Christmas tree a dazzling pyramid of white lights among the luxuriant green.

She was convulsed with rage.
Dragging herself unsteadily to her feet, she felt the bile fill her throat, and spat on the pavement.
Then wildly, pushing and shoving her way through the theatre-goers, pleasure-seekers, shoppers, office workers, she made her way up towards the Aldwych.

'Hey! Look where you're going!' A man caught her arm.
'Piss off,' she hissed. 'F***ing Bastard!' and then shouted in his face,
'F***ing Bastard!'

She tipped all her change out on the counter of the off-licence in
Burleigh Street. There would be 4p over for a bottle of Bulgarian red.

Amrit Singh, neat and clean in light brown suit with wide lapels, red
tie and cream shirt, watched her with discomfort.
She was a regular, counting out her pence in little piles.
He thought perhaps he should not serve her.
Tonight her fair hair darkly wet against the ashen face.
Outside the icy sleet polishing the pavements.

How did a young woman like her come to be like this?

He thought of his daughter, Soraya — her long black plaits, gold-
bangled wrists, head bent over her books.
She was studying law at London University.
He was so proud of her.
He sighed, wrapped the bottle in a sheet of tissue paper, and gave
her back 50p.

'Thank you,' she said. 'Thank you very much', and picking up the
bottle she went back to the streets.

The Lilac Bowl

She had laughed at him. Her thick brown hair falling across her face.

'Don't you want to kiss me then?' she had teased, and as he came towards her, laughed again and ran back down the hill, the full skirt swirling round her legs.

He felt his throat constrict with anger and despair — turning slowly to follow her.

'Floozy,' his mother had said, thumping the plate of stew, shining with dumplings, in front of him. His father continued to read the *Mirror*, asking for the salt.

'I saw you with her, so it's no good you denying it. She'll come to no good that one.'

She sat down at the table without removing her apron.

'Leave the lad alone,' said his father. 'She's pretty enough.'

He had won a place at Trinity College Cambridge. It was unbelievable. Mr Stone had been overjoyed. 'I knew you could do it,' he kept repeating.

There was a special lunch at school. The headmaster gave a little speech commending his achievement, and wishing him well.

His friends were grudgingly admiring. Not many boys from Holsford Grammar aspired to Oxbridge.

Therese went to boarding school. Coming home in the holidays — throwing stones at his window, racing him up the hill, flinging herself enticingly on the grass, her hands behind her head, always teasing.

Her father was the village doctor, in brass buttoned blazer and flannels, he sped down the country lanes in his dark blue Jaguar. Her mother, vaguely wispy, absent-minded, her cardigan inside out, presided over the local Women's Institute meetings, providing the stall at fetes with many jars of transparent jelly and painted fir cones.

There were not many young people in the village. The few boys of his age went to the Secondary Modern School, and spent their spare time kicking a ball round the bald field behind the garage. The even fewer girls sat and gossiped in the bus shelter.

The boys eyed Therese cautiously, but never approached her, emitting the occasional whistle. The girls said she was stuck up — envying her smart clothes and easy assurance.

Unable to resist the glamour of Cambridge she came often, sitting in his rooms, silken legs crossed, smoking — permitting him sometimes to kiss her — flirting shamelessly with his friends. She glittered among the peasant skirted, fringe-bagged undergraduates, with their messy hair and thonged sandals.

Punting lazily on the Cam with a basket of white wine and crisp ham rolls.

Wandering the abundant scented flower garden of Clare.

She walked with head-turning ease.

Dancing the night away at the May Balls in shimmering taffeta. Walking back to his room carrying her satin shoes.

He got a 1st.

She went abroad whilst he was studying for his PhD. Now and again he received a card, from France, Switzerland, Italy — 'Wish you were here!!!' She returned to England, and took a job with an advertising agency in the City, and became engaged to a stock broker.

One night she came to his flat in Swiss Cottage, demanded a drink, sat on the sofa with her legs tucked under her, and asked him to marry her.

'I've done a lot of thinking,' she said. 'And I have decided I want you.'

When he asked about the stock broker, she laughed and shrugged, and then got up and went into the bedroom, stripping off her clothes as she went, calling him to come and join her.

That spring they were married. It was a grand wedding. Alec's parents uncomfortable in their new unaccustomed clothes. Therese's mother caused a stir by turning up at the church still wearing her old gardening raincoat. Somehow she had missed the hired limousine, and arrived in her old orange mini.

It did not matter. Nothing mattered on that wonderful day.
Therese floated in white silk and lace, and flowers — so many flowers.
Pink champagne and lobster mayonnaise.

The honeymoon in Paris — wet lamplit streets, flowering chestnut trees, flowering cherry trees, the pavements soft with petals. The flower stalls yellow with spongy mimosa.

The house in Kensington. Their white bedroom, all lace and fine linen. Thick towels in the white bathroom.
His study with tooled leather desk top and the bronze figure of a rearing horse. Therese said it gave it a dignified look.

She had laughed, standing at the window of the white-carpeted drawing room, pushing him away. 'You'll miss your train,' she had said.

Robby found the sleeper, throwing his briefcase onto the upper bunk. He always took the upper bunk. Alec, his tall lean frame bent with fatigue, sat slumped on the lower bunk.

Robby had whisky in his briefcase, but he knew Alec would not want it. 'Shall I hunt out some coffee sir?' he asked.

Alec said yes that was a good idea, leaning back and closing his eyes.

Robby slid open the door and went down the corridor to find the Night Attendant.

He hated seeing Alec in this state. Working so close to him, it was impossible to avoid the pain in his face. He was only too well aware of the cause. The beautiful, sexy Mrs Ross. She was probably playing around. She had probably always played around.

Alec lay in the bunk and tried to sleep. He had rolled his jacket up under the small pillow to raise him up a little.

He had not slept the night before, lying restlessly awake in the extravagant bed in his suite at the Castle Towers — seeing Therese laughing, wondering who she was with.

She had a way of leaning forward — of lifting her grey eyes — of crossing her silky legs, seductive, challenging.

Soon it would be their fifth wedding anniversary. He wondered how long it had been before she had first been unfaithful.

How many lovers — how many adulterous afternoons, fictitious friends, hairdressers appointments, charitable occasions?

A terrible jealousy made him shake with cold. The thought of someone else touching her was unbearable, had always been unbearable. He turned on the shaded overhead light, and re-read the article in the newspaper.

"On finding his wife in bed with her lover, Mr X had beaten her to death with a hammer he had taken from his tool box in the garage. The lover had escaped, clad only in his vest. He had called the police. When they arrived, Mr X was sitting by the bed, his wife a bloody mess, clutching the hammer. They had had to prise his hands from it before taking him away."

It was morning. The steely cold fogged outside the window. He shivered in the warmth of the compartment.

Robby had gone again to fetch coffee from the Night Attendant, sitting in his booth at the end of the carriage. They would arrive at King's Cross on time at 6.55.

Alec drank his coffee...

He could always tell. The suppressed elation — the lazy acquiescence to his love-making. The heightened atmosphere as she came in.

There had been no children. He had not wanted any. He could not bear anything to come between them, and yet he had been betrayed for years, perhaps always.

What would Mr X do now he had destroyed his tormentor? Would he be sent to a merciless prison? When he was released, what would he do?

'More coffee, sir?' asked Robby.

Alec had managed the meeting with his usual expertise, countering Hank Kreisler's aggressive questions.

They had had a preliminary breakfast meeting. The American boss forking large mouthfuls of scrambled egg, his coffee high with cream. His assistant Theo Masters in pale jacket and buttoned down shirt tried the kippers, making notes in his important folder.
Robby made notes too, and enjoyed his eggs and bacon.
Alec had coffee and orange juice and fiddled with some toast and honey.

Later they had the proper meeting in their Edinburgh office, presided over by Ian McIntosh, the Scottish Director.

Alec was the youngest Research Director the company had ever employed. They were anxious about investing large sums of money in what might be an unsuccessful research programme. Alec's integrity and knowledge completely reassured them.

Robby shaved, asking if Alec had been pleased with the meeting. It had seemed to go very well.
Alec raised his eyes from the newspaper. He hadn't heard what Robby had said. He nodded briefly, and went out in the swaying corridor to the toilet. He saw his drawn face in the scabbed mirror, the greying hair. He shut his eyes. He was mounting the curving, gilded staircase, the bronze horse in his hand — beating her until she no longer laughed — the faceless lover rushing away behind him.

He pulled himself together and returned to the compartment.

"Mr X had broken down in court and wept, covering his face with his hands. He had been unable to bear his wife's ridicule, her amusement at his distress.
    The defence lawyer pleaded diminished responsibility. His client had been driven beyond reason by his wife's blatant infidelities."

Robby looked at Alec anxiously. He seemed really strange. He had phoned Sara, Alec's secretary, to say they would be on the overnight express.

Sara was in love with Alec, fiercely protective — loathing Therese. Alec never noticed her as a woman. He appreciated her efficiency, and relied on her absolutely. Unobtrusively well dressed, her long fine hair coiled in a polished knot, she ran the office calmly and firmly. Nothing was allowed to trouble Alec.

She had been working for Alec for about three months before she met Therese.
She had told Jane, her flatmate, that her new boss was really 'dishy' and a gentleman, treating her impeccably.
In her past jobs the bosses' wives had generally been a dull bunch. Well bred, conservative clothes — smart little suits, Jacqmar scarves,

sensible heels and discreet jewellery.
She was not prepared for Therese.
She had swept into the office in a trail of expensive perfume, wearing a cream silk suit with an excessively short mini skirt. The cream silk shirt unbuttoned almost to the waist, showing soft flesh and a froth of lace underwear. She had a fine cream wide-brimmed straw hat with a large floppy cream silk rose.
She appraised Sara quickly with cool grey eyes, drawled a greeting, and went straight into Alec's office.

That was three years ago. She hadn't seen much of the fabulous Mrs Ross since then.

She made an annual appearance at the classy dinner at Grosvenor House.

Her clothes were always stunning. A black décolleté, deeply frilled. Red chiffon with a back so low that her partners were at a loss where to put their hands. A shimmering sheath of crystal-trimmed white.

Alec became increasingly thin, streaks of grey in his dark hair. Sara had to look away from the pain in his eyes, her heart aching for him. What a bitch!

Robby had phoned Sara from the hotel lobby. Hank and Theo had taken the five o'clock flight to Amsterdam, where they were to attend a meeting of the Dutch office.

Alec was sitting in a capacious leather armchair in the cocktail lounge, an untouched whisky on the round glass table in front of him. His eyes were shut. He was mounting the stairs, the bronze horse in his hand. Therese lying in the crumpled sheets, her hair tumbled on the pillow — laughing.

Sara was just leaving the office.
Robby liked Sara, and was aware of her feelings for Alec. She was too tall, cool and blonde for his taste, but she was a nice girl.

He told her the meeting had gone well, and everything was fine. She was concerned about Alec. 'Was he alright?' She thought he had seemed rather distraught before he had left for Scotland. Robby was noncommittal. He avoided discussing Alec with anyone. Both he and Sara knew that Alec was deeply unhappy, but it was, after all, none of their business. Therese was Alec's wife.

They dined at the hotel. Alec had soup and an omelette, neither of which he finished, and glass of red wine.

Robby ate hungrily, enjoying the steak, the stilton, the fudge ice cream.
They had coffee in the lounge before setting off for the station.

Alec was edgy and pale. He stalked Therese with the bronze horse, ready to strike.

Now in the chill light of the new day he tidied the bunk. They would be in London in about half an hour. He had a splitting headache, a throbbing pain down one side of his face. He asked Robby if he had any aspirin.

Robby had. His girlfriend Elspeth, a practical young woman, insisted he had aspirin, Alka Seltzer and Elastoplast in his shaving bag, also throat pastilles and a pair of scissors.

Alec lay back on the bunk, tense and exhausted. He had not told Therese he was coming home this morning. She would not expect him until this evening.

He wondered what sentence Mr X would receive. Would the judge be lenient? The Prosecution had claimed some premeditation. Why had he taken the hammer upstairs? Alec wondered if he had planned it. Watched and waited until he knew they were there together, his wife and her lover.

He took a taxi from the station.
Her car was parked outside the house. The bedroom curtains were

closed. He felt his heart leap, and then became still as he walked into the white tiled hall. There was a mass of white lilac in the two tall Chinese vases outside the dining room, filling the air with fragrance. He stood listening, holding his breath, and then noiselessly mounted the stairs.

He stopped on the landing outside their bedroom door. There was a sigh, a moan… a small moan. She was not alone.

He saw the bronze horse in his hand. He saw the creeping red stain spread across the white bed, he saw her hair tangled with blood — a sound screamed in his head.

He found himself standing rigid outside the door, his hand clutching the knob. She moaned again.

He almost ran down the stairs — into the study. He opened his desk drawers and emptied the contents into his briefcase. When it was too full to close, he stuffed the rest in his overnight bag.

He was gasping — deep sobbing breaths. For a moment he stood looking at the bronze horse, its elegant head stretched forward. He picked it up, holding it, cold and heavy, the little moan sounding in his ears.

Then, with all his strength, he threw it across the room, smashing the glass-fronted bookcase, shattering the glass, splinters flying.

As he came out in the hall the bedroom door opened, and she was there at the top of the stairs, her white lace nightgown clinging revealingly, the straps fallen from her shoulders.

'Alec!' she exclaimed, almost in relief. 'What are you doing?'

He didn't answer. Picking up his bags he left the house.

Sara had come to work early anticipating an early start. There was always a lot of work to do after such an important meeting.

She was shocked by Alec's wild dishevelled appearance. He was unshaven, the dark stubble accentuating his pallor.

Muttering a greeting, he left his bags, and went upstairs to the executive suite to shower and shave.

Sara fetched coffee and croissants, standing wretchedly, wondering what to say, and then when he made no attempt to speak, left the room and started sorting out the day.

Alec did not know how long he sat there. His head full of red zig-zags, Therese's laughter, the little moan, the smell of the lilac.
Surprisingly hungry he drank the coffee and ate the croissants. He called Sara on the intercom, and asked her for aspirin and an *Evening Standard*.

"Mr X was found guilty as charged, but because of the extreme provocation he had suffered, temporarily of unsound mind. The Judge thought that no useful purpose would be served by giving him a custodial sentence. He gave him a three-year suspended sentence, and recommended he should receive psychiatric help…"

Alec folded the newspaper on the desk in front of him. He rose and went to the window, the sheet of plate glass with its sweeping view of the river.

He had to let go — to let her go — to release himself. He had to release himself.

He called Sara again on the intercom.

'I would like you to find me a lawyer,' he said. 'A divorce lawyer.'

Toccata

Diana took her hat off in the hall, taking care not to disturb her hair, newly set — rinsed silvery blonde.

She put it down on the hall table by the pot of mauve cyclamen, black, the crown swathed in velvet.

She noted the whiteness of her throat in the ornate gilded mirror, the soft curves, subtle beneath her prim tucked blouse.

She turned sideways, pulling it down, admiring her round swelling shape.

Somebody was playing the piano quite wonderfully.

It certainly wasn't Anthea plodding through her Grade 3 Clementi, and Theo had given up the piano years ago.

She crossed the deep-piled carpet, scattered, like everywhere else in the house with Chinese rugs, pink and cream and red, and opened the drawing room door.

The Bosendorfer Grand was at the far end of the room. A young man with long dark hair in an untidy pony tail was playing. Thick columns of sound — clear jewelled notes, filled the room.

She stood, holding her breath, not wanting to break the spell.

She was pleased with her room, the heavy gold velvet curtains, vases full of white chrysanthemums, white tulips, a scented jasmine. The discreetly lighted pale misty flowered landscapes. The squashy indulgent sofas.

She backed out quietly, hearing her heart beating, unusually disturbed by the intensity of the music, and went down the passage, lined with sporting prints, to the kitchen.

It was a utilitarian theatre of white and steel. In the centre an eating area, a high white bar, with white leather-topped stools and trailing plants. Stylish and horribly uncomfortable.

Anthea was seated. Her school bag open on the floor, dog-eared books scattered.

She had a tin of coke, and was spreading Nutella thickly on a slice of bread. The sliced loaf loose from the packet, a collapsed house of cards.
She had an exercise book open in front of her.

Diana could never get used to Anthea.
She was guiltily pleased that she was quite plain — long straight mousy hair, the nose too long, the mouth too wide.
She had nice long legs, which Diana envied — *her* legs were not her best feature — but such large feet!
Diana took great care of her appearance. she had kept her figure. Her skin pampered with expensive creams.
Teddy adored her.

Anthea was totally disinterested in her looks, dressing like a tramp in grubby jeans and sweat shirts with crazy slogans, and awful trainers.
Her school uniform would have won a medal at St Trinians.
Her hat folded and stuck in her blazer pocket as soon as she was out of the school gates.
'Nobody wears hats nowadays,' she said scornfully, tying her hair back with a soiled black and white handkerchief.

Theo was the same. He was nice looking like his father, not quite as tall or broad — but fair and open-faced.
It was different for boys. It didn't matter if they looked scruffy.

She had absolutely nothing in common with her daughter.
She didn't even think she liked her very much. She found her cleverness intimidating. She was really quite impossible. Independent and opinionated.
'Where's Theo?' she asked. For some reason she was reluctant to ask who was playing the piano so beautifully.
'You shouldn't do homework while you're eating — you'll get your books all messy.'

Anthea said she thought he was upstairs, and it was only ghastly Maths, so she hoped she did get it messy.

Diana turned away. What should she wear tonight? Freda was always so smart. Perhaps the jade silk. No. The black velvet with the butterflies embroidered on the jacket, and the short, short skirt. She had specially sheer stockings.

'I don't think Coca Cola is good for the stomach,' she said, and then, feeling suddenly hot, 'Who is that playing the piano?'

'Oh that's Josh,' said Anthea spreading Nutella on another slice of bread — leaving the sticky knife on the shiny white surface of the table.

'Really Anthea! I do wish you wouldn't make such a mess, and where is Ingrid?'

Diana filled the kettle. She wasn't very pleased that Ingrid took so much time off — all these classes… Still, she rarely went out in the evenings, and she was wonderfully clean and tidy.

Freda had warned her about having these fresh young girls, especially young Swedish girls, as au pairs. 'Asking for trouble,' she said. 'Men can't resist their youth, and Theo is just at the age to be seduced.'
She wasn't at all worried about Teddy. He had no cause to wander. She looked after him too well, besides, he worshipped her.

The bushes outside the kitchen window shone darkly in the light from the kitchen.
She would have to speak to Edmund. Surely there were less dismal bushes — early flowering or something. There had been an article in Homes and Gardens about bushes. She would look it up and prime herself with a few names before approaching Edmund.

She pulled down the white blind. It was printed with a Japanese woodcut of a woman, her mushroom of black hair impaled with long prongs of bamboo. She held a bowl.

Freda was having their whole house redesigned.

Basil de Groot, 6ft 2ins of dove grey suiting, a pale blue silk tie to match his eyes, gold monogrammed cufflinks, blonde hair thinning on the top. He had a Dutch father, and spoke with clipped precision. His assistant Cosmo, shorter and also blond, favoured denim with pink shirts and white suede shoes with crepe soles.

They had papered the hall with red brocade, with marble busts on lacquered tables, a tapestry of a hunting scene taking up one wall, the dying stag tormented by hounds.
The drawing room, by contrast, was elaborately draped and frilled, with soft-porn portraits of women in various postures, their clothing disarranged or non-existent.
Oscar's collection of weird objects collected on his many travels arranged artistically on small tables.

The dining room curtains were made from antique French bedspreads, hung from arrow-headed brass poles. Everything was red, even the ceiling.
Both Diana and Teddy disliked it.
'The safety of the womb,' Oscar would murmur, exchanging a conspiratorial look with Freda, who responded with a twist of her scarlet mouth.
Oscar always made her feel uneasy. She felt he was laughing at her.

Freda had very thin legs and a straight body. Her face, despite the creams and lotions, yellowed and lined.

Diana took her tea and went upstairs, pausing outside the drawing room to listen to the silken runs.

Smugly, serenely secure in her marriage. Completely in charge, manipulating Teddy as she wished. He was always attentive and caring, concerned with her pleasure.
She never had to do anything she didn't want to, except sometimes entertain Teddy's business associates, sitting through interminable operas or dirgey plays.
Teddy always complimented her on how well she managed everything, bringing her roses or a piece of jewellery in a velvet-

lined box, to show his appreciation.

She put a lot of bath oil in the bath. Whilst she was luxuriating in the thick foam, Theo came into the bedroom.

'Can Josh stay tonight?' he asked.

'Don't come into my room without knocking,' she said, annoyed at having her self-cosseting interrupted.

'Sorry,' said Theo. 'Is it OK?'

'Yes, yes...' She felt suddenly vulnerable, as if Theo would sense the tremor in her limbs. Really this was ridiculous!

Freda had young lovers. Artistically limp young men — the occasional medical student.

Oscar encouraged it, said it did her good... did their relationship good.

Freda said she should try it. 'It does wonders for your ego darling,' she said, 'and your skin!'

Teddy seemed quite tetchy in the car. They should take a holiday, go down to Martha's place in Nice, have a rest... get some sun.

Oscar took her hand, massaging it between both of his. 'And how is the lovely Goddess Diana?' he said. 'As beautiful as ever.'

Somehow Diana didn't find his attentions flattering. She felt he was mocking her, playing with her.
Freda was wearing a black crepe trouser suit. She liked to wear trousers. Her slightly hooked nose gave her the appearance of a predatory bird, her cropped black hair winged above her ears.

Oscar had a round head and a small fleshy mouth, his greying hair crisply wavy. Women flocked to his plush consulting rooms in Harley Street, paying large sums of money to divulge their most intimate secrets.

Seated in his swivel chair, waistcoat neatly buttoned over his ever so slight pot belly, he exuded authority and sexual power.

His Dynasty lookalike nurse, Eve, in her figure-hugging uniform, soothed their way with her husky, honeyed voice.

Diana was sure she was Oscar's mistress.

They had also invited an American couple, a fellow psychiatrist and his wife — Fanny and Mo — on their first visit to London. Mo, bullet-headed, with thick sandy eyebrows and creased brown suit. Fanny overdressed in gold lurex, her hair rising like pink candy floss above her pallid face. She wore purplish lipstick.

There was Freda's latest young man, in grey flannels and hairy tweed jacket. He had a gingery beard and closely bitten nails.

Oscar introduced him, expansively laying his arm across the young man's shoulders.

'This is Grant,' he said. 'A poet! Ah, what it is to be young with a heart full of poetry!'

Diana was uncomfortably aware of the sarcasm behind his smile.

Freda sucking on her long black cigarette holder, eyes narrowed, kissed Grant on the mouth, leaving a long smear of scarlet lipstick.

'Darling boy!' she said. 'Take no notice of Oscar. Nobody takes any notice of Oscar.'

Yvonne arrived.

The statutory single female, invited to make up the numbers. She had a crush on Oscar.

She wore lace dresses with batwing sleeves, rattling with beads and bracelets. She had smelly breath.

An ardent opera fan — a singer manqué — needing little encouragement to burst into song. Snatches of this or that aria, a little Schubert. Her voice reminded Diana of an old vacuum cleaner.

Oscar handed Diana a drink. He undressed her with a swift glance, lingering briefly on her bosom — Freda had no bosom — and then

turning to Teddy, said everybody should experiment with their sexuality. It was healthy and natural...'
Teddy asked if anybody had been to the Magritte exhibition at the Hayward, it was really worth a visit.

Diana was so relieved at the change of subject, that she didn't think to wonder what Teddy had been doing going to the Hayward Gallery. She knew nothing about art. Of course she always went to the Royal Academy Summer Exhibition, and she had been to the Monet. Everybody had been to the Monet.

They had kidneys in red wine, braised salsify, rosti potatoes. A runny camembert, Stilton, crème brulée, vanilla ice cream spiked with candied fruits.

Teddy's normal easy going good humour had left him. He was tired. He had never liked Freda and Oscar. Diana's perfume was overpowering. He wished she was not so vain. The way she preened in front of any reflective surface, the small sounds of simulated pleasure during lovemaking, her feminine softness — the things he had found so endearing, now merely irritating.

He had become increasingly aware of his growing children.
Their brains and independent views.
Theo was reading Satre in French. Anthea had written a long essay on Franco's Spain. They both wore many badges — CND, Amnesty International, Greenpeace, Friends of the Earth...
Diana uninterestedly unaware, complained of their untidiness, the loudness of their pop music, for watching too much TV, for smoking! Ingrid tidied up.

Teddy found it deeply offensive when Diana had laughingly warned him off having any 'designs' on Ingrid.
He was not the sort of man who made passes at the au pair, however pretty. He treated them all with the same dispassionate affection he had for his daughter.

He had met Kay at the Hayward. She worked in the PR department.

He knew her vaguely.

They had both been surprised to see each other there. They went round the exhibition together, enjoying each other's company.

They had had tea in the coffee shop.

They found they had many things in common.

He liked her smile, her wide set eyes.

She was unobtrusively well-groomed, smelling faintly of scented soap.

Since then they had lunched together several times.

He knew it could go no further.

Sometimes, lying next to Diana's softness, his mind wandered to Kay, wondering how it would be with her.

He felt so easy with her. She was so natural and straightforward. He had to keep his emotions in check. It would not do.

Oscar was being particularly odious, discussing the importance of pornography — making people face up to their deepest desires — the dark currents of eroticism.

'Well balanced people have no need for that sort of thing,' said Yvonne, sucking up a piece of angelica.

'There *are* no well-balanced people,' said Oscar smiling, his fleshy lips moist and pink.

Grant fiddled with his cutlery, pushing the dessert fork back and forth on the cloth.

Fanny said she thought those soldiers with their funny fur hats were 'real cute'. She had bought several models to take home to her friends.

Mo drank Bourbon.

Yvonne said she had been to the most marvellous production of Traviata at Covent Garden. She hummed, wheezily, a little from the famous Aria in the second act. 'So moving!' she sighed.

Freda said she thought Garbo was the ultimate Camille.

'They say she wore loafers under her gown,' said Teddy, forestalling Oscar, who looked as if her were about to make another embarrassing statement.
He wished he could take Kay to Traviata. Diana disliked opera, going on sufferance if it was socially necessary.
Teddy loved Puccini.
He thought of Kay in her grey silk blouse, and the skirt with the pleats.

They did not speak much in the car going home.
Teddy was tired and disgusted.
Diana complained about Ingrid taking too much time off. Yvonne was perfectly ghastly, and really Oscar *was* a bit much...

Josh was still playing. The myriad colours of Debussy tumbling together, a rain soaked garden.

Teddy felt some of the tiredness leave him. Suddenly calmed and refreshed.
He said he would get himself a cup of coffee and leaving Diana standing in the hall he made his way to the kitchen.

Diana, unaccountably nervous of meeting this friend of Theo's started upstairs.
Freda had said the young an inexperienced were the most fun.

In the morning she would get up early. She would put on her robe with the peonies, and go down and meet Josh properly. Usually she never went down until they had all gone.

Teddy sat at the white 'breakfast bar' sipping coffee. He had held Kay's hand, had wished so much to touch her...
Theo came in with Josh.
They shook hands, Teddy complimenting him on his playing.
Nice looking lad, he thought.
Teddy said he was too tired.
She shouldn't have wasted the extra perfume, the slippery satin nightdress.

She lay frustrated — tingling — staring at the ceiling — seeing the back of a dark head and long white hands...
She had not expected him to be so tall — much taller than Teddy and so thin — so pale with fine features.

The sleeves of his blazer were too short — his long hands sticking out from frayed shirt cuffs, his collar and stringy tie also frayed.

She had done her hair and put on some pale pink lipstick, and a hint of eyeliner. She wore her housecoat with the pattern of red and pink peonies.

He was very polite and had a lovely smile. She felt her heart flutter.

He and Theo ate an enormous amount of toast and marmalade. Anthea noisily devouring a plate of Sugar Puffs. Teddy just had coffee. He was reading *The Times*.

He wondered what Diana was up to. She never came down for breakfast.

*　　*　　*

Fran sat at the kitchen table, mending Holly's leotard.

The old wooden table mapped with scars and stains, barely visible among the clutter. A brown teapot, mugs, a saucer of cigarette ends, a half-eaten KitKat, a plate of orange peel, smeared with pickle, a pile of sketches spread out, held down by a milk bottle and a bowl of dusty sugar.

Fran sat with her back to the tall dresser, hung with assorted cups, equally cluttered with jars of pencils, spoons and dried flowers, bent books and a pile of raffia table mats from Oxfam.
Her sewing basket, open on the table, spilled wools and cottons in a tangled mess.

They had bought the house when they were married.

It had been a bargain.

The two elderly spinster sisters who had lived there had gone quietly mad — rushing into the street waylaying passers-by with tales of hauntings, headless ghosts...

In the end, alerted by the gas man, the Social Services found one old lady dead, and had removed the other one to an Old People's Home.

The house had been in a terrible state.

Mike's father lent them the deposit, and they scraped and cleaned and painted it into a reasonable condition.

Since the divorce it had slid backwards, neglected.

The blackened bricks needed repointing, the woodwork split and blistered, the garage doors hanging precariously.

The gravel in the front was full of weeds.

A depressed conifer, the bottom branches shaggy with dead brown needles stood among shrubs, small leaved evergreens with spiky thorns — the kind that grow on railway embankments.

All the houses in the street had the same shambling air of neglect, some had little turrets with broken tiles, and arty porches ringed by milk bottles.

The hallway was dark, with balls of fluff.

The high-backed black upright piano in the 'dining room' had seen better days. The keys loose and rattling — chromatic passages really bizarre.

A heavy legged table took up most of the room, laden with music, bills, school reports, bank statements, all were chucked on the table with the tarnished condiment set, swimming cups, Holly's life-saving medal, bowls of paper clips and old coins, and a jar of uneatable sweets congealed to a solid mass.

Josh walked home, down to Abbey Road and up West End Lane.

He had forgotten his coat and it was beginning to rain.

The brilliant run at the start of the third movement rocketed upwards into the night sky, splitting the clouds with a shaft of light.

He went through the dark hall smelling the familiar smell of shoes, damp and cigarette smoke.

'Where the hell have you been?' said Fran, screwing up one eye to avoid the smoke from her cigarette — her hands were short and stained with nicotine, her hair scraped back untidily, strands falling round her face — her shirt and jeans spattered with clay.
'You're supposed to phone if you aren't coming home.'

'I tried, but there was no answer,' said Josh, sitting down and taking a cigarette from the packet.

'So where have you been... and kindly don't smoke my cigarettes.'
'At Theo's,' said Josh.

'And where is that?' said Fran, biting off the thread and examining her handiwork with displeasure.
'St John's Wood,' said Josh. 'They have this fantastic Bosendorfer.'

Holly appeared in the doorway. She moved with studied grace, standing with her feet in third position.
Delicately boned, her dark hair smooth and shiny.

'I shall be late,' she said.
'Well it's your own bloody fault,' said her mother. 'You should have given it to me before.'
'I really need a new one,' said Holly.
'Ask your father', said Fran. She got up. 'I shall be late too, I'm meeting Lenny at 7.30.' Oh God, she would have to change!
'I'll give you a lift,' she said. 'I'll just go and change.'

Josh felt the teapot — it was stone cold.
'Is there anything to eat?' he asked.

'You'll have to go and get something,' said Fran. 'There should be some money on the dresser.'

He got himself a large bowl of cornflakes. He couldn't be bothered to go out again.

Theo's mother had said he could come and play the piano whenever he wanted. She had said he must call her Diana, pressing his hand, praising his playing.

She was very perfumed.

He thought of his mother in his old pyjamas and his father's old woollen dressing gown, cigarette dangling, clearing a space on the littered table to put her mug.

Theo's mother smiling at him over her white cup, her nails the same pink as her mouth, a pale square of toast on the white plate.

Anthea had made a face at him, and Teddy said he was welcome any time. Josh liked Teddy, he was a grown-up version of Theo.

Fran clumped about above — hunting among the heaps of crumpled clothing for a clean T shirt — shirt — sweat shirt — throwing the duvet over the disordered bed.

Josh heard her swearing and calling Holly to hurry up — coming down the stairs, her feet noisy on the uncarpeted treads.

She opened the kitchen door. 'Get your homework done!' she said.

Josh never thought about his father. He seldom saw him. He and Holly had visited him regularly when they were younger. Holly had always cried. He had just felt angry and uncomfortable with this smooth man and his smooth woman in the smooth characterless flat.

He had distant memories of his mother's distress, but had been too young for articulate understanding.

Now they refused to go.

He never even remembered their birthdays.

The front door slammed and he heard the unhealthy sound of the old Vauxhall reversing out of the garage.

Holly had ballet class twice a week. On the other days she stayed late at school to practise in the sports hall, using the climbing frames for a bar.

Dancing was her life. The music flowed effortlessly through her fragile elegant limbs.

Madame Simianovsky thought her very promising. A natural talent.

She was puzzled by Fran's lack of interest. She was besieged by other mothers, demanding this and that — pushing their daughters, fiddling with their hair, carrying their spare shoes and leg warmers. Occasionally she glimpsed Fran disappearing in a cloud of filthy exhaust fumes. She rarely came to the regular performances… and there was always a problem over costumes, and the late payment of fees.

The shop had been Christine's idea.
She had got fed up seeing Fran sitting at the kitchen table, among the accumulated debris, consuming endless quantities of Jaffa cakes and hot chocolate, her face swollen with lack of sleep and weeping, Holly crawling round the floor in food-stained pyjamas (another mother took Josh to school, otherwise he would have been crawling round as well).

When Mike had gone off with synthetic Phyllida — bell-like hair, small even teeth, not too high heels, no laddered tights, frilly pillowcases, mugs with no mould — Fran had gone to pieces.

She and Christine had been students together at St Martins.
Fran would have liked to have been a sculptor, but settled for pottery as a more practical alternative.
She found the whole process immensely satisfying.
Transforming the greyish bags of clay into fat pots, long necked vases, the soothing rhythm of the wheel, the moment when the painted, glazed dishes were taken from the kiln.

Christine made jewellery from scraps of metal and glass, her boyfriend Duncan contributed carvings of serious animals, salad servers, bowls made of polished wood blocks.
They just about broke even.

And there was Lenny.
Lenny was a plumber who had dealt with the water supply at the shop, installing new pipes. There was an outside loo which had needed attention. The place had been pretty derelict.

Their relationship was casual, undemanding.
They would have a few drinks and go back to his place.
He never came back to hers.

Josh had a scholarship to the Junior Department of the Royal College of Music, where he spent his Saturdays.
Serge had entered him for the concerto prize. He was to play Rachmaninov's 2nd piano concerto.
The winner would have the honour of performing their chosen work with the National Youth Orchestra at St John's Smith Square.

Josh started going home with Theo every day after school.
The piano was irresistible.
Nobody minded how much he played.
They were all very kind and helpful.
Theo's mother, charming and enthusiastic.
Teddy interested and encouraging.
There was always plenty to eat.
Theo made terrific spaghetti bolognaise.
Ingrid made pancakes.
He often spent the night.

He sat on the long tapestry stool, the sounds already gathered in his head, hardly daring to put his hands on the key to bring them to life.

Upstairs, Diana sat at the dressing table, smoothing L'Oréal anti-wrinkle cream round her eyes.
She heard the spine-tingling chords, sweeping her into dreams.
Her feelings for Josh were irrational and uncontrollable.
She was overcome with longing for him.
She told herself again that it was ridiculous. He was the same age as Theo. She wasn't like Freda.
She flirted, of course, but had only had intimate relations with one other man besides Teddy, and that was when she was 20.
She tried to convince herself that it was just his music, his talent, that attracted her, but it did not explain this terrible weakness.

Fran had to let the large room on the top floor.

There was also a basic bathroom — for the servants of a bygone era — the bath chipped, the high cistern rusty and gurgling. The window firmly jammed, neither shut nor open, leaving an icy gap at the top.

They had had a succession of lodgers — anonymous regimented beings — secreted quietly above.

Pauline was almost invisible. She left the house at 8.45 every morning, returning at 6.35 every evening — except Thursdays, when she had an Italian evening class.
Saturdays she went to the launderette.

'I wish to God she wouldn't creep up on you,' said Fran, who had suddenly encountered her on the landing. 'She bloody well nearly gave me a heart attack!' She kneaded a lump of clay on the pastry board — nobody ever used it for pastry, she didn't make pastry. She was working on the lid for a coffee pot, part of a coffee set specially ordered by Mr Carpenter. He wanted it decorated with green dragons, their tails twined round the handles, the knob of the coffee pot a fire-breathing dragon's head.
She worked the clay into the shape of the lid.

'I expect she's lonely,' said Holly.
'All the more reason not to creep about,' said Fran. 'Where's Josh?'

Holly said she thought he was at Theo's, he was always at Theo's.
'He should move in there,' said Fran sourly, and rolled the clay into a ball.

The concerto prize went on all day.
Josh was to play at 5 o'clock after Tasmin Thoroughgood, who was playing the Elgar cello concerto.

Neither Fran or Holly were there.
Fran was still struggling with the coffee set.
The dragon-tail handles were quite a problem. Holly was doing her Saturday job at the Spar supermarket.

All the Carmichaels were there.
Teddy casual in soft suede jacket.
Diana in black velvet with frilled blouse.
Anthea and Theo in jeans and sweatshirts.

Theo had asked to borrow one of his father's dark suits — Josh had nothing suitable to wear.
'Poor boy,' said Diana, exaggeratedly commiserative.
'He must have a dinner jacket of his own.'

She insisted she should buy him one. Silencing his protests. It was sponsorship. All artists needed sponsors!

They went to Harrods.

Josh was uneasy.
He teetered on the edge of a precipice — cascades of stones clattered and pinged down the broken sides onto the pointed rocks far below.

He had not told Fran about the dinner jacket.

The silent damask-lined lift was full of Japanese — black suited beetles with long umbrellas and heavy cases for their video cameras.
The lift man — a displaced bandsman in his braided suit, intoned the contents of the departments on each floor, his adam's apple rising and falling in his stringy neck.

Josh was not sure that this was a good idea.
Diana in black patent high heels, and flesh coloured stockings, held his arm.
She was talking — what about? He was not sure. He hadn't been listening — something about peacocks?

The carpet was thick and spongy — tall silver vases of red gladioli — tall silver ashtrays.

He should have tried to borrow a dark suit from someone at school.
He only needed a dark suit.

Hot air wafted from gold mesh panels.
His feet felt large and heavy.
'It was made of ice cream,' said Diana. 'Wonderfully clever!'

She sat on the red velvet seat of the spindly legged gilt chair, watching the Brilliantined assistant help Josh try on jackets. She was airy with smug satisfaction.

'Sir is very long in the arm.' The assistant smelt of mothballs.

Diana exuded pleasure.
She took Josh's arm.
There was till the pleat-fronted dress shirt — the black tie — the shoes.

She brushed carelessly against him as they emerged from Harrods, carrying their purchases in the gold embossed dark green shiny bags.

'Thanks a lot Mrs Carmichael,' said Josh, not knowing how to disengage his arm without seeming rude. 'It's really great of you.'

'Nonsense,' she said 'It's nothing. I'm pleased to be able to help — and *do* call me Diana, Mrs Carmichael is *so* formal!'

They went to the hairdressers, chokingly warm and scented — Diana's skin delicate, papery after years of extravagant moisturisers and age-defying creams, flushed uncomfortably in the hothouse atmosphere.
Marco tut-tutted over Josh's hair, and assured her he would do his best.
'Just a trim,' said Diana. 'He has such lovely hair!'
The tapes of the initialled cape were secured round Josh's neck.

Warning lights flashed — a huge articulated lorry bore down on him, its radiator emblazoned with silver flowers and pneumatic pinky-blonde pin-ups.
The roar of its engine pounded in his head.

The long blades of the scissors flashed. He shut his eyes.

Diana leafed through a copy of *Harpers & Queen*, studying the society photographs — the opening of a restaurant in Kensington, a grinning group of celebrities, the Hon. Gerald Colt and wife in idiotic hat, clutching a Siamese cat with jewelled collar — the wedding of the Hon. Lucinda Braithwaite — in white crinoline with tartan — kilted page boys. Her mother and father stern and unsmiling...
Briefly, with irritation, she tried to envisage Anthea in white crinoline... she would probably never get married...
She was so gauche.
She watched with pleasure, as Marco carefully clipped Josh's thick dark hair. He was so handsome!

He won the competition.
Teddy opened a bottle of champagne.

There was no-one home.
The kitchen light with its art deco shade of brown and yellow glass petals illuminated the messed table — the saucer spilling cigarette ends — marmite crusts — Holly's knitting a shapeless length of blue wool.

Josh went straight upstairs to his room — taking the steps two at a time — he could hear the faint murmur of Pauline's TV.
He wanted to take off the dinner jacket before Fran came in.
He presumed she was down the pub with Lenny, and would not be back until closing time — perhaps later.
He didn't mind Lenny. He was quite a decent bloke.
Holly was probably over at Clarissa Jenkins'.
They had a video of the Russian ballet dancing the Sleeping Beauty.

He changed into jeans and lay down on the bed.
Coloured stars danced before his eyes.
He had not eaten since lunchtime. He should go and find something to eat.
His head concertinaed with sounds.

*   *   *

Theo was making toast.
He consumed large quantities of toast and butter.
It was his favourite food, apart from Chinese take-aways.

Anthea had propped her book on a pot of fern and variegated ivy.
She was measuring a diagram.

'Whatever have you done to your hair?' said Theo, looking at her
once straight hair, now a wildly tangled frizz.

Josh was playing Brahms — densely dark, spiked with colour. A
sumptuous box of chocolates — soft centred pink, violet and orange
— brittle butterscotch — aromatic marzipan — a whole liquid
cherry…

Anthea could almost taste them.

'You do realise Mum is gaga about Josh,' she said. 'I hope Dad hasn't
noticed.'
Theo realised she wasn't joking.
He crammed his mouth with toast.

Josh started the same passage again.

'So what am I supposed to do about it?' he said. 'I can't very well
ask him not to come anymore because my mother is harbouring an
illicit passion for him. It's ridiculous!'

He didn't sound very convincing. He too noticed his mother's
heightened awareness when Josh was around. Her choice of clothes,
the way she talked too fast.
Jesus! What should he do?

That ghastly woman Freda had breathed heavily on him once.
She was definitely peculiar, like a snake that swallowed its prey
whole before slipping away into a putrid swamp.

He would keep on the alert. Try and forestall anything ghastly.

*   *   *

Fran had a problem starting the car.
She was still fuming from her telephone conversation with Mike.

Both the children had scholarships to their schools, and Josh had his
scholarship to the Royal College, but Holly's dancing classes had to
be paid for.

Mike said Phyllida was going to have a baby.
Fran said she didn't give a damn if Phyllida was having an
Orangutan, what about his existing fourteen-year-old daughter, who
needed new ballet shoes, a new leotard, and money for her dancing
classes?
She heard the elongated sigh, and furiously banged down the receiver.
Even after all this time, she still shook after any communication
with him.
He had not bothered to ask about Josh.

They jerked forward, the gears grating.
'What's with Theo?' she said.

Holly sitting neatly beside her — Fran could never make out how
Holly was always so neat and tidy, certainly didn't take after her —
said, 'It's the piano. They have this fabulous piano. Josh can play it
whenever he likes, that's all.'

She looked sideways at her mother's set face — her coat collar askew.
'They're very rich. They have burglar alarms. Theo's father is really
nice. His mother is a bit of a pain', she giggled.
'I think she's got a crush on Josh.'

The car stalled at the traffic lights.
'Oh really,' said Fran. Bloody cheek! she thought, irritably restarting
the engine. 'What makes you think that?'
'Well, she's bought him a dinner jacket and taken him to her

hairdressers,' said Holly, wishing she had kept quiet.
'Why the bloody hell has she bought him a dinner jacket?' Fran was
very angry.
'It was for the competition. She said it was sponsorship. She said all
artists have to have sponsors.'
Fran swore at a car turning in front without signalling.
'Bloody idiot!' she shouted.
'So why didn't he tell me?' she asked.
'He thought it might upset you,' said Holly.

Fran snorted.

The workshop was cold.
It had been the kitchen.
There was a paraffin heater — hissing quietly — smelly and
unconvincing. Cobwebbed shelves stacked with bits and pieces, an
old metal filing cabinet containing trays of coloured glass, silver
chains, bits of broken china.

She had to finish the coffee pot.
She kept her coat on — pulling the light towards her across the table,
she studied her sketches.

She felt inadequate.
What was she supposed to do?
She knew Josh was very talented — but to her he was just a boy who
left his clothes on the floor — was always hungry — irritatingly
unpunctual — smoking her cigarettes.
School work neglected — little sarcastic notes from his teachers.
God knows what his A level results would be like.

She certainly couldn't provide him with a Bosendorfer, dinner jacket
and designer hairstyle.
She got up and fetched a can of lager from the rickety plywood
wardrobe. She lit a cigarette and drank the beer from the can. Damn
this stupid coffee pot!

*   *   *

Vicky was complaining about her mother.
'She sits about all day watching Humphrey Bogart films, smoking pot and then totters out half stoned to fetch Timothy from school.'
'At least she doesn't dress up as an ageing Femme Fatale and try to lure his friends into her "tender trap",' said Anthea and they collapsed with mirth, rolling helplessly on the floor of Anthea's room.

Downstairs Josh started the second movement again — the tempo wasn't right.

*   *   *

Freda had persuaded her to buy the dress.
They had been lunching in Harvey Nichols.
It was displayed in the 'Evening Gowns'.

Diana thought it was too daring.
'Rubbish,' said Freda. 'Why not show off what you've got?'

It was deeply décolleté — caught on the hips with a large bow — a wonderful sea green — deliciously floating.

She tried it on thinking of Josh — the young supple length — quickly she turned away from the mirror...
It was very expensive.
The seats in St John's Smith Square were bare and hard.
Diana wore her mink jacket over the new dress.

Anthea and Theo sat several rows behind in protest at her fur.

There had been a fierce argument about clothing — Anthea finally changing from her torn patched jeans into a long black wool skirt and governess boots — her newly permed hair in dramatic disarray.

Teddy said she looked like a Millais. He kissed her on the cheek and smiled. 'You should have some flowers in it,' he said.
Diana was annoyed. She didn't like Teddy making references to art.

It made her feel insecure.

He had come in late — didn't even notice her dress.
She was particularly pleased with her appearance this evening.
Soft white shoulders emerging from the gentle sea-green folds.
He couldn't find his cufflinks. Didn't say a word about how lovely
she looked. He had noticed his scraggy daughter though.

Anthea saw Fran and Holly arrive.
Holly beautifully poised in black leggings and long black sweater, her
dark hair smoothly combed.

Fran, untidy, uncombed, her strong face bare of makeup, wearing
an old brown cableknit sweater and jeans under an anorak, its sleeve
torn, the zip broken.

It was Josh's old anorak.
She had grabbed the first handy garment, forgetting to change the
dirty split trainers.
They had had a pub lunch. The pickled onions had not been a good
idea, they hadn't mixed well with the beer.

One of the coffee cup handles had broken in the kiln.
She had had to leave it.

She sent Holly to the patisseries on the corner for a coffee cake, and
to Oddbins for a bottle of Champagne.

She had not had time to change.

Holly was stiffly upset that they were late, and that Fran looked such
a mess.
She swallowed back the tears.
She loved Josh more than anybody. This was his evening.
She mustn't let anything spoil it.

Discreetly she pointed out the Carmichaels to Fran.
'My God!' said Fran. 'That woman with the mink jacket? Why are

the kids sitting so far away?'

Holly wondered what Mrs Carmichael would think of Josh's mother.
Diana found the Mendelssohn overture tedious.
She was glad they would be leaving at the interval after Josh had
played. She wouldn't have to put up with the symphony.
Josh stood completely self-possessed, easily handsome in the black
dinner jacket, one hand on the piano.
The vibrating chords still filling his bones.
He bowed to the applause.
The conductor shook his hand.

They stood in an awkwardly polite group in the coffee bar in the
crypt.

'We're taking Josh to supper,' Diana smiled kindly at Fran... what a
sight! 'We thought it would be a nice way of celebrating.'
She put a proprietary hand on Josh's arm.

Teddy said, 'I hope you don't mind.'
'Not at all,' said Fran. 'Stuck up bitch,' she thought.
Anthea and Theo were uncomfortably aware of the sudden tension
and Holly felt the tears rise again... what about the cake and
champagne?

'We'll celebrate another night,' said Fran.

'We've booked a table at the Savoy for 9.15,' said Diana, still holding
Josh's arm, 'so we'd better get on. I expect this wonderful boy is
starving!' She laughed, a light little laugh.

'I'll bring him home,' said Teddy, wishing Diana would be quiet.

'Thanks,' said Fran. 'Have a good time,' and she turned abruptly and
went out up the stairs. Holly followed miserably.

Diana was pleased with the table, by the window, banked with
creamy camellias.

She sat between Josh and Teddy — Theo joking — Anthea stonily disdainful as usual.

They ate Foie Gras — Scallops à la Newburg — fillet steak — salad — Bombe Surprise. Anthea a vegetarian — vegetable soup, courgettes in tomato sauce, a dish of sizzling potato and onion…

Diana had had too much to drink. She was delightfully light headed. She rested her hand casually on Josh's arm.

Josh had followed Fran and Holly up the stairs from the crypt to the door leading to the square.

They stood on the steps, the sounds of the symphony muted by the heavily curtained doors. Fran grim — Holly tearful.

'I'm sorry Mum,' he said. 'I didn't know they were going to take me out for supper. It was a surprise.'

'That's OK,' said Fran. 'Don't worry about it.'

He was still suffused with the music.

He would have liked to walk away across the dark rain-wet square — the puddles gleaming oily mauve in the dim glow of the street lights — the shiny bug bodies of the parked cars in a watchful circle.

He felt distant — rising to meet the chasing clouds — holding the strands of the melody in his hands, the notes escaping through his fingers, scattered by the wind — mingling with the weeping sky.

'You were great,' said Holly, swallowing the tears that threatened.

Josh gave her a quick hug.

He ate his meal in a dream. The glittering lights, attentive waiters, silver-domed trolleys, flaming flambé dishes. Theo talked a lot. Diana laughed a lot — a shrill high laugh. Anthea ate carefully — disapproving of the surrounding opulence. Teddy had suddenly become aware of his wife's attention to Josh… the absurdly revealing dress — her shrill laughter — the hand on his arm. My God! She was flirting with the boy.

They took Josh home.

*   *   *

Anthea was in the kitchen drinking tea.

Theo was doing *The Times* crossword.

'Can't you get Mum to get rid of this ghastly bar thing?' said Anthea perching on one of the stools. 'It is *so* uncomfortable. Why can't we have a table and chairs?'

Teddy grunted. He was still thinking of his wife's behaviour. She had pretended the dress had been for him. Hanging it in the cupboard in their bedroom, she had asked coquettishly if he had found it attractive.

'I have to stay desirable for you,' she said meek in the lacy underwear. Teddy had felt unaccustomed anger. He didn't answer. Didn't trust himself to speak.

He went downstairs.

He poured himself some Perrier water and pretended to look over Theo's shoulder at the crossword.

He thought of Kay — the neat collared blouse — her hair curling over her ears.

If only he had the courage to go to her.

'Dad,' said Anthea, 'why don't you get Mum to do a course in something — learn a language. What about French? You are always going to France.'

Teddy avoided her eyes — there was a vibrant silence.

He turned and looked out into the darkness — the black shapes of the bushes illuminated by the lights in the kitchen.

'I'll ask her to get rid of the bar,' he said. What would they say, these two new grown up people if he said he wanted to leave?

'I'll get a syllabus from the Adult College on my way home,' said Anthea, not to be put off. She could hardly say to her father, 'Mum is making a fool of herself over Josh, and it is absolutely sickening.'

Diana got into bed, her heart pounding. She was whoozy from the champagne. Had Teddy noticed anything? She would be especially nice to him when he came to bed.

She could always wind him round her little finger.

He wouldn't be able to resist her in this nightdress with the lace bodice.

She turned on the small bedside light and lay expectantly waiting. She dozed.

Teddy came in quietly, took his pyjamas, and went down the passage to the spare room. He felt unable to lie beside this foolish shallow woman — trapping him with her soft hands. He felt no love for her, that had gone a long while ago, if it had ever existed. He doubted it now... just youthful fervour and natural desire. She had played hard to get — teasing and tantalising.

He had been so proud to have won her — but who had won in the end?

The spare room was cold. He got tiredly into bed, and lay and thought of holding Kay. What it might be like to kiss her...

*   *   *

Josh heard Diana come in.

He had been playing Debussy — the sonorous beauty of La Cathédrale Engloutie — the submerged bell moving weightless in the rocking water.

He got up slowly — still immersed — feeling the sand — the fronded sea weed — the solid salty waves.

She approached across the thick softness of the carpet.
'That was beautiful Josh,' she said and kissed him full on the lips.
Her mouth was wet.
He recoiled. She pressed herself against him.
'Dearest darling Josh,' she murmured, her hands clasping his neck.
He stepped back quickly, catching his funny bone on the edge of the piano lid.
What the hell should he do?
Theo's mother! Oh my God!
He remembered with a shudder tales of the 'older woman' initiating young men in the mysteries of love — 'tea and sympathy' — all that rot.

Theo had come in.

He stood silently in the doorway, eyebrows raised in alarm.

Diana released her grip. 'Well,' she said briskly, 'I'll leave you to get on,' and without looking at Theo, she left the room.

Josh started to apologise — to explain — but Theo cut him short.

'Don't worry,' he said, 'I expect it's the menopause — that ghastly hag Freda tried it on me once. I expect they are trying to recapture their lost youth and all that crap.'

He shook Josh's arm.

'You'd better get that lipstick off before anybody sees you.'

*   *   *

Vicky passed a note up the row, scribbled on a torn piece of envelope. 'Mac' the Headmistress, droned on — she wore her gown untidily over her sludgy green coat and skirt — her glasses, hanging from a chain, slipping off her nose. She peered at the pile of papers in front of her.

'Barney wants me to come to her room at break!! Noooo Way! Meet you in the lab.'

The girls viewed Barney's desire to be All Pals Together with suspicion, and some hilarity. Heads bowed to conceal the giggles as she let her hand linger on someone's shoulder, whilst perusing their work. If they worked things well they could talk all through the History lessons. 'Free discussion' Barney called it, earnestly replying to their questions.

'I just don't understand,' someone would wail.

'What is the *point* of learning the dates of all these sea battles?'

'Please Miss Barnes, do you think President Kennedy was really Marilyn Monroe's lover...?'

'Do you think Queen Victoria was really having a "thing" with the gamekeeper...?'

She never questioned their innocent bewilderment.

At least three of the girls were already on the Pill, and pot smoking was pretty routine.

Let's go up to Clarke's and get some really wicked doughnuts,' said Vicky.

They were not allowed out during school hours, but there was already a queue at the bakers.

The doughnuts were marvellous — large and sugary — oozing jam. Vicky ate two. 'They're all sexually deprived,' she said. 'My mother — your mother — Barney — probably old Mac as well…' She spread her arms despairingly. 'I hope to God we don't get like that.'

Theo said he had caught Diana kissing Josh.

'Oh God!' said Anthea. 'What did you do?'

'Well she sort of stopped and went off as if nothing had happened.'

'What about Josh?' said Anthea.

'He was absolutely rigid with horror.'

'Damn,' said Anthea. 'I suppose he will stop coming now. She is a stupid cow.'

'I expect that ghastly Freda encouraged her,' said Theo.

They sat gloomily in the kitchen dipping biscuits in their tea.

Ingrid was peeling potatoes — she appeared not to listen.

Anthea found the thought of her mother trying to seduce Josh completely disgusting. She was *so* vacuous!

She felt like saying something to her father, but she didn't want to hurt him. He was a dear!

Anyway Josh wouldn't come anymore now, so that would be the end of that.

Teddy didn't comment on the silent piano. He missed it.

The house seemed hollow, empty and echoing like the chambers of his heart.

He didn't ask Theo why Josh didn't come anymore.

He had a very good idea.

Diana was full of honeyed sweetness. He found it impossible to respond. She said they should take a holiday… go down to Martha's villa in Nice... it would be lovely this time of year.

She was still 'in love' with Josh, hoping he would come back.
Perhaps Theo would persuade him, or the ultimate temptation of the
Bosendorfer would lure him back.
Theo said he had been asked to do a recital of Debussy at the Purcell
Room.
She had had to trust her instinct that Theo would not tell his
father what he had seen in the drawing room that day. It had not
been mentioned, but she was pretty sure he would say nothing. He
wouldn't want to upset his father. She was uncomfortably certain
that he had told Anthea. The atmosphere between them was
increasingly cold and distant.

There had been a unanimous decision to get rid of the breakfast bar.

'We are all fed up perching on these awful stools,' said Anthea. Theo
said they were not the right height for anybody, and gave him back
ache, and Teddy said it made the kitchen look like a snack bar.

Diana went to order a table and chairs in thick natural pine. She
would have the kitchen redesigned in pine, she was tired of the white
anyway.
She spoke to Basil on the phone. He would come and measure up.
She went to have her hair done.

*   *   *

They walked in Kensington Gardens.
The opaque February light suspended between the trees.
It was a beginning and an end.
He had resolved to tell her that it was no use.
Nostalgia trod on his heels — the warmth of her hand in his already
a memory.

Teddy was an honourable man, respected and liked by colleagues,
friends and children. He was unable to behave in a dishonourable
way.

They had taken a taxi from the offices in Throgmorton Street. He didn't want Kay embarrassed by office tittle tattle.
They had lunched at La Perle Noire in De Vere Gardens.
He tried to tell her how he felt, but could only comment on the freshness of the salad.
He wanted to ask her to come with him to a hotel, but could only ask if she wanted more coffee.

He saw Freda — a black witch — with the ginger-bearded poet in baggy cords and rubberised jacket, coming towards them.

He led Kay away from the bare-earthed flower beds edged with green metal hoops — the cruelly pruned rose bushes — up the path among the heavy-trunked trees.

Of course Freda would tell Diana. He was not concerned. Her absurd infatuation for the boy Josh, egged on by Freda no doubt, left a nasty taste. She lived such a useless life. If it were not for Anthea and Theo he would ask her for a divorce.

It was Kay who said goodbye.

Diana met Freda for coffee at Fortnum's.
Freda broke pieces off her iced Danish Pastry, eating mouthfuls between puffs on her cigarette in the long black holder.
She drank herbal tea.

Diana had cream in her coffee.
Freda shook her head. 'You should cut out the cream darling,' she said. 'It will settle here', patting her non-existent stomach.

Diana fiddled with her croissant — aware that hers was not non-existent.

'You'll never guess who I saw walking in Kensington Gardens darling,' she drawled. 'Teddy... with a woman.' She sipped her tea, exhaling a thin strip of smoke.
'Grant and I had been to the Serpentine Gallery... There is a

fascinating sculpture exhibition by this young Austrian... very sweet... bowing, hand kissing, wonderful blue eyes... She paused. 'And there was Teddy hand in hand with this woman... in that bit of garden behind the Albert Memorial.'

Diana felt a flush spread up her neck into her face. She put a hand to her throat to disguise it. 'What did he say?' she asked.

'Oh he didn't see us,' said Freda. 'Much too absorbed, darling!' She picked a sultana from the plate with her long scarlet nails.

Diana was dumbfounded. Teddy with a woman. It was unthinkable. She felt vaguely guilty. Her mind was so full of Josh that she had almost forgotten Teddy existed. Since the concert she had hardly noticed him, politely distanced.

She was incensed. How dare he! It was too humiliating. Her devoted adoring Teddy. She didn't believe it. Perhaps Freda was making it up just to be spiteful.

Teddy wandered in the clipped garden.
The sadness a physical thing.
His limbs heavy — his head aching.
Green-veined snowdrops in milky clusters decorated the damp rough grass.
The doors had swung shut on spring — separating him from the distant hazy-green hills.
A cold wind blew round his feet — stirring the fallen leaves — now crumpled and brown.

There was to be no wandering between sweet-smelling hedgerows.

He went into the house. Picking up his briefcase he went into the study.
He had to work on the Parthenon-Klaus merger.

Teddy was not yet ready.

It was really too bad... what was he doing?

They would be late.

She had said nothing about the woman in Kensington Gardens. It was probably nothing — Freda liked to make trouble and she didn't want to stir things up — just in case he found out about Josh.

Besides, she couldn't believe that *her* Teddy would do anything stupid.

He was too devoted to her.

She was looking forward to this evening.

She always enjoyed Horace and Sybil's receptions — Sir and Lady Caulfield — Horace was 'something important' at the Foreign Office, his white hair touching the collar of his masterly cut dinner jacket which hung loosely from this coat-hanger shoulders, an unlit, half-smoked cigar always between his fingers.

Sybil's brassy hair lopsidedly high above her rouged face, a noose of pearls tight around her neck, moved from group to group in yards of trailing patterned chiffon.

Terence, the aged butler, as skeletal as his employer, creaked slowly about the impressive lounge — the mountainous chandeliers hanging from dusty velvet ropes.

Butter pats in a bowl of ice — black shiny beads of caviar in silver dishes — carefully arranged triangles of brown bread and butter.

Tonight there was to be a string quartet, and they were going to be late.

She went down the passage to the kitchen to see if Ingrid was back from her typing class — she thought it was typing on Thursdays...

She could hear the loud thump of pop music.

They were all in the kitchen, sitting at the white breakfast bar — the pine furniture was still on order —

Ingrid was wearing a large Snoopy T-shirt, the blonde hair falling around her face.

They stopped talking as she came in.

'You're all in here then,' she said feebly, feeling the wretched flush warming her face. 'I just wanted to make sure Ingrid was back...'

Theo said they were quite old enough to be left on their own.
Anthea said nothing.
Diana said the music was too loud. She left the room, more annoyed than ever. What was Teddy doing? She better go and find out...

Teddy lay on the bed fully clothed, the legs of his city suit sharply creased — fine striped shirt — sober tie.
He made a strange gargling sound.

Diana attempted to rouse him — his breathing shallow — bubbling.
She rushed screaming from the room...

Anthea phoned the ambulance.
Theo held his father's hand — talking to him. 'You'll be OK Dad. Hang on. Ant's called the ambulance... Don't worry.'

Teddy was unconscious.

The doctor said he was a lucky man.
He needed rest — a nice long holiday...

Diana phoned Martha — as soon as he was well enough they would go down to the Villa in Nice.
Oscar could drive them down there and fly back.
They could stay as long as they liked.

The children would be alright with Ingrid. There were plenty of people to turn to if they needed any help.

Theo had asked Josh to come and play.
'Dad likes to hear the music,' he said.
Diana was grateful that Teddy had not died.
She didn't know what she would do without him.
He had always done everything for her.
She had thought she could incorporate her passion for Josh within her normal boundaries — but it was not to be.

She quelled the pangs of longing.

There would be other opportunities.

She was already lazing on the Mediterranean sands in her white bikini. She could even go topless. Everybody did down there. Bronze limbs, lapping water, wine and long warm evenings.

She put Teddy's tea on a tray and took it upstairs.

A Trip to the Moon

'"Brief Encounter",' she said, and smiled, a warm, wide smile.

They sat by the lake in St James's Park, the ducks chuntering busily, a column of ducklings anxious behind their mother, the reeds thick and green.

He had just rescued her hat — sent dancing down the path between the brightly ordered flower beds, by a sudden gust of wind.

A pretty wide-brimmed hat with long ribbons and daisies.

He smiled back — the sun was hot — dust from the path coated his shoes.

She wore a dark blue cotton frock with small pale flowers, and blue suede shoes.
Her legs were bare.

Her hair was thick and shiny — golden brown — swept back from her face in a tumble of curls. She was deliciously tanned.

'Except I haven't got a smut in my eye.' She laughed. 'They must have been incredibly dirty — steam trains, I mean. Incredibly romantic though — you can't imagine being ravished by Rachmaninov on an Inter-City!'

Robert agreed — her eyes were brown, flecked with green. He wanted to say something witty and interesting to delay her going, but it was too late, she was already on her feet.

She thanked him again and went away down the path in the direction of Whitehall. She didn't turn back.

He picked up the W. H. Smith carrier bag which contained his plastic box of sandwiches, and went slowly back to the office.

They were digging up the road on the corner of Richmond Terrace.
The noise of the pneumatic drills dulled by the double-glazed
windows.
Outside the huge vats of black tar bubbled and shone in the glaring
sunlight — the pavements shimmering with heat.
The workmen, stripped to the waist, dark from the sun, dripping
rivulets of grime, whistled at the passing girls with the mini-skirts,
swinging skirts, trying to avoid the pools of black softness — and
drank water from plastic bottles.

Alan sat on the edge of the desk smoking. Smoking was frowned
upon, but not banned in the office. He wore shirts with wide stripes
and American style light weight suits.

Alan had retained his carefree life-style — chatting up the women
in the office — discussing his work problems with Sir Cuthbert —
wheedling extra biscuits and slabs of fruit cake provided especially
for Sir Cuthbert, from Elsie, the dour sallow tea lady — her hair tight
grey corkscrews.
He lived with his girlfriend Mandy in Blackheath.
Mandy worked in Whitehall Place. She was sharply clever —
executive smart — polished and shining.
'We're going to Paris for the weekend,' he said.

Robert stared at the papers on his desk.
He walked hand in hand with the girl in the park up the Champs
Elysées, under the rustling green arbour of the chestnut trees. The
sky pale, pale blue… He had never been to Paris…

He had shrunk — was diminished — weighed down by the
oppressive tedium of his existence — his empty stupid marriage.

He had met Laura at a tennis club dance.
In those days he danced and played tennis.
He played nearly every weekend with Stephen who lived just outside
Horley with his parents, and was a member of the Tennis Club.
He lived in a bed sitting room off the Cromwell Road, in Longbridge
Road.

A high bare, dusty room, the window sashes broken, the frame rotted — the mattress thin — the pillows lumpy.

The other occupants of the house mostly quiet and invisible.

He heated cans of soup and baked beans on the gas ring, crouching yoga-like on the splintered floor, and drank a lot of tea.

He was perfectly content. He had a lot of friends, and was nearly always out in the evenings.

Laura, a pretty fluffy blonde, her full skirts swirling about from her tightly belted waist, the bodice low and revealing, danced close, her perfumed hair against his face.

She was a mixture of sophistication and helplessness.

They did a lot of kissing — but that was all — rousing passion abruptly halted.

In the end he did what was expected, and asked her to marry him.

So they got engaged — a small single diamond ring was purchased, a small stuffy party given by her stuffy parents.

They drank Pomagne and Cyprus sherry from glasses printed with marigolds, and ate crisps and cubes of cheese and tinned pineapple on cocktail sticks.

They were lower middle class Tories. There was a picture of the Queen in her Coronation robes over the mock electric log fire.

'We're flying Air France Friday night,' said Alan, and hummed 'Isn't It Romantic'.

So they got married — bought the ugly bungalow in the ugly street in Horley and filled it with ugly furniture. He was caught.

In the seldom-used dining room — on the cheap veneered sideboard, next to the imitation silver fruit bowl — was a wedding photograph in an imitation silver frame.

Laura pert in her ballerina-length sticky-out skirt.

Himself stiffly anxious.

Her mother in powder blue jersey — feet planted squarely, holding the matching handbag. Her father, a small man, barely visible behind her shoulder.

His parents were not there.

His father had taken a job in Canada when Robert was nine.
He was going to send for them — but he never did.

His mother was dead.
She had started drinking after her husband left — unobtrusively
— just a glass or two. She was rarely sober — the corners of her life
blunted — the restricted boundaries of day to day routine softened,
blurred.

Her friend Joyce had found her, on the floor, an open whisky bottle
in her hand, the spreading stain dried and pungent, when she came,
as usual, on Thursday for tea.

Robert gave Joyce most of her belongings — a pathetic collection of
odds and ends — even the few spoons didn't match.
He threw out the shoe box of photographs.
He stood in the shabby spotless living room — the carpet patched
with stains — the brown check upholstery — the brown shade of
the overhead light split on one side — the polished brass fire irons
redundant beside the gas fire.

His childhood had been very much like this room — shabby, clean,
oddly stained with loneliness and boredom.
It had been hard for his mother. There had not been much money.
They had had to be very careful.
He had done well at school — good at games as well as lessons — he
had plenty of friends.
He did well in the Civil Service exam — going directly to the office
in Whitehall as an Executive Officer.

On their honeymoon she had been surprisingly expert.
They had gone to Exeter — the hotel a square white building with
mangy lawns and wind-flattened bushes.
The Sandy Cliffs Hotel.
There were no cliffs and the beach was unpleasantly stony with
sharp black rocks.

The dining room overlooking the car park, full of silent couples and argumentative families.
The food lukewarm and overcooked, served by a slovenly girl with a none too clean apron on which she wiped the cutlery.

Soon it became a routine, performed weekly like the dusting and the laundry — a wifely chore to be accomplished as quickly as possible.
He felt clumsy, inept, inarticulate.

'A hotel on the Left Bank,' said Alan.
Robert looked from the window across the sloping rooftops, the evening light casting pinkish shadows.
There were tables on the pavement outside the cafe opposite.
Long glasses of Pernod and ice.

The girl stood beside him — he could feel her warmth.
Behind them the wide bed — heavy linen sheets.

'We'll breakfast in the Tuilleries under the trees... Fresh squeezed orange juice...' Alan closed his eyes, blissfully envisaging the scene.

They sat with the sunlight dappling the table through the leaves.
Warm crusty croissants — thick white cups of hot chocolate, a white dish of cherry jam.
Her bare golden legs touching his.

He walked to Victoria — the austere buildings clasping the heat.
He almost missed his train.

*   *   *

They had kippers for breakfast.
They always had kippers on Saturdays.
Robert didn't like kippers very much. They gave him a terrible thirst, the thready bones sticking between his teeth.

Saturday was always the same.
He took Laura to the hairdressers in Reigate, and then went to

Sainsbury's to do the weekly shopping.

The list was almost identical all year round.

Shoulder of lamb or chicken for Sunday — Laura liked fatty meat — Special K, pale green toilet paper, a piece of cheddar, a pound of best mince.

Then to pick up Laura from the hairdresser and go to the mock tudor tea shop for coffee — a neon edged teapot over the door — a place of milk-curdling gentility.

Coffee was served with a plate of cardboard biscuits — those with a circle of hard jam in the middle, and asbestos filling.

Lunch was chopped pork sandwiches.

In the afternoon he was supposed to *do* something — mow the lawn, weed the scruffy flower beds, sweep the path.

Occasionally they went for a little drive — even more occasionally to visit friends.

At least Horace and Marlene went to the Costa Brava every year, bringing back a curious-shaped bottle of acid rosé as a gift.

Laura was afraid of flying, suffered from seasickness, and coach travel gave her a migraine.

Every year they drove slowly to Teignmouth to spend two weeks at the same dismal one-star establishment.

The rooms were too low, he bumped his head.

The springs of the beds rattled and wheezed, causing Laura to ban 'any of that' whilst they were on holiday.

Laura was still girlishly pretty — filled out to a knitted plumpness.

She was very proud of her small feet.

She took a three and a half — favouring high wedges with peep toes.

He had suggested going to France for a change. He had never been to France. They could go to the Loire valley, visit some of the chateaux. The crossing from Dover to Calais was only an hour and a quarter, hardly time to get seasick. They would have the car, and could stop where they wanted.

It was no use.

Laura had been on a day trip to Boulogne — a school outing. She hadn't enjoyed it at all.

The toilets were disgusting — she had been ogled by persistent unsavoury-looking Frenchmen — and the food had upset her stomach. The boys had drunk too much and were sick all over the place.

She had her own white mini, but apart from driving the short distance to work in Horley, she went nowhere.

Sometimes her mother would fetch her, and they would go shopping in Crawley or East Croydon.

They had the same food on the same days — Mondays, mince — Tuesdays, sausages — Wednesdays, frozen lasagne — Thursdays, pork (or lamb) chops with frozen peas — Fridays, frozen cod with parsley sauce — Saturdays, cheese on toast eaten on trays watching Blind Date and Casualty.

Fish and chips for a treat.

Laura was always complaining about being chained to the stove.

She worked part-time at the Electricity Board, filing things, typing a few memos, answering queries.

She was home by half past four.

She would bring home a creamy pastry to eat with her tea whilst she watched TV.

Robert had offered to help with the cooking.

He was good at egg and bacon, or smoked haddock.

What about a baked potato?

Laura ignored him.

She didn't want him messing up her kitchen, thank you very much.

She had enough to do without having to clear up after him.

*   *   *

On special occasions they went to an Italian restaurant in Horley.

It wasn't a very good Italian restaurant.

The food thickly disguised with glutinous sauce — the cheese sweaty — the sweets artificially bright.

He took sandwiches to work — one of Laura's 'little economies'.
'Somebody's got to watch the pennies.'
Cheese and pickle.
He didn't care much for cheese and pickle.
Sometimes there was some cucumber.
He didn't care much for cucumber.

There was no tennis or dancing.
They never even went to the cinema.
Laura said you 'picked up things' in the cinema.

They went to the garden centre to buy a swing for the garden. They already had a round plastic 'wrought iron' table and chairs, placed beneath a single silver birch in the middle of the lawn.
Laura couldn't decide between the yellow/orange or blue/green flowers — or the mauve and pink stripes.
It was very hot and crowded — beach clothes and bare flesh out of place beside the busy road, the stream of cars crawling — the smell of hot metal and petrol fumes.
Couples argued and the children squeezed in and out sucking lollies, scuffing their toes in the dust.
She finally chose the yellow/orange.

Robert thought of the girl in the park.
She had the colour and scent of warm apricots.
He wondered what her name was.
Of course she would have a boyfriend.

There was a pile of bright blue swimming pool shapes beside the 'leisure furniture'.
They swam together, long clean limbs in the clear blue water, their shadows dark on the white tiles of the pool.

He waited for Laura as she arranged delivery of the swing seat.

Her strapless sundress was too tight. She had put on weight, her plump arms flabby.

On the way home they dropped in to see Horace and Marlene.

They were sunbathing on the patio, spread-eagled on their cushioned sun loungers, their skin already an angry red.
They both wore shorts, Marlene heavily drooping in her bikini top.
Plastic ivy coiled up the trellis, there was a large plastic pot of wilting petunias and plastic foliage.
They had a small round slimy pond which attracted the flies — the water plants yellowed and dying.

The deckchairs were very comfortable.
Horace and Marlene believed in being comfortable.

Marlene went indoors to fetch some ice cream.
Two scoops of vanilla in glass dishes, bottled chocolate sauce, woody chopped nuts.
Laura licked her spoon clean with the tip of her little pink tongue.
She loved ice cream.

Robert felt a wave of revulsion.
Part of him had already left.
He wandered densely wooded valleys — clear streams — icy waterfalls — beside him a soft golden girl with bare feet and loving arms...

The heat was a good excuse for putting off the weekly 'better now darling' ritual.

It was so hot they were allowed to remove their jackets in the office, an unprecedented relaxation of the rules.

Alan came back from Paris boasting — gloating, and went round whistling 'I Love Paris'.

Robert could think of nothing but the girl in the park.
He looked for her everywhere.

Each lunchtime he set off full of anticipation — returning dejected — sandwiches uneaten — to the stifling heat of the office.

He walked around the lake in St James's Park, up the path to the Hyde Park Corner gate — up Whitehall — along the Embankment as far as Waterloo Bridge — up Horse Guards Road, Carlton House Terrace to the Haymarket — among the tourists taking each other's photographs with the pigeons in Trafalgar Square.

There were many girls with bare legs in flowered dresses — many straw hats with flowered brims…

He went to the National Gallery.
He stood in the dim, air-conditioned room, calmed by the serenity of the Leonardo da Vinci.
He discovered with a jump of the heart, Monet's picture of the Gare St Lazare — the black shadowy engines, the puffed billows of smoke and steam — blues, whites, greys.
Next to it Renoir's languid girls rocked their orange boat gently on the bluish haze of the lake. One vaguely rowing, the other reading. They both wore ribboned hats.

He returned, time after time, ending each day's fruitless search in front of Monet's magical station.

*   *   *

They had new neighbours. The Bartons had retired to Eastbourne. Cyril and Betty — expensively cheaply smart. They were invited to drinks. They had ornate patio furniture including a drinks trolley. Cyril poured them large vodkas. They both wore gold bracelets and gold chains. Betty had an ankle bracelet.
She wore white peddle-pushers tied round the waist with a flowing red scarf — Cyril in loudly patterned Bermuda shorts. Of course they had been to Bermuda, and Las Vegas, Miami, Disneyland. They were thinking about a cruise to the West Indies, but Betty wasn't sure she would like to be stuck on a boat, however luxurious, for such a long time.

Her arms and neck were shiny with suntan oil.

The glasses were real crystal.

Betty handed round smoked salmon and cream cheese on little biscuits.
Cyril insisted on them trying some Californian wine.
Laura crossed her little feet and giggled a lot.
Cyril was elaborately gallant. Complimenting her on how cool she looked.
Laura shook her blonde curls coquettishly and giggled.

It was as if he had swallowed a stone — it obstructed his breathing, made speaking difficult.

Laura was not very pleased with him, although she had absolutely no desire for him, she expected him to desire her...

He could not bring himself to touch her.
He would have to leave.

*   *   *

He had known almost immediately that his marriage was a terrible mistake, but until now it had not occurred to him to do anything about it. 'For better or worse...'
He had been too young — too inexperienced.
The purring kitten swished her tail, the sharp claws drawing blood.
The girl who had danced soft and yielding a petulant, shallow stranger.

Jostled and squashed on the 7.58 to Victoria, the stone grew heavier.
The unavoidable proximity of armpits, necks, nostrils.
His head swollen with fatigue, he began to plan his escape.

He scoured the Appointments Vacant in *The Times* and the *Guardian*, and every night in the *Evening Standard*.
He didn't know what he was looking for.

He would know when he found it.

*   *   *

And then she was there!
Coming down the steps of the National Gallery with a tall blonde
girl in bright pink.
She was wearing a silky black dress with large white spots.
The stone lurched within him.
'Why! How nice!' she exclaimed, and held out her hand.
In spite of the heat it was cool and dry.
'My Sir Galahad!'
He said, 'What about a coffee, did she have time?'
His voice sounded strange.
She said 'Oh dear!', they were terribly late already.
Robert was dimly aware of the tall blonde in pink.
There were so many tall blonde girls.
He was still holding her hand.
'Perhaps some other time! That would be lovely.'
He could still feel the pressure of her long fingers.
The stone fell bruisingly back into place.

*   *   *

The hot days dragged. He was restless and hopeless.

Alan said why didn't he take Laura to Paris for the weekend — he
looked as if he needed a change, put a bit of romance into his life!
He blew a kiss at Kathy.
She was a graduate as well as being rather a smasher — Sloaney but
good natured. Another tall blonde.
She actually said 'Yah!' and 'Super'.
Alan said he wouldn't mind getting in there!
'It's you she fancies you know. Why not have a bit of a fling?'
Robert was embarrassed. He hadn't even noticed her.
'Rubbish!' he said, and longed for the girl in the park.

It was a relief when Cyril and Betty suggested a weekend in Brighton.

They would stay at The Ship, they always stayed at The Ship.
They would go in Cyril's car.
'Only a short drive,' Betty said, patting Laura's hand.

The 'girls' sat in the back so they could have a good gossip. Cyril
droned on about widths and depths and cubic capacity. His firm
made cardboard boxes — there were so many different shapes!
They had just installed automatic folding machinery. It would mean
laying off a few people, but you had to go with the times.

It continued to be stiflingly hot. Tarmac melted — sheep died on
the Welsh hills — the grass burned biscuit brown as the reservoirs
dried up.
The stony beach was sticky with crude oil.
Betty wore a figure-flattering black tailored bathing costume.
Laura had a yellow bikini. She needed to lose some weight.
Robert wore his old tennis shorts.

'*Well!*' said Betty, nudging Laura. '*Who's* got sexy legs then?'
Laura giggled. She didn't look at him.

It was stultifyingly dull.
The beach was hot and crowded with reddened bodies and tar-
smeared legs.
Betty and Laura rubbed each other with sun tan lotion and spread
themselves on their towels — face down — Laura unfastened her
bikini top, Betty slipping her arms out of her costume straps.
Robert felt deep disgust, and went for a walk along the front as far as
the King Alfred swimming pool.

The hotel, facing the sea, took the full force of the sun all day.
It was unbearably hot and airless, smelling of dusty upholstery and
fried fish.
It was impossible to sleep.

Robert's dislike for Cyril and Betty was tempered with relief at
not having to spend the weekend with Laura in the claustrophobic
confines of the ugly bungalow.

Laura had changed her hairstyle, bought a gold ankle bracelet and several 'jogging' outfits.
She had agreed to go on a day's shopping trip to Calais. Betty had told her there was a wonderful new remedy for seasickness.

They had also persuaded her to join the local Amateur Dramatic Society, the Reigate Players.
Cyril and Betty had been leading lights in the dramatic society in Carshalton where they used to live — appearing in many productions including 'South Pacific' and 'Oliver'.
The Reigate Players were going to do 'Guys and Dolls'. Rehearsals would start in September, every Thursday.
They tried to get him to join.
'We're always short of *goodlooking* young men…,' Betty had wheedled, clutching his shoulder with her long fingernails.
He had muttered about evening classes.
Walking hand in hand in the lamplight among the fallen leaves, soft rain powdering her hair.

The city sweltered in the heat.
The parks scorched to parchment dust.
Water rationing was threatened.

He leant on the parapet by Charing Cross Pier, watching the pleasure-boats chug their way through the scummy sulphurous water, leaving trails of petrol-green and black smoke.

He could still feel the coolness of her touch.
They stood together on the polished deck of the blue-funnelled liner — white spray thrown by the wind — the taste of salt — the throb of distant dance music.
She was almost as tall as him.
He hardly needed to bend his head to kiss her.

The young homeless benefited from the long spell of hot dry weather.
They smelt terrible, the heat bringing out the stench of deep dirt.
He held his breath passing a group sitting with their backs against the wall.

One of them asked for change. He wore woollen mittens.
Robert fished in his pockets, and handed over two one pound coins.

He sat in the Embankment gardens and listened to the band playing
Viennese waltzes.
They played every Friday lunchtime.
He had thrown his sandwiches into a waste bin. He wasn't hungry.
The stone blocked his stomach.

The kiosk had cold drinks. He bought a lemonade, trying not to
think of the impending two weeks in Teignmouth.

He was still looking in the Appointments Vacant columns —
perhaps he would find something in time.

He looked for the girl everywhere.
In the streets round Covent Garden, and up New Oxford Street. He
bought himself a tape of the Rachmaninov Second Piano Concerto
from HMV — keeping it in his desk drawer in the office.
Cyril and Betty wanted them to go to the Seychelles with them.
It was much too expensive.
Laura sulked. She wanted to go — amazingly overcoming her life-
long fear of flying. Betty knew of some marvellous pills to calm you
down.
Robert tried to persuade her to go without him.
They could afford one.
She was adamant, she wasn't going as a 'single' — nobody went as a
'single' — except those poor misfits who couldn't find a partner. Not
that he was any use except as an accompanying male, a necessity no
self-respecting girl should be without.

There was no escape from Teignmouth.

He walked the red cliffs — perspiration soaking his shirt. The sun
beat a gilded pathway across the rumpled surface of the sea —
patched dark with seaweed.

Laura complained that he was always leaving her on her own,

stamping her little feet in vexation.
She bathed cautiously, wading knee deep in the sea and flopping into the water, arms flapping like a startled starfish, managing a little uncoordinated breast stroke, holding her head stiffly to avoid getting her hair wet.

The girl swam beside him, long brown arms slicing the larch green water — tasting the salt on her lips — floating motionless rocked by the waves. He had only to reach out to touch her.

*   *   *

The merciless heat continued into September, branding the city with red hot irons. Buildings wilted in the searing sunlight.
Glass-walled office blocks — earthbound spaceships — flashed glittering signals.

The buoyancy of early summer had gone.
The fresh dresses, casual shirts and sandals tired and limp. Bare arms and legs dusted with grit. A persistent smell of smoky bacon crisps.

Welcoming the dank-tunnel breeze — tweaking skirts, sending empty cigarette packets and sweet papers scurrying — which preceded the furnace heat of underground trains.

Commuters enduring the daily misery brought clean clothes in their briefcases and changed in the office.

Once he thought he saw her, coming out of the stationery shop opposite Charing Cross station, but she was gone — if it had been her — before he could cross the road.

*   *   *

Rehearsals for 'Guys and Dolls' started in the second week of September. Suddenly it was cooler, the fierce intensity of the sun mellowing to comfortable warmth.

Sleep and thought were again possible. There was dew on the grass in the mornings when he left to catch his train.

He had still not seen anything suitable or interesting in the Situations Vacant columns.
He was anxious to leave as soon as possible — but had to get things properly sorted out first.
There would have to be financial arrangements for Laura — there was a mortgage to be considered.
Depending on what sort of job he got, she might have to work full-time, move to a smaller place…
Perhaps he should just leave now and then sort it out.

He stood at the bar of the Clarence with Alan.
Blissful Thursdays!
They were waiting for Mandy who was working late, and then might go for a Chinese.
Alan said there was a great place in Wardour Street.
He was telling Robert about the house they were thinking of buying.
'It's OK I suppose,' he said. 'Of course Mandy insists we will have to rip the kitchen out — and there's no central heating.'

She came through the door with a short girl wearing a floppy emerald green velvet hat, and two young men in dark suits and sober ties.
She had a honey-coloured coat draped round her shoulders.
They were laughing.

The stone caught fire — scorching his chest.

They sat down at a table in the corner.
One of the men came over to the bar.
She was talking to the girl in the green hat — and then she saw him.
A pleased look of recognition lighted her face. She smiled, and with a brief word to the girl, got up an came towards him.
'It must be fate,' she said, 'us meeting like this. I'm Natasha…'

Somehow they were alone.

Making excuses to the others.
Leaving hand in hand.

They went to the cocktail lounge at the Savoy.
It had to be somewhere really special.
They sat in the civilised luxury of the cushioned seats, and drank martinis served with little dishes of fancy titbits.
A young man in a dinner jacket played Cole Porter and Gershwin on a white grand piano in a white pergola entwined with greenery.

He put his hand out across the table and took hers. She did not move it.
She looked down at her glass, her eyebrows soft and brown as sable paint brushes.
'We should ask him to play "Just One of Those Things",' she said.
She put her other hand out and touched his face.

The stone was softened, diffused, a glowing ball.

She told him about Crispin, her fiancé. An engineer, working for a year in Saudi Arabia.
He told her about Laura, his plans for escape.

Later they walked up the Strand.
They stood at the bus stop outside Charing Cross.
He kissed her cheek — smooth and cool.
She got a number 9 bus.

Until next Thursday — an eternity!

Alan was seething with curiosity.
'Who is the beauty?' he said. 'You're a dark horse — hiding a secret passion!'
Alan had a very low opinion of Laura. He thought her stupid, narrow and uneducated. He had, of course, never actually said so, but it was pretty obvious from his attitude.
'No wonder you weren't interested in our Kathy! What a stunner!'

Robert wished he had Alan's ease and experience. What would happen if he messed it up? Saying the wrong things, doing the wrong things? The stone hurt.

They met on the corner of Northumberland Avenue. It was a cold night, the frost lightly sugaring the pavements.
She suggested going to her place.
They took a taxi.
It was so easy — as if they had always been lovers.

He caught the last train.

*   *   *

Laura was totally preoccupied with her new role as Musical Comedy star.
She went round the house singing snatches of 'Luck be a Lady Tonight', practising unsteady pirouettes.
She spent a lot of time over at Betty and Cyril's.
Betty spent a lot of time at their house.
They gossiped about the other members of the cast — eulogising over Sean, the Producer.
Laura's face flushed whenever he was mentioned.
Betty said they were terribly lucky to have got him — and they argued about whether he was 'one of those'.
Betty said he was — he lived with a friend, Dominic, in Earl's Court.
They both wore black polo necks and gold necklaces.
Dominic wore mascara!

She didn't object when Robert moved into the spare room.

'Don't expect me to make up the bed,' she said tartly, and went to phone Betty about her clothes for the scene in the Diner.
Casting had been a problem — getting a tolerably matching chorus line virtually impossible.
There were tall and thin and short and fat. Tall and fat and short and skinny.

Sean ran his hands through his hair until it looked as if he had had an electric shock — dividing them up into those who could sing and not dance — those who could dance but not sing — and the few who could do both.
Betty was cast as Adelaide, the star of the Hot Box night club.
She was too old — but she could sing and dance, and from a distance, with plenty of make-up, could pass for thirty.

Laura was one of the chorus line at the Hot Box, a 'Moll' in the gambling scenes — Sean had had to substitute women for men in these scenes as there were not enough men in the company — she also appeared in the Street, the Chapel, the Diner and a South American Bar — wherever people gathered.

She would have frequent costume changes, and was experimenting with different ways of doing her hair.
She could talk of nothing but 'Guys and Dolls'. And Sean…

Cyril got the part of Nicely Nicely Johnson — singing 'Sit Down, You're Rocking the Boat' with considerable gusto.

Cilla, a busty dark girl with a loud laugh and flat breathy voice, was cast as Sarah. She could see little without her glasses, but was enthusiastic, good humoured and quite pretty.

Nathan was to be played by Jason — a tall emaciated youth with shoulder-length black hair and several gold earrings. He moved stiffly, speaking his lines in a nasal monotone.

Casting someone to play Sky was even more difficult.

Sandy, who wore braces and denim shirts was finally chosen.
Ferrety short with gingery hair and pale eyelashes, he sang surprisingly well.
Wearing stacked heels, he would be about the same height as Cilla.

'Sean thinks I have lots of natural talent,' said Laura. 'He thinks it's absolutely amazing the way I cope with all the different parts.'

Now she wore a leotard to go to rehearsals — carrying a towel, stretchy headbands and dancing shoes in a duffle bag she had bought from Miss Selfridge in Croydon.
She tapped her foot as she stood by the telephone in the hall.
She was talking to Betty.
'Sean thinks we should do "A Woman in Love" as a samba... Well it is supposed to be in Havana... No, I don't know if they samba in Havana,' she giggled. 'Perhaps it should be the rumba, I've never really sorted out the difference. See you later.'

She hardly noticed him.
'You'll have to get yourself beans on toast or something,' she said, going upstairs. 'I haven't time to think about supper.'

They were having a script reading and movement rehearsal at Betty and Cyril's.

He phoned Natasha.
There was no reply.

*　　　*　　　*

She had got up to answer the phone.
She stood in the doorway of the living room, her gold brown hair falling loosely on the collar of her short dark blue towelling robe—
— slender bare legs — delicate feet.

On the wall opposite the bed, Degas dancers in their powder-puff dresses bent to fasten the ribbons of their silken slippers.

Over the dressing table Toulouse Lautrec's poster of the dashing Aristide Bruant — dramatic in wide-brimmed black hat and nonchalant red scarf.

'Yes,' she was saying. 'A June wedding!' She laughed. 'Very conventional!'
There was a pause. 'Of course I shall wear white!'
She made an amused gurgling sound. 'OK, I'll have a scarlet garter...'

The stone was spiked with fear and jealousy.
They never spoke about Crispin — or her engagement — and now she was standing there chatting about her wedding. *Her* Wedding!

When he said he loved her, that she was wonderful, beautiful, it sounded remarkably silly.

She never said she loved him — traced his lips with her fingers and smiled…

*   *   *

Laura had the sewing machine out. She was making costumes. The living room was littered with fabric and patterns and boxes of pins. She had a tape measure draped over her shoulder in a business-like way, and a printed list of everybody's measurements on the table beside her.

'You'll have to go to Sainsbury's on your own,' she said. 'I changed my hair appointment to Wednesday. Mum's coming over later. She's bringing some raffia to trim shoes.'

He rang Natasha from the kiosk outside Boots.
There was no reply.

'You're looking a bit peeky,' said Laura's mother, licking a piece of thread and pushing it through the eye of a needle.
'I don't like this colour much,' she said to Laura.
Laura was hunting for something among the piles of material.
'Things have to be bright for the stage,' she said in a long-suffering voice.
'Why don't you go up to the golf course?' said her mother. 'Get a bit of fresh air. It's quite nice now its stopped raining.'

He took the car and drove to town. He went up to Kenwood and walked across the Heath to Highgate Ponds.
The Coach House was serving teas.
He sat thinking of Natasha.

He stopped at Swiss Cottage and phoned her again.
She was there.
She said she was going to the theatre, but he could come if he wanted, she didn't have to leave until seven.
He bought a bottle of champagne — proper stuff — Dom Perignon and two dozen pink roses.

It was the first time he had been to her flat in the daytime.

The street was lined with plane trees filtering the autumn sunlight through the bare branches onto mottled bark.
She buried her face in the pink roses and kissed him — going into the little kitchen to find a vase.

He said, 'I'll leave after the show — I don't want to cause a fuss now...'
She put the champagne in the fridge.
'We'll let it cool a little,' she said, and took his hand — leading him into the living room.
They stood by the window without speaking.
He thought she must be able to hear his heart beating.

Later they drank the champagne.
Later still they went out to get something to eat.
She missed her theatre date, phoning to say she had a headache.

It was nearly one o'clock when he got home.
Laura was watching an old movie on TV. The room was very untidy.
She was annoyed. 'Where do you think you've been?' she demanded, the black and white figures moving silently across the screen behind her.
'I went to see Alan,' he said.

*   *   *

'I told her I was with you,' he told Alan.
Not that she was likely to enquire. She didn't like Alan, thought him a 'bad influence'.

They were having a lunchtime drink in The Clarence.

'I'll tell her as soon as this damned show is over — she's completely obsessed with it.'

Alan lit a cigarette and blew a column of smoke at the ceiling. 'And Natasha?' he asked. 'Happy ever after?'

Robert tried to keep his voice steady, casual.

'I don't know,' he said. 'I just don't know.'

She had turned the handsome photograph face down on her dressing table.

'I don't think we want him watching us,' she said, unbuttoning his shirt.

*   *   *

They were to lunch with her parents at their house in Sunningdale.

It was easy to get away.

Laura had gone to Croydon with Betty to look at shower fittings.

She wanted a shower like Cyril and Betty's, with frosted glass and gold and white lilies.

Betty had suggested they convert their third bedroom as the bathroom was too small to take a shower cubicle, and the third bedroom was hardly more than a box room.

The house was grey stone with a pillared doorway and wrought iron bootscraper.

The gravel sprouted weeds.

There were steps leading down to the lawns, guarded by two dilapidated lions, one with no feet, the other with no muzzle.

Beds of mauve Michaelmas daisies bent by the rain.

There was the clean earthy smell of autumn.

It was Natasha's father's birthday.

She had bought him a jar of Gentleman's Relish and some pickled walnuts.

Her father was a good looking man, tall and slim with thick hair and a sensual mouth.

He wore a camel hair cardigan with leather patches on the elbows.

Mrs Pemberton, working on a framed tapestry, was dressed in blue and grey, her faded hair held by a blue slide.

Both had the deeply lined dehydrated skin of people who had lived in a tropical climate.

Lunch was served in the dark mahogany dining room.
Two girls in white, waving paper lanterns among dark foliage, adorned the wall behind Mr Pemberton.

Opposite Robert a severely-bosomed lady with a long train and feathered toque glared grimly at the diners.

They were served by a maid in a grey woollen dress and bedroom slippers.

The pheasant was unbelievably tough, the game chips blackened, the bacon rolls salty.

'What about Crispin?' said her father.
'He's in Saudi Arabia,' said Natasha.
'Dreadful hole,' said her father. 'Just a lot of teetotal Arabs and sand.'
He ignored Robert.
Mrs Pemberton cut her food into small pieces, and pushed it to the side of the plate without eating.
'I thought you were engaged,' said her father.
'We are,' said Natasha.
'Bad tempered things — camels,' said her father.

The maid shuffled in with an apple pie. The pastry brittle, heavily spiced with cloves.

'Did you order stilton Alicia?' demanded Mr Pemberton.

Mrs Pemberton had the vacant look of someone summoned from afar.

Robert had noticed the way she had walked into the dining room —

each step carefully in front of the other.
His mother had walked just like that — as if walking an invisible tightrope.
Too many 'gin and "its"'.

'I don't remember dear,' she said vaguely.
She rang a little bell by her plate, and asked the maid to bring the cheese.

Under the elaborately decorated lid of the cheese dish was a wedge of blue-veined cheese.

Mr Pemberton was enraged. He speared the cheese and brandished it across the table,
'So what do you call this?' he asked. 'This apology for cheese?'

Afterwards they walked in the garden between the high glistening hedges — the path thick with fallen leaves.
They kissed — but she pushed him away laughing.
'Don't be so serious,' she said.
The stone lodged coldly in his chest.
He wanted to tell her how much he loved her, but she took his hand and pulled him down the path to the square goldfish pond full of sinewy waterlilies — a moss covered fountain feebly spouting water.
He tried to kiss her again — but she avoided his mouth.

He wanted to ask her how she really felt about Crispin. The tall figure, always in the background, jaunty in Old Harrovian tie and cricket flannels.
Did she love him? Was she really going to marry him?

*   *   *

Mandy's office celebrated Christmas early.
Their annual party was held in the superb reception rooms on the first floor, at the beginning of December — giving the Heads of Department and assorted V.I.P.s ample time to disappear for the Christmas Hols — to Klosters — Mustique — their Country Estates

— leaving the Affairs of State in the hands of their astute underlings.
'Why don't you come?' said Alan. 'Bring the beautiful Natasha.'

She wore something black and silky with ropes of pearls.
Mandy elegant in wide-legged chiffon trousers and tunic.

The magnificent room with moulded ceiling and brocade curtains
roped with gold — the heavy crystal chandeliers dimmed for the
occasion — was normally used for superior functions, meetings
of the boring and the blustering, greeting each other with false
bonhomie. The men uniformed in Saville Row suits — their stature
and wealth denoted by the colour and pattern of their ties — stood,
drinking shorts, grunting comments on 'Funding', 'Expansion',
'Urban Development', 'Bangladesh'…
The scattering of women discreetly smart, keeping their opinions to
themselves, sipping tonic water with slices of lemon.

Attempts had been made to create a festive atmosphere.
A web of tinsel and baubles covered a vast gilt-edged mirror over
the marble fireplace — filled with tubs of greenery and silver stars.
Mistletoe hung in the doorway of the anteroom, where food was laid
out on long polished tables decorated with candles and bowls of gold
and silver fruit.
A tree reaching the ceiling stood at the far end — a mass of blinking
coloured lights.
There was a temporary stage on which a group of young men in
jeans and shirtsleeves were playing 'Basin Street Blues'.

'Gervase and his Peterhouse Stompers,' said Mandy. 'They were all at
Cambridge together. The trombonist is head of an ecological Think
Tank.'

It was very crowded.
White-gloved waiters moved with difficulty among the dancers
carrying trays of drinks.
Mandy and Alan were swept away by eager friends.
'Hey! Mandy! Alan! Over here!'
'Hey! Over here you two!'

They danced — they had never danced together before — never
been to a party.
He held her close, oblivious of the crush.
The band played 'Up the Lazy River'.
They swayed, hardly moving — her hands flat on his back — their
faces touching — soft hair, soft arms, soft perfume.

A very tall girl with a lot of bare shoulder and long black gloves — a
mass of black hair swept elaborately to one side, came shrieking
towards them.
'Natasha! How simply marvellous to see you! Where have you been?'
She looked Robert up and down with narrowed eyes. Natasha
introduced him, without moving from his arms.
'So where is Crispin? Still digging holes in the sand?'
'Hey, Vicky!' A balding man with protruding eyes was waving a
glass at her from above the dancing heads.
'Have to go darling! See you later!'

Natasha put her arms round his neck and kissed him gently.
'Take no notice. Vicky is a frightful bore!'

A serious young man with glasses and a black velvet bow tie
approached them. He greeted Natasha with pleasure.
'Didn't expect to see you here! Crispin still eating sheep's eyes? Can
we dance? You don't mind, do you old chap?'
He whisked Natasha away to join Alan and Mandy who were jiving
with abandon — other couples clearing space for them, clapping.
Natasha and the young man jived with rhythmic ease. The band was
playing 'Sweet Georgia Brown'.
Alan danced with Natasha.
Robert danced with Mandy.
The band played 'Everybody Loves My Baby'.
Alan sang — whirling Mandy away.
They ate asparagus tips rolled in wafer thin brown bread, and little
warm cheesy tarts.
People began to drift off, calling goodbyes.
The night was cold. Alan kissed Natasha goodnight.
Mandy kissed Robert on both cheeks. 'Take care!' she said.

Robert hailed a taxi — the sky was full of stars.

He phoned Laura at work from the office in the morning.
She sounded as if her mouth was full — she was very fond of chocolate Bourbons.
'We went to a party,' he said. 'I missed the last train.'
'Who's we?' she said. He could hear her swallow.
'Alan and Mandy,' he said.
There was a pause. 'Why didn't you phone?' she said.
'It was very late.'
'Well! Sean has called an extra rehearsal tonight, so *I'll* be late,' she said. 'He's not happy with the gambling scene, Jason is having trouble with the song. You'll have to get your own food.'

He arranged to view two flats.

He had given up looking in the Situations Vacant columns.
It was better that he kept his job. Natasha wasn't used to being short of money.

He had not asked her to live with him. He knew instinctively that she would say no. He couldn't bear the hurt. Perhaps if he found somewhere really nice she would say yes.

He had a sense of increasing urgency, as if his time was running out — like the sand in an hour-glass.

The first flat, not far from Notting Hill Gate, was much too pokey — the bedroom barely big enough for a double bed, and the bathroom had an unpleasant smell.
The second, nearer Queensway, was nicer, bigger and more airy, but it did not compare with hers.

He phoned her from Victoria Station.
There was no reply.

*   *   *

They had quarrelled about Christmas.
Sitting in the neon-lit office, trying to concentrate on the work in front of him, the taste of wine sour in his mouth.

They had met for lunch at Le Verre Rouge in Tavistock Street.
Here they played tapes of Bix Beiderbecke and Sydney Bechet.
They sat at little round tables lit by flickering candles, and ate Quiche Lorraine or thick pea soup with chunks of ham, and drank wine.
They met there often.
They could hold hands, sometimes kiss, unobserved in the semi-darkness.

He was making plans to leave in time to spend Christmas with her. The two of them together — they could go away somewhere, anywhere she liked,
He thought about Paris. A city of shimmering promise, even in December.
They would stay in the very best hotel, with tubs of hydrangeas and bay trees by the carpeted steps.
They would walk by the Seine, eat in intimate little restaurants, absorb the beauties of the Orangerie, wander the streets — the houses slate grey in the winter sunlight, with curly balconies and high slatted shutters — admiring the opulent windows of Fauchon — amber, orange and crimson fruits glittering in glass jars, and mountains of chocolates festooned with coloured satin ribbons. The elegance of the clothes in the Rue du Faubourg St Honoré, the designers' names picked out in gold. Climb the many wide steps to the Sacré Coeur to gaze out over the city below — the rhinestone belt of the river. He could hardly voice his longing...

She was going to St Moritz — with friends.
They were going skiing for two weeks.
They had already booked the chalet.
Six of them — old friends.
They went every year.

'Don't make a fuss,' she said, withdrawing her hand, pouring herself more wine. 'It was arranged ages ago. I can't back out now. Anyway, I don't want to. It's always great fun. I look forward to it.'

It was somebody's birthday. He was given a glass of sweet sparkling wine and a plate of cake with pink and white icing. The neon lights gave it a greenish tinge.
Everybody sang 'Happy Birthday'.

What gift could he give her for Christmas?
Taunted by the expensive beauty of her engagement ring — a square emerald set in diamonds — the gold earrings chipped with topaz.

Alan said get her a book. She looked the brainy type.
Something about the Pyramids — Amazonian Rain Forests — Wildlife in Chile.
What about a CD? Something romantic! Verdi, Tchaikovsky, Frank Sinatra?

He and Mandy were going to Tenerife for Christmas.
He said he wasn't surprised Natasha was going skiing.
'Who wants to stay here for Christmas?' he said, avoiding Robert's taut unhappy face. 'Cheer up, old chap! It was arranged before she even knew you.'

He bought her a book on the Impressionists.

*　　　*　　　*

She said she couldn't see him this Thursday.
'I'm going to a dinner party,' and 'Don't look like that — I can't always be available.'

She was looking particularly lovely — her hair pulled back into a smooth thick coil. She wore a white shirt and long black jacket and skirt.

There had been a subtle change in their relationship since she had been away.

Two empty, arid weeks without her.

The dreary stretched tedium of Christmas.
Lunch with Laura's parents and her disagreeable Aunt Phoebe
— bready stuffing, frozen sprouts, crackers which refused to pull.

Boxing Day with Betty and Cyril and a collection of their overdressed
friends and business associates. Mulled wine, mince pies, boring
talk about the state of the economy.

There was a dinner-dance at the Cresta Hotel on New Year's Eve.
They went with Betty and Cyril.
Anything was better than sitting in their ugly living room watching
TV, gnawed by miserable thoughts of Natasha.
What was she doing? *Who* was she with?

The band wasn't bad.

'Well, Robert!' said Betty as they glided into a quickstep. 'Laura
never said you could dance! What a pity you didn't join us in the
show — we could have done with a good-looking young man who
can dance.'
She brought her face close to his — 'Do you sing as well?'

The band played 'I Can't Give You Anything But Love'.

Laura pressed against him. She was slightly drunk.
She wore too much make-up and a sparkly red dress that was too
short. Her hands were clammy.

He tried not to think of Natasha, dancing close in someone else's
arms, cheek to cheek with a tall handsome blond, tanned from the
mountain sun. Would he try and kiss her? Would she kiss him back?

'You're treading on my foot,' said Laura. She had new red shoes.
'You're so clumsy.'

Balloons and streamers rained down from the ceiling, entangling the dancers as they joined hands for Auld Lang Syne.

Happy New Year!

*   *   *

When he saw her he thought his heart would burst.
He hugged her to him — not caring who saw them — not caring
about anything except that she was here.

'Don't go away again,' he said, kissing her, holding her tightly.
She didn't answer — disengaging herself — taking his arm.
'It's cold here,' she said.
They went for a coffee at Milo's in Bedford Street.

His longing for her had become unbearable.
He wanted them to find somewhere together. Now.
'I can't bear being away from you,' he said.
'No,' she said. 'I don't want to live with anybody.'

'I love you,' he said, feeling stupid — but he persevered — 'I love you
— I want to be with you — that's all — I just want to be with you.'
'Please,' she said. 'Please don't be so serious.'

Between them hovered the wispy figure of Crispin.
The stone sprouted thorns.
He closed his eyes — taking her hand, brushing her fingers with
his lips.

*   *   *

The dancers sashayed unevenly across the stage — twirling long
strings of beads.

Robert had brought some of the finished costumes.
Preparations had reached fever pitch.
There were not enough Dice — striped straws and cocktail parasols
were needed for the scene in Havana.

'The drink has to be RED,' said Sean. 'RED! It's not lemonade! The audience has to SEE it...'
He sat at the back of the hall and watched the untidy chorus line singing 'Take Back Your Mink, Take Back Your Pearls'.

Sean clapped his hands sharply. 'Darlings! Darlings!' he expostulated, approaching the stage with arms upraised. 'Keep together! Don't slouch Fiona! Hold your heads high. High, Michelle! Betty luv, you're not Dick Wittington, let's have some *oomph*, darling!'

The pianist stubbed her cigarette out in the oversize 'Guinness Is Good For You' ashtray on top of the glass-ringed upright, and struck several jangling chords.
She wore shiny navy serge and jumpers knitted from old balls of wool. Her name was Dorothy, and she played for the dancing and keep fit classes which were also held in the church hall.
'Let's start again,' said Sean. 'Please, darling,' turning to Dorothy. 'There is a rallentando at the end of the second verse...'

They started again.
One two three — right leg across.
One two three — left leg across.
Kick right, kick left, kick right, kick left...

He would soon be able to leave. Just a few more weeks.
He had not yet found a nice enough flat that he could afford. Since she had said she didn't want to live with him — with anybody — he could just move in anywhere and keep looking — hoping she would change her mind — before it was too late?
Why should he feel so desperate — so insecure?

'Relax your arms!' cried Sean, in exasperation.
'Keep together! You're glamorous showgirls, not the Raggle Taggle Gypsies!'

He was hollow with longing for her.

Sandy — carroty hair tied in a bunch, accentuating his sharp features, the legs of his jeans bagging over his trainers — was singing in his surprisingly pleasant voice, 'Your Eyes are the Eyes of a Woman in Love'.

'Look at Cilla, darling,' said Sean, rapping the back of his chair. 'How are you going to know what her eyes look like if you are staring into space? Cilla — come in closer.'

They stood together, awkwardly, without his special shoes Sandy only reached her shoulder.
Sean sighed. 'Right! Let's try it again. Try and look as if you are being swept away by a crazy passion. You're not taking your washing to the laundrette!'

Of course she wanted to see her friends. That didn't mean she didn't love him...

*   *   *

The evening had been almost perfect — if she had said she loved him it would have been perfect.

She had made some tea — bringing it on a round painted tray to the side of the bed.
'Bliss!' he said, pulling her down to kiss her, feeling the steady beat of her heart.

She sat up and put sugar in the tea, dropping in the lumps one by one.

'Crispin is coming back,' she said. 'He will be here on Sunday.'
It was as if she had struck him. The world went into slow motion — a record at the wrong speed.

'I'm sorry,' she said. 'I expect we could work something out.' And as he didn't speak, 'We should be able to keep seeing each other — for a while...'

'You want me to SHARE you with him?' Robert could hardly control his voice. The stone shattered into piercing fragments.

'Well, he doesn't have to know,' she said.

'Why can't you tell him about us,' he said. 'Why can't you tell him? Oh God, Sasha, I love you so much…'

'We're getting married in June,' she said. 'It's all arranged — the church, reception, my dress, the honeymoon… I'm sorry, really sorry. We could go on seeing each other.'

'I can't share you with anybody,' he said. 'And how could you consider sharing yourself? One night with me, one night with him. For God's sake, Sasha!'

A wave of nausea hit him.

He stood in the bathroom shaking with cold, struggling with his clothes. She didn't love him. If she loved him she would cancel the wedding, she would tell Crispin, she would live with him. She didn't love him.

'Please,' she said. 'We've had lots of fun — it's been great — really — you're a terrific lover' — and 'I'll miss you, really. I'll miss you a lot.'

It was raining heavily when he left the house in Cranley Gardens — a fine beaded curtain — coloured by the lights from shop windows, traffic lights, headlamps.

His whole body wept — the wetness of the rain on his face indistinguishable from tears.

He took the back streets to Victoria oblivious to the drenching downpour. Up Cale Street, Elystan Place, across Sloane Square to Chester Row, Eccleston Street, down Buckingham Palace Road, his feet treading the familiar route without guidance.

He went into the bar on the station, and ordered a double brandy.

He was soaked, water ran down his neck, pools forming on the table from his coat sleeves.

He sat there a long time, unable to move, and then like a blind man groped his way out into the icy wet night.

He walked, all the way along the river to Fleet Street, alive with printers and journalists, and men who worked the cumbersome inky presses, stamping out tomorrow's headlines.

He walked to St Paul's, and on down to the Monument, trying to cope with his misery and pain.

He took a taxi to Alan and Mandy's. It was five in the morning.

Alan answered the door, bleary and crumpled with sleep.
'Good God!' he said, standing aside to let Robert in. 'Whatever has happened?'

They were kind. Alan insisted he should go to bed. 'I'll tell them you're ill,' he said.
Mandy brought him sweet strong tea.

Alan told them Robert had flu. He went to Horley to speak to Laura and fetch Robert's things.
Laura phoned, sobbing, to say she was going to get a divorce.

He spent the days walking the streets, being careful to avoid anywhere he might run into her. Nights he lay sleepless, staring into the dark.

Twice he tried to phone her, once there was no reply, the second time a man answered. He replaced the receiver without speaking.
He wrote several letters and tore them up, and then wrote to say he loved her — would always be there if she changed her mind, and that, and that, he loved her.

'Stay as long as you like,' said Alan.
But he needed to be alone.
He found a small flat at the top of a house in Sutherland Avenue. It was shabby, but had all he needed. The tops of the plane trees almost brushed the windows.

Alan and Mandy helped him move in, bringing groceries and linen.

They stood uncertain. 'Are you sure you'll be alright?' said Alan. 'Do take care,' said Mandy.

He wrote telling her of his new address, and how much he loved her.

Sheila phoned from Personnel to say they had not had a 'sick' note.

He returned to work, empty and rotten, like a decaying tree trunk, the stone embedded in the crumbling mess. He was glad of the winter darkness, hiding his pain from the dimly surging crowds, turning his eyes away from the first tentative signs of Spring.

He started looking again in the Situations Vacant columns. He would have to get away from here. He couldn't bear the thought of perhaps bumping into her, of being again a stranger...

Kathy brought fragile narcissi into the office, the scent overwhelmingly fresh and poignant.

Alan found him in the cloakroom, leaning against the wall, ashen-faced.
'Are you OK old chap?' he said.
'Yes,' said Robert. 'Yes thanks, just felt a bit dizzy.'
Alan fetched him strong coffee, and sent one of the juniors to get a sandwich from the canteen.
'When did you eat?' he said. 'You'll make yourself ill. Look, I know it's tough, but try not to take it so hard.'

*   *   *

He saw the ad in the Domestic and Catering Situations in *The Times*, next to Rentals and Births and Deaths.

WANTED:
Capable person to help run bar/restaurant on French Atlantic coast.
Some French useful. Interviews London.

He came out of the Underground at South Kensington into the grey drizzle of a February afternoon. People hurried, hunched under umbrellas, collars turned up, eyes down to the rain-greased pavement.

The interview was at the Queens Hotel in Clareville Street. It meant going past Cranley Gardens. There was no chance he would see her. she would be at work.

He had to pass the little restaurant where they had so often come to eat.
He stopped outside — the lighted interior friendly, welcoming — woven together, a single heartbeat, his arms holding her.
The stone melted into a molten, tingling stream.
Reaching for her hand, he had knocked over the carnation in its little vase on the table. She had picked it up, holding it to her face, her lips soft as its petals, her eyes full of love.
The waiter had mopped up the water and brought her a long-stemmed red rose, which he laid by her plate, with a little bow.

He wanted to shout his misery — to punch his way out of this cage of hopelessness.
He walked away, an injured man, almost limping, crossing over to avoid Cranley Gardens.

The interview went well. Imogen and Chris Lewis, a hearty couple in their forties. They were expanding their restaurant — very busy in the summer, and off-season business increasing all the time.
It was arranged that he should fly over as soon as he could, and have a look at the place before deciding.

He tried to phone her from South Kensington.
Standing in the smelly, scrawled phone box, sweating, his head thudding, he dialled her office number.
'Miss Pemberton is not in her office at the moment,' said the operator. 'Can I give her a message.'
'No,' he said. 'Thanks — no message.'

He wrote to tell her of his plans — and how much he loved her.

He sent in his letter of resignation.

Alan was appalled. 'Don't do it old chap,' he said.
Sir Cuthbert's secretary, Enid, came looking for him.
'He wants to see you,' she said. She was unobtrusively well-groomed, as if she had just come from the hairdresser. Robert followed her up the corridor to Sir Cuthbert's office, the thick red carpet deadening their footsteps.

Sir Cuthbert was standing at the window. It was raining. The white plumes of the Queen's Life Guard on duty opposite, hung bedraggled against their gold helmets — the black horses restive — shaking the water out of their eyes.

His letter lay open on the leather-topped desk.

Sir Cuthbert turned and looked at him.
He was a big man — tall and muscular.
He wore pink shirts and his regimental tie.

'What's this all about, Fellowes?' he said, indicating the letter, and gesturing for Robert to sit down.

Robert eased himself into a leather-armed chair by the desk. He didn't answer.

'I understand you are having some kind of domestic difficulties? He paused. 'We really can't afford to let good men like you go.' He frowned, and looked down at the letter.
'I can arrange for you to have up to a year's sabbatical — on full pay, of course. That should give you time to put your affairs in order. Don't want to do anything hasty, do we?' He picked the letter up and tore it into little pieces, dropping it into the waste-paper basket with the departmental crest on the side. 'We'll just forget all about that,' he said. 'Let me know when you want to go.'

Enid said she hoped everything was alright. She stood nervously clutching a folder — her pleasant face puckered.

'Yes,' said Robert. 'Everything's fine.'
'Oh, I'm glad,' she said, and 'I do hope everything works out for you.'

He didn't go back to the office, but straight out into Whitehall.
He had been reprieved. He did not have to make irrevocable decisions. He could go away and try to put his life back together.
He turned left towards Parliament Square, crossing over at the Cenotaph and down Great George Street to St James's Park. The lake was scabbed by the rain — the ducks huddled, dishevelled among the scrubby bushes.

The seat where they had first met was wet and dirty.
He sat down. Nothing mattered anymore.
He felt remembered sun on his face — her presence, warm and golden, beside him, smiling the wonderful smile as he retrieved her flowered hat.
He put a hand over his eyes.

*   *   *

The salty wind came tearing across the sea, whisking the rolling waves to a tumble of foam.
The pale, clean sand stretching its moon path, way into the distance, scattered with thick, tawny seaweed.

The beach was deserted — the holiday flats shuttered and empty, the cafés along the promenade closed, the chairs stacked behind their glass doors, hotel signs switched off. He walked in the pine woods — feet sinking into the mounds of fine, soft sand. There was no-one.

Here he could heal — perhaps.
He would be able to return stronger — perhaps — after the summer when she would officially belong to someone else.

It was too soon to believe he would ever stop loving her.

The Food of Love

She was to meet Godfrey in the foyer of the Royal Festival Hall. It was a Brahms concert. Godfrey was crazy about Brahms. She wished he was not called Godfrey. It wasn't the sort of name that could be shortened. She could hardly call him God...

She went into Waterstone's Bookshop and looked at the current bestsellers. She did not read much. She enjoyed the occasional thriller, and bought the *Daily Mail* every day on the way to work.

Godfrey fetched salt beef sandwiches and a glass of sour wine from the sandwich bar. The sandwiches were cumbersome, bits of yellow fat sticking out from the sides. She cut hers carefully into small pieces. Godfrey wolfed his down. She avoided looking at him. He was over-tall, and over-thin, his sinewed neck at a loss in his over-large shirt collar. He had tied his tie in a strangulated knot, the ends uneven, the narrow end hanging some way below the thick end. His cheap suit irrevocably creased at the knees and elbows, was a light brown check, his shirt a washed out blue. His enthusiasm for music was boundless.

Her mother had named her Joan after Joan Fontaine. At the age of 17 in the turbulent unsettled year of 1940 she had seen her and Laurence Olivier in 'Rebecca'. Thereafter her dream was to find someone as broodily romantic.

Joan's father could not have been in more striking contrast. Small and dapper with thin sandy hair smoothly combed, and shirtsleeves kept in place by rubber bands, diamond-patterned socks and a spotless ironed white handkerchief. His name was Sydney, shortened to Sid by his friends. Her mother always called him Sydney.

Her mother had joined the ATS and worked as a typist in the Communications Section at Sevenoaks. Her father in the army, rose to the rank of Corporal, serving in the desert, invalided out after being wounded on the Normandy beaches.

They met after the war at a reunion dance at the Regimental Headquarters in Aldershot. By that time her mother, beginning to be concerned about being left on the shelf, was prepared to relinquish her dream of a dashing Olivier look-a-like, and settle for the steady affection of a 'good man', and security.

They became engaged in 1950, but did not marry until 1953 when they were allotted a council flat in Edmonton. Three years later Joan was born.

Despite her mother's efforts, Joan remained unalterably plain. Edna's hopes of her daughter as another Shirley Temple, or perhaps when she was a little older, Deanna Durbin, were not to be fulfilled.

Joan attended dancing class every Thursday afternoon after school. In white socks and pink woollen knit, her steel-curlered hair limply corkscrewed, she was ungainly and unrhythmic, driving the ever patient Miss Grimswold to exasperation. Rotund and greying, in short red pleated skirt and black leotard, she demonstrated the steps, one hip jutting incongruously higher than the other.

Miss Grove, her pianist, sucking mints, pounded her way through the repetitive music, smiling vaguely at the class from her elevated position on the dusty platform at the back of the hall. She wore decorated jumpers and fur-lined boots, her face made up like an elderly doll.

They progressed through Fairies in the Dell to the Gay Gordons, encompassing Bulgarian folk dancing and the intricacies of the Quick Step.

Joan tried hard. She really wanted to be a good dancer, but never seemed to get it right. The other girls' hair stayed curled and their socks stayed up.

Then there were the elocution lessons. They were worse. The gimlet-eyed Miss Hatton, owner of several bad tempered cats, in her bead-curtained drawing room, threatening to fill her mouth with marbles from the dish by her chair, whilst the green-eyed Prinnie watched her malevolently from a tapestry pouffe by her feet. Here she had to recite suitable verse, enunciating and articulating to produce a cultivated sound.

At school she sat at the back of the class hoping nobody would notice her. She spent most playtimes in the cloakroom. She made few friends.

By the time she was eleven her mother had given up the struggle. She put the money saved to better use — new curtains for the lounge-diner, bus rides 'up to town', occasional visits to the cinema.

Godfrey had spilt greasy juice on the lapel of his jacket. She did not like to point it out, chewing politely with her mouth shut.

The strip-lighting in the office gave her a headache. They had knocked down the protective walls, and made it open plan.

She had enjoyed her cosy office, with the worn desk, calendar of the Lake District, and holiday cards of Benidorm and Crete. Here she had eaten her sandwiches instead of going to the canteen, and had her tea from her brown Thermos flask.

Now exposed to the flourescent-lit edges of the room, privacy was no longer possible.

Mr Carstair's secretary, Miss Bean, sat by the glass door to the Executive Suite, vetting visitors and distributing work among 'the girls'. Joan had been there longest, apart from Miss Bean, who wore grey flannel and a monogrammed gold brooch. Her nails polished pearly pink, and fine colourless stockings.

The other girls came and went, never staying very long. Thin or fat, uniformly mini-skirted, high booted, with studs or outsize earrings, chewing gum, or smoking Rothmans Lights, and their hair!

Joan wished she could emulate their casual attitude. Their instant familiarity. Mr Carstairs and Miss Bean — Hugh and Susan. Chatting on the phone, chatting to each other, extending their lunch hours, arriving late, leaving early, eating at their desks.

'You won't mind staying late Joan, will you?' Miss Bean would say, handing her last minute letters to type.

Godfrey was telling her about a new recording of Beethoven's 9th Symphony.

Godfrey lived in a boarding house in Kentish Town. Meals were provided, except at weekends, and the rooms were cleaned and sheets changed. Each room was numbered, and there were two bathrooms on each landing. Guests could be invited to supper, if advance notice was given.

Joan had had supper there. Lamb stew — carrots and pearl barley, the small pieces of fatty meat concealing sharp pointed bones. Bowls of gritty rice pudding decorated with circular blobs of scarlet jam. Nasty grey coffee. She added three lumps of sugar.

Godfrey ate nervously, coyly served a second helping of stew by the formidable landlady, who from her size must have had an alternative supply of food. They ate in silence, with the other assorted residents.

Godfrey had a number of flexi-shelved bookcases, shakily overburdened with records. His room had a down at heel Do-It-Yourself appearance, the odd pictures scattered at strange heights, hiding holes in the wall where fixtures had fallen away. There was an ineffective radiator under the window, which ran with condensation, leaving dirty streaks and sodden curtain ends.

She had gone to tea one Saturday to hear some of his records. The tea was weak, the milk rising to the top in rancid strips, the cake which he produced from a tin under the bed, stale.

She had sat primly on the edge of the one armchair, whose springs had long ago gone into retirement, sipping the unpleasant brew, and trying to show the proper enthusiasm for Mahler's 6th. Godfrey had a magnificent and expensive hi-fi system, and sat, eyes closed, fingers drumming in isolated ecstasy.

She had met Godfrey at a Tchaikovsky concert. Unable to get a seat, they were standing next to each other at the side of the auditorium. Godfrey had become very excited, beating time with his feet and waving his arms. He had bumped into her. Apologising profusely he had offered to buy her a drink at the interval.

They met regularly now, sharing an interest, overwhelming for Godfrey, enjoyable and restful for Joan.

Joan had never really had a boyfriend. She wasn't at all sure that she wanted one. She turned her mind away from the thought of what a physical relationship would mean. She couldn't imagine herself unclothed, or any of the men of her acquaintance either. To be actually with someone unclothed was unimaginably awful!

Once at an office party, one of the men had forced her into a corner fondling her with searching hands — sloppy lips on her neck. She had kicked him hard on the shins, and then gone to the ladies cloakroom to retch in a basin.

Apart from Godfrey there had really only been Robin.

After her mother had finally agreed, reluctantly, to her leaving home — after all she was nearly thirty — they had gone for a week's holiday in Brighton.

Joan's father had died two years previously, succumbing to the long-term effects of his war wound and an over-zealous intake of medicinal brandy.

After the initial shock Edna had settled down to a comfortable widowhood. It was a relief really. She preferred her romance from the pages of Mills and Boon. It was more satisfactory, and less messy.

Joan suggested the week together in Brighton to show there were no hard feelings about her leaving.

It was out of season. The stony tar-stained beach deserted. The ice cream and candy floss stalls shuttered, except for one on the border with Hove, which sold tea in thin plastic mugs as well as ice cream, and sticks of rock. The outside decorated with limp flags and hats bearing jaunty slogans. Joan and Edna huddled together in the draughty concrete shelter watching the brownish waves slop onto the beach.

Elderly couples battled against the wind, and ladies in old-fashioned furs promenaded their dogs.

The West Pier, a rusty skeleton, the ballroom tipping towards the sea, was chained off with a notice warning of the 'Dangerous Structure'.

The Palace Pier, scrubbed and bare, music blaring stridently from the depressingly garish Amusement Arcades. A few youths, much-buckled, with shaven heads and ringed ears, disconsolately feeding their dole money into the fruit machines.

Tattered posters announcing the end of Pier Entertainment flapped against the blistered railings. A group of men obscured by woollen hats and scarves fished over the side.

The hotel was also practically empty. Their narrow room with blue flowered bedspreads and skimpy matching curtains overlooked the neighbouring wall and fire escape. It was possible to glimpse the sea, if you leant far enough out of the window.

Robin and his mother were also staying there. They lived together in Raynes Park. She had the stiff demeanour of a body restrained by corsetry. Her feet bulged in her white K shoes.

Robin was fair and slightly chubby. He wore short sleeved shirts, pale fawn slacks and a light brown ribbed cardigan with leather buttons.

The mothers had eyed each other suspiciously over the tinned grapefruit segments — passing swift, critical judgement on each other's offspring.

Robin was a careful eater, slowly chewing the stringy bacon and pale tasteless sausages. He used a lot of ketchup.

There were two other guests. Miss Montagu, who was a permanent resident. She had her own napkin with a raffia napkin ring, and her own jar of marmalade, labelled with her name. She spoke to no-one and read a closely printed hardback book with a leather bookmark.

The other guest was a paunchy elderly gentleman, who sucked on a pipe and propped the *Daily Telegraph* against the teapot.

Mrs Cousins provided breakfast and dinner. At lunch they would have a film-wrapped sandwich at one of the cafés on the Front.

One day they had fish and chips.

One day they took a bus to Rottingdean and had poached egg on welsh rarebit in a beamed Tea Shoppe.

Edna bought cards of the Pavilion to send to her few friends, and her brother and sister in law in Sunderland. She talked about taking a package holiday to the Costa Brava the next summer. Everybody she knew went to the Costa Brava.

They had supper in the chilly dark dining room. It was full of knick-knacks and dusty plastic flowers. A string of fairy lights ornamented the mantelpiece. Mrs Cousins served the meal herself, it was not worth her while to employ anybody to help after the season was over. She presented the food with a flourish, a white serviette over her arm. Tinned soup, gristly stew, grey slices of lamb, indistinguishable vegetables — tinned fruit and custard. After supper they would gather in the 'lounge' to watch television.

On the last evening Robin suggested they should go out for a drink, and get a last breath of sea air.

The mothers, pretending a deep interest in a programme about Tibet, (they would both have preferred to watch 'Boon' on the other side), avoided looking at each other.

Robin's mother was knitting a long green garment. Edna didn't knit. She had given up hope of Joan getting married, she was really too old, still there was always a chance she might find someone.

Robin worked in Insurance, in the claims department of a big firm with offices near Smithfield Market.

They started spending the occasional evening together, going to a film at the Barbican, or an Indian meal, which gave Joan terrible indigestion.

Robin was very bound up with his mother. They went everywhere together. She resented the few evenings he spent with Joan, and on the few occasions she had visited their dismal semi on Sunday for tea, constantly used the proprietory 'we'.

'We are thinking of going to Ibiza next year.'
'We are going to get a new three-piece-suite in the Arding & Hobbs sale.'
'We are going to redecorate the kitchen red and cream.'

Robin seemed well pleased with his situation, being fussed over and admired. His mother attended to all his comforts, cutting the crusts off the bread and sugaring his tea, laying out his freshly ironed clothes.

She watched them carefully for any 'dangerous' signs, and remembered to develop a painful limp when any activity was mentioned that didn't include her. She would smile a syrupy smile and go on about 'You young things!' in a wistful voice.

They really had nothing to say to each other, nothing in common.

Their meetings gradually petered out.

Godfrey seldom went home. His parents lived in Leicester. He explained that they did not care for music. His mother liked Frank Ifield, and his father didn't mind Peter Dawson singing the 'Floral Dance', but that wasn't music!

As a young boy he had gone with his class from school to a performance of Handel's Messiah, and had been completely overwhelmed. Music had become his great passion.

There had been nothing remotely sexual about her relationship with Robin, any more than there was anything remotely sexual about her relationship with Godfrey.

Edna nagged her on the telephone, warning her about 'time flying' and how it would be nice to see her settled before she died. She obviously did not hold out much hope for her daughter, but felt it her duty to try.

Thinking of Robin's clammy hands and plump thighs, Godfrey's bony agitated swallowing, Joan shuddered.

The performance of the Brahms 4th Symphony was particularly exhilarating. They had seats in the Grand Tier. Godfrey rose to his feet to applaud, shouting 'Bravo!' and 'Encore!' as the conductor returned for the third time, bowing deeply, tossing his hair back, gesturing to the Orchestra to rise, shaking hands with the Leader.

They travelled together on the Northern Line to Charing Cross, where Joan changed to the Jubilee Line for Finchley Road. Godfrey walked fast. She had to hurry to keep up. It had been raining and she tried to a avoid treading in the puddles with her best black court shoes.

A few wet bundles crouched under the bridge. Joan stopped to give something to a dripping flute player.

Godfrey was talking as they hurried along.

There was to be a performance of Traviata on the television. Of course he would not be able to see it. There was a television in the communal sitting room, but nobody would want to watch Traviata. Nobody ever watched anything serious apart from the News.

Joan said perhaps he could come and watch it on hers, and then felt uncomfortable. He had never been to her room. She didn't want him getting ideas. Why had she suggested it? It was already too late. Godfrey greeted the idea enthusiastically. Joan said perhaps he would like to have some supper.

She was very pleased with her bedsitting room. On the first floor of a square house in a leafy street behind Finchley Road, it had its own kitchenette with small fridge and cooker. She shared the bathroom with the two people on the 2nd floor. A handsome freckled girl with red tangled hair. She watched late night movies on the television, sounds of screams and gun fire the music swelling to a dramatic crescendo, the ceiling alive with imagined incidents.

On the other side of the landing was a Japanese student, noiselessly polite, bowing with lowered head when passed on the stairs. His presence only detected by the pungent aroma of dried fish.

The ground floor was occupied by Bridget McCahon. By the amount of sodden bags of empty bottles by the dustbin each week, it was apparent that she drank a great deal. Mostly sherry. She had two black cats, Montagu and Nixon, for whom she left saucers of mouldering rabbit on the front step.

She lurked drunkenly — ready to intercept anyone entering the house.

It took some skill to avoid her.

She had made her room as homely as she could, buying her own curtains and cover for the bed in a Laura Ashley print with little pink flowers. She had a rather nice framed photograph of the Alps, and a small print of a bowl of apples. There were two uncomfortable easy chairs and a scratched bookcase. She had a boxed set of Jane Austen, which she had never read, a few nondescript novels, several Agatha Christie, *Cooking for One*, which her mother had bought her, a book on the care of house plants — she had a small pot of ivy, and straggling Tradescantia — and the *Penguin Lives of the Great Composers* that Godfrey had given her for her birthday.

She decided to make a casserole. She was not a good cook, but you couldn't really go wrong with a casserole. She would prepare it the night before, and get a nice bit of Danish blue and some crème caramel from Safeway's.

She had her hair done at Eve's Hairdressing Salon in Fairfax Road. Every six months she had her hair tightly permed, so it would last, and then set it herself.

As this was a special occasion, she went for a rare shampoo and set.

Sharon's pink nylon overall was a size too small — combs and scissors sticking out of the torn pockets.

She chewed gum as she pinned Joan's hair, the bangles on her wrists rattling against each other. Her long red nails scratching Joan's scalp.

She emerged frizzed and hot-faced, her hair stiff with lacquer. She bought a bottle of Hock in the Victoria Wine.

They sat together on the divan, the cushions artfully arranged to give the appearance of a sofa.

The meal had been successful. Godfrey had gulped down the food and wine with relish. They did not speak much as the opera had already started.

There had been an awkward moment when Godfrey arrived. Joan had been watching from the window ready to rush down before

Bridget could waylay him. Unfortunately Godfrey had tripped over one of the cats, bringing Bridget swearing into the hall. He brought Joan half a pound of Cadbury's Milk Tray.

She served coffee in her blue Denby cups. She had remembered to get a box of After Eights.

He said the whole evening had been delightful. He hadn't cared much for the soprano, she was too fat. But the production had been first class, the orchestra well balanced, and the tenor very acceptable.

Suddenly, turning towards her, he embraced her fiercely. Joan was filled with horror. The wet lips on hers, hands fumbling with her blouse. She pushed him off — forcibly holding him away from her.

He was breathing deeply — slightly taken aback. He got up abruptly, and took his drab gabardine raincoat off the hook behind the door, sticking his long bony arms into the too short sleeves. There was a button hanging loose.

'Well… Goodnight then,' he said, and 'Thanks very much…'

She heard him stumble on the dark stairs. She took a Kleenex and wiped the strange saliva from her mouth. She was trembling, filled with disgust. Never again, she thought.

She took the cups into the kitchenette. There was enough casserole left for tomorrow. She transferred it to a smaller bowl.

Of course she should never have asked him to her room, but she'd been to his room and it had been alright. She felt unaccountably guilty. She hadn't wanted to upset him. Her mother was right. She was not the marrying kind. She was better off as she was. She preferred it that way.

She washed the dishes, putting everything away in its proper place, before turning out the light.

Shadows

So this was how it was to be — the Sister, kindly, slightly greying, said they would have to try for a vein in the other arm, it was difficult to find one in the much-used left arm to put the drip in.

In the bed opposite, Mrs Kerr was complaining again. She tried not to listen, groping painfully for her earphones which had slipped down the side of the pillow. She was very weak. Mrs Kerr was saying she was going to refuse to take any more pills, they were trying to poison her. She had a bottle of whisky in her bedside table with which she enhanced the plastic cups of tea and coffee, wheeled round by the large gloomy dark-skinned ward orderly.

She had this strange feeling of not belonging to her own body anymore, as if it was a separate person that had to be looked after separately.

Patricia had brought flowers and a pretty bottle of moisturiser. The back of her arms were flaking where the skin had rubbed on the sheets. Pat sat on the brown plastic chair beside the bed, and told her how slow the buses had been. She could see the sky outside, grey and overcast, and wished to sleep. Her arm hurt and somewhere the pain inside moved making her wince.

Pat talked on, her eyes worried. The thin nurse with the spiky hair was on duty, she came to check her drip. Pat got up to leave. 'You're better off here in the warm' she said brightly as she put on her coat, and bent briefly to kiss her friend.

She managed to pull the bed table towards her. The orderly had put the supper tray down, but had not pushed the table near enough. There was fish and a round mound of mashed potato and carrots under the metal cover. She used a spoon, breaking the fish into small pieces and eating it very slowly. There was a plate of sponge pudding with custard. She enjoyed the comforting sweetness, but couldn't finish it. The effort was exhausting and she needed to go to the bathroom. She swung her legs round and pulling the drip behind on its wheeled base, she managed to make her way across the small ward. The pain made her sweat and shake — she eased herself carefully back onto the bed.

There were five beds in the ward. Opposite Mrs Kerr made up her face, ravaged by illness, bizarrely highlighted. The wide ribbon at the top of her nightdress drawing attention to the shrivelled neck. She kept up an endless chatter, mostly complaining. Fortunately she was a smoker, and made frequent sorties out of the ward to have an illicit cigarette.

Gladys, next to Mrs Kerr wore turquoise jogging pyjamas. She had many visitors, noisy women in tight black pants and mock ocelot coats, jangling many gilt chains. They came laden with cellophane wrapped baskets of fruit, fluffy bedroom slippers, beribboned boxes of chocolates. They stayed for many hours eating sandwiches, leaning together to gossip.

Next to her, Mary — younger with dark curly hair. She wore short flowered nighties and her visitors brought quantities of magazines, tins of sweets and perfumed sprays.

She knew she would be transferred soon. Mr Carruthers had said it would be best. This ward was for people passing through, on their way back hopefully to better health and a prolonged life. She was not sure how she stood, but she was to go to a more permanent ward. They would try to contain her illness and then send her home. She closed her eyes and saw her blue room — her pictures — her pillows. She was very tired.

Cynthia came, awkward and hot in her sensible tweed suit and pearl-buttoned blouse. She asked if she would soon be coming home, and told her that neither of her boys had done any revision, and would fail their exams, and that Michael was very angry. They had spent so much on their schooling.

She had had difficulty parking the car. It was ridiculous not to have planned a car park when they built the hospital. Still, there were nice shops downstairs, and a hairdressers. Quite a surprise!

She avoided asking Celia about the operation. She had brought grapes in a brown paper bag.
She asked about Anthony, and how Derek was coping.
She couldn't stay long. She had to go and pick up the boys from a rehearsal. They were both in the school play. Only small parts, but at least it pleased Michael that they were participating and not sitting at home in front of the television, littering the carpet with crisp packets and Coca Cola tins, or smoking in their rooms whilst listening to Punk or Funk Rock, whatever it was called.

Derek was annoyed. His plane had been delayed, and the hotel dining room was closed. The hurriedly eaten beef and cheese sandwiches heavy on his stomach.

He came into the Ward in his pin-striped business suit carrying a bunch of chrysanthemums.

She wondered why he bothered to come. He could have made an excuse and gone home to bed. He treated her illness with the same irritation he had shown with everything she had done throughout most of their married life. It was an inconvenience, as if she had done it on purpose.

His trip had not been very successful. His Italian counterparts unpunctual and badly informed. The airless hotel room, jarred by traffic noise. The restaurant expensively nondescript. He voiced his complaints and left, patting her briefly on the arm.

They had not really said how ill she was. She surmised from the kindly consideration she received from Mr Carruthers and his young earnest Registrar Dr Coombes, that she must be quite bad. They stood unhurried by her bed, not asking how she was, Sister silently holding her clip board.

She wondered if they had told Derek. He only seemed concerned about the lack of socks in his drawer, and that the fool milkman had not read his note, and there was all this stale milk to throw away.

She had hoped Anthony might come. Since he and Emma had moved to Leeds last year she had only seen them once.
He had sent flowers and a card. Get Well Soon, love Anthony and Emma. She had wanted to weep.

Illness was a lonely business. In the increasingly bitter years she had yearned for solitude, but not like this. She had never thought about dying. Life took up all her time.

The pretty staff nurse came round with the drugs trolley. She tried to persuade Mrs Kerr to have a sleeping tablet. She was in the habit of constantly ringing her bell during the night, disturbing the rest of the ward.

Mary said they ought to insist. Selfish old woman!
She complained about the uncomfortable bed. The mattress was too thin. Her husband brought in pillows from home.
Her children had been to see her. Bouncingly healthy teenagers, the boy serious, the girl laughing, even white teeth in her rosy face, leaning to whisper, bringing clean nighties in a Sainsbury's carrier bag.

The male nurse, Chris, efficient and helpful, came with the night drinks. She was grateful for the tea, drinking it very slowly because of the pain.
Chris asked if she needed anything, noting her wince, straightening the pillows deftly, easing her gently against them.
He was younger than Anthony, his hair dark and curly, a gold chain on his wrist.

He had taken her on the high 'Theatre' bed in the lift for the operation, her hair hidden by the white cap.

Now he fetched a plate for the grapes and a vase for the chrysanthemums.

She welcomed the long darkness of the nights — had begun to live in dreams — to wake choked and tired to the next day's emptiness. The aching burden of the morning weighed her down.

In her dreams she searched in vain, wandering dry-throated through gossamer woods and sky-scrapered cities — stumbling in crowds, always searching, always late, always lost...

The desert stretched behind her, dotted with oases, the silent glint of water and green-palmed trees. In front of her, rolling, shifting sands.

She slept fitfully — lurched into wakefulness by the spreading pain. She rang her bell and Chris came. She needed help to go to the bathroom. She could hardly speak.
When he had got her back to bed, he gave her a painkilling injection.
He stood by the bed holding the empty syringe.
'Try to sleep,' he said.

She closed her eyes to contain the pain. Images flickered and faded, like an old home movie — jerky — disconnected.
A soft fragrant mound of newly mown grass, seductively green, warm to the touch.
Splitting open the cotton wool pods of broad beans, dropping the smooth pale beans into a white bowl.
Anthony on his red tricycle.
The Spanish Steps cascading azaleas.
Round golden gnocchi for lunch at the Pensione on the third floor of an old Palazzo, a glass dish of parmesan to sprinkle on them.
Derek playing cricket with Anthony on the lawn, showing him how to hold the bat.
Real strawberry ice cream.
The fountains in the Piazza Navona.
Walking arm in arm with Derek in the Galeria Vittoria Emanuele in Milan. The cold wind lifting the cafe tablecloths.
Hand in hand on the bus to Lake Maggiore in the driving rain. The wide windscreen wipers sweeping the water from side to side.
Stopping for overpriced hot chocolate and crumbly macaroons at a shiny plastic cafe by the lake.

The sulpherous glow of factory chimneys as the Night Express slowed through Lyon.
Champagne on the flight from Paris, wearing an expensive primrose yellow coat and matching gloves.
Derek bought her yellow roses.
The hotel room high up, overlooking the Arc de Triomphe.

Mary came and stood by her bed. She was wearing a new white towelling dressing gown and blue quilted slippers. She spoke kindly, comforting. It's bound to be bad for a few days — it would get better.

Celia drifted again.
Anthony on the beach, a little crab in his sea-filled bucket. His small body brown from the sun, his feet making wet imprints on the sand.
Derek carrying her over a bramble-tangled ditch.
They had grown apart. The strands of communication snapping — ever diminishing — until there were only memories and misunderstanding.

For years now they had occupied separate rooms. She had wanted it that way, withdrawing into defensive solitude.
It was too late now for regrets. The tenuous thread of contact had been broken forever.
They treated each other politely, as strangers…

Dr Coombes was doing the rounds on his own, anxious and distracted. He studied her chart, and asked if she was feeling any better.
She tried to smile.
He inspected the dressing and pronounced everything fine, and could she try to take more fluids. He told Sister to give her another injection.

She closed her eyes, the film flickering on.
With her brother Peter cycling down a hill, his feet on the handlebars, the hedges frothy with white thorn.
His wedding to Pamela. She awkwardly behind in pink puffed-sleeved satin and white net gloves, holding a bouquet of freesias, a

coronet of artificial rosebuds in her hair.

She wished he would come. Another Get Well card, a lavish bunch of carnations.

He only lived in Surbiton. Pamela had become increasingly stodgy, blinkered and smug. Amanda and Kate were now strapping teenagers, clever articulate girls, disdainful of their parents, particularly Pamela.

Chauffeured by their mother in the company Volvo Estate, from their privileged private school to various extra-curricular activities. Amanda to tap dancing, piano lessons and extra French. Kate to swimming, flute lessons and karate. She had also taken up rowing which meant early morning and weekend training.
Then of course, there was the dry ski run, to prepare them for their annual winter holiday in the French Alps.
Summers spent in a villa in the Algarve.
Pamela coped magnificently. Clothes bought from Principles, hair washed and set at Manuel's in the High Street, organizing Cheese and Wine parties and clothing sales for the PTA.

The spiky nurse came to say that Derek would not be coming this evening. He had a meeting.

Derek turned his back to speak to Cara in shimmering scarlet gown, placing a languid diamond-studded hand on his arm.

She could never be sure about Derek and Cara.
Sonny, Cara's husband, a large blond jovial man — wealthy — Saville Row suits — silver grey Mercedes.
He played squash with Derek every weekend, drinking back the weight they had lost at the bar of the plush Club.
Cara would join them there in her Designer casuals and much real jewellery.
Celia had been once — to the Christmas cocktail party. She had never enjoyed communal jollity, reluctantly donning the cardboard hat trimmed with tinsel.

Derek kissing Cara under the mistletoe, an unnecessarily lingering kiss. Their hands stayed clasped.
Slim, sequinned, her black hair a sleek cap. Cara was extremely lovely.

She made Celia feel drab, mousy, nondescript.
Later she noticed they were absent...

Mrs Kerr was shouting at young Dr Crisp. He had been instructed to replace her drip. The curtains drawn around the bed an ineffective privacy.

Gladys had been told she could go home in the morning.
'Thank God,' she said, 'I've just about had enough of *her*' — waving towards the heaving curtains. Her leather-clad visitors sniggered and carried on gossiping, helping themselves to Gladys's chocolates.

That weekend Derek had stayed on in Birmingham after a conference.
She knew Sonny had been in New York.
She was never sure... and then there was the business trip to Paris when Cara had gone to visit her mother in Exeter.

Cara in miniscule white bikini by the pool in their extensive garden in Esher — golden tanned, laughing in Derek's face, splashing him with water — pulling him down into the pool with her — their heads close, limbs entwined.

Celia hadn't cared to swim. She sat in the shade of the striped sun umbrella, cold spots of water splashing her legs, and pretended to read a book.
Sonny was indoors on the phone.

The Spanish maid brought drinks and a bowl of ice, placing them on the white wrought iron table under the umbrella.
Derek and Cara chased each other round the pool, flopping down beside her on the spread towels.
When Cara wrapped in a vast white towel, went into the house, Derek followed her...

'I don't know what you ordered for lunch,' said Mary, 'They seem to have forgotten my vegetables.'

Celia felt sick. Mary came over and pulled the table towards her.
'Can I help you sit up a bit?' she said.
Celia grasped her arm and managed to pull herself a little higher against the pillows.
'You should try and eat something,' said Mary.

She had asked for fish again — there was a white sauce — the effort was too much — she drank a little water and closed her eyes.

Sonny and Cara had gone to live in New York.

Now there was Derek's secretary Lisa — razor smart — impeccable groomed to the last blonde hair — silk shirts — shoes from Hobbs — discreetly perfumed.
She frequently accompanied Derek on his business trips.
One step behind, carrying his briefcase? Celia thought not.
She was always very polite.
'Mr Curtis is in a meeting I'm afraid, Mrs Curtis.'
'Mr Curtis says he will call you back Mrs Curtis.'

She dozed.

The perfume of crushed currant leaves.
Her birthday lunch at Gennaros — the small perfectly iced cake with pink candle, her name in pink sugar. Pearl studded earrings in a dark red box lined with red velvet.
If she could only bring back the touching and the laughter, gradually eroded… now gone.

Anthony in his school blazer.
Anthony in his graduation gown.
Derek was still disappointed he had not gone to Oxford.
He had met Emma at Manchester University. She was a pretty girl with curly dark hair and brown short-sighted eyes. She was always mislaying her glasses. She had very definite opinions, and was not

afraid to voice them. She had a 1st in Physics.
Anthony had only managed a 2:2 in Maths.

Derek was against the marriage. *Student romances never last — she
was bossy and looked like a gypsy.*
She wore long cotton skirts, ragged T-shirts, trainers and thick
woollen socks.
She made Celia nervous.

The wedding had been a small affair — only close family and a few
friends. They were married in the Registry Office in Devizes, which
was near Emma's home. There was a nice lunch at the local Country
Club, and then they went for two weeks' honeymoon to Crete.
Emma had bowed to convention, wearing a cream satin ankle length
dress, with high neck and long sleeves.
Her parents had seemed nice enough. Derek looked very
distinguished, but was in a hurry to return to London. He had an
important meeting.

Celia moved restlessly, bending her knees against the pain.

She walked by the Serpentine, the steady rain peppering the surface
of the water, delighted ducks shaking out their feathers.

She had come from the hospital, getting off the bus at Hyde Park
Corner, and walking into the park.

Mr Carruthers had said, 'I'm afraid it doesn't look very good,' and
then, 'Don't worry, we will do our best,' and instructed his Nurse,
crisp in the dark blue uniform, to get her admitted as soon as
possible.
She hadn't wanted to go straight home. Derek and Lisa had left for
Madrid the day before to attend a Conference, and would not be
back until Friday.

She walked, oblivious to the rain, breathing the wet leaves, calmed
by the familiar stretch of water, ignoring the niggling pain, crossing
the little bridge, turning down the other side to get a cup of tea at

the Serpentine Café…

As the afternoon darkened, Anna came. Cheerful and comfortable in her camel hair coat, her umbrella dripping.
She carried a dark green bowl of dark blue hyacinths, their wonderful fragrance surged with memories.
Anna had brought her hyacinths like these when Anthony was born.

It had been a difficult birth. They had got domestic help, but she still found it hard to cope.
She had resented Derek's absorption with his work, his late hours, the frequent phone calls from Diana, a 'business colleague', taken in the study with the doors closed…

Anna sat by the bed and took Celia's hand. For the first time the tears rolled slowly down her face.
Anna said, 'You'll be OK. They can do wonders nowadays,' and squeezed her hand.

Mrs Kerr had slipped getting out of bed to go for her smoke. She fell, a small heap of grubby quilted housecoat, dragging the tube of her drip, her cigarettes scattered on the floor. She lay groaning, calling feebly for the Nurse.

Anna went to help pick her up.
'I'm very ill you know,' said Mrs Kerr, pathetic with draggled self pity. 'They're trying to get rid of me, giving me all these pills.'
Anna said she was sure it wasn't true, gathering the cigarettes and replacing them in the packet.

Celia's arm hurt. Sister had said tomorrow they would remove the drip if all was well.
Anna said she would speak to Anthony — 'He must be able to take some time off' — took her nightdresses to wash, and said she would be back on Thursday.
She stood a moment, awkwardly unable to voice her feelings, she managed a reassuring smile.

Celia dozed again.

Anna had helped her get ready for her wedding. She had worn an oatmeal wool suit and small veiled hat with velvet bow.
Her mother had been there, frosty and disapproving, afraid that her daughter might already be pregnant, otherwise why the rush, why the registry office? She needn't have worried. It was three years before Anthony was born. Wearing a purple feathered hat and short mink jacket she remained unsmiling throughout.
Her father was tactfully absent, sending a cheque from himself and Rita.

Derek's mother and father objected to the Registry Office, saying it was not a proper marriage, and that it was much too far to come. They lived in Devon.

There was a commotion outside in the corridor. Two Indian gentlemen were arguing with the Sister. They were in the wrong ward. One of them had a heavily bandaged head, the other shouted and waved a handful of papers.

It was too painful to reach her earphones. She turned her head towards the windows... the hollow darkness.

The hotel bedroom had a balcony overlooking the lake.
The young waiter brought them breakfast. Fresh squeezed orange juice, coffee with cream in a fluted jug, warm rolls wrapped in a napkin, a dish of amber coloured jam.

It was too early in the year for real warmth. The air was clear and bright — the Lake — sapphire blue glass.

They had lunch in Verona with Derek's boss, Mr Pringle and his wife.
They ate in the overheated hotel dining room veal escalopes, pears with chocolate sauce.
Mrs Pringle drank a lot of wine. Her face was flat, her eyebrows plucked black arches, expensively coiffed blond hair.

She stared out of the window at the camellia flowered gardens, shiny with the rain that had started to fall, a fine persistent pressure on the glossy-leaved bushes.

Derek had been very pleased with the meeting, but not very pleased that she had talked so little, hardly speaking to Mrs Pringle, and was really annoyed when Celia intimated that she thought she was drunk. They returned to their hotel in frosty silence.

Was that the beginning of the distancing...?

The night staff had come on duty. The pretty staff nurse took her temperature, and studied her chart carefully, and then left the ward, taking the chart with her.

Mrs Kerr was complaining that nobody had come with the night drinks. 'You'd have thought she's had enough to drink,' said Mary sourly.

The staff nurse came back with a treacly liquid in a little glass. She said Celia had a slight temperature, and this would help to settle it. It was nothing to worry about.

Chris was discussing baking with Mary. He enjoyed cooking, particularly cakes. He thought he might go to Cake Decorating classes, but he never had the time. Mary said she had made all kinds of cakes when her children were young. One of the most successful had been a hedgehog. Chris said he was well known for his fruit cakes. It was the icing that was the problem.

She refused a sleeping tablet. She asked Chris to put the earphones where she could reach them. She would listen to the radio. She had all day to sleep.

They had gone to the Opera with the Pringles.
Mr Pringle had a box.
She had known the green dress was a mistake.
As she got in the car, Derek said she looked washed out, and then,

abruptly starting the car, 'Why on earth don't you use some make up?' Celia had applied her usual amount of pink lipstick. She had even brushed her lashes tentatively with mascara.
He took her arm as they mounted the red-carpeted staircase.
Mrs Pringle stepping with a drinker's care in her diamante embroidered shoes, her black velvet wrap trailing over her arm.
Mr Pringle bent to beam, noting Derek's affectionate support.
So many public showings of togetherness.

They moved her to a side ward. Her fever refused to come down. Mr Carruthers said not to worry, they would soon sort it out. They removed the drip and gave her another injection.

The side ward was stark and silent. There was a hand basin and a TV, as it was sometimes used for private patients.
She was shivering. A young nurse, who she didn't know, brought her a blanket, tucking it round her, covering her feet.

Gladys crept in to say Goodbye, and 'all the best'. She left a box of crystalised fruit on the side table next to the wondrous dark blue hyacinths.

She became worse during the day. The pain fused in an intensity that was overwhelming. She drifted in and out of consciousness, her dreams confused, overlapping past and present.

She had seen Derek and Annabel Cohen in the Burlington Arcade.
They were holding hands in front of a jewellers.
The shock hit her an icy blow.
She dodged quickly into the doorway of a knitwear shop. They hadn't seen her, it was lunchtime and the Arcade was crowded.

She had been on her yearly visit to the Summer Exhibition at the Royal Academy. It had been quite fun.

Berny Cohen, Derek's partner, clever, thin, serious. Annabel in skin tight cat suits, jewelled belts and extra high heels had never seemed a very compatible wife.

The mock Tudor house in Golders Green, furnished with leather, stainless steel and musical cigarette boxes.
The dinner parties. The food supplied by Harrods — jellied consommé, glazed ham, profiteroles — eaten by the light of silver candelabra, incongruous on the glass-topped, spiked-legged table.

Berny had come to see her. He had sat and wept. Annabel and Derek were having an affair, Annabel had taunted him with it.

Bernie had resigned. Celia never mentioned it to Derek, expressing surprise at Bernie's resignation.

What a coward she had been.

She longed for Anthony to come. She should have told him the truth. Perhaps Anna would tell him.

Lunch came, but she didn't even try to eat it. She sipped a little water, clenching her hands at the effort.

Mary came and sat with her. She was to go home the next day. She told Celia of the holiday they were planning, Greg had suggested a cruise. Her son was going on a skiing trip with his school to Austria, kids had so many opportunities these days. The new patient in the ward seemed quite nice.

Celia tried to say she wanted to see her son, but she didn't seem able to speak. She drifted.

They had hired a car, driving up into the hills behind Florence, and ate chicken and mushrooms at a restaurant jutting out over the rocky valley with silvered slopes of wizened olive trees.
Sister came with Dr Coombes. She couldn't understand what they were saying. She wished they wouldn't mumble.
Chris came and held her hand.

As darkness fell Mr Carruthers came, but she could not hear what he said either... his face kept fading into the wall.

She was in her own bed. The leafy branches of the silver birch outside her window transparent green in the sunlight. There was a round bowl of mauve and dark red pansies on the dressing table. Anthony laughed at her from the silver framed photograph, holding the tennis cup.

Derek and Anna came together. She tried to smile... to speak. They sat on either side of her. Anna was crying. Derek a stiff blurred outline.

She walked the chalky cliff path, fighting against the tearing wind. Huge tawny waves curled and crashed on the rocks below. Seagulls whirled and swooped. She was very cold.

The pain had gone. She felt light and strange.
Anthony was there in the jeans and red lumberjack shirt that he had worn on holiday in Germany... and Peter in cricket flannels, tanned from the sun. Her mother stood behind them in flowered cotton dress, slim and young... and Derek... why was he wearing a Paisley dressing gown? He was smiling at her... with his eyes.

She held out her hands to Derek... to Anthony.
The tiredness weighed down on her, dragging her back into the pillows... into silent darkness.

When the Sister came, she stood quietly by the bed for a few moments before gently pulling the sheet over her face, and going to fetch young Dr Crisp.

Griffin

His head was razor sharp — the thin colourless mouth scummed with saliva — the nose a raw bone — a ragged scar across his cheek from a pub brawl.
There had been broken glass, and a lot of blood. He had been too drunk to remember.

He put his foot, smart in the new Adidas trainer, on the tip-up seat at the bus stop — balancing his can of lager.
He had earphones — slipping against his gristly ears — translucent in the late October sunlight. The music was very loud — numbingly loud. Griffin liked it very loud — the crashing drums and shrieking synthesizers taking over his head — inciting violence. Gouged eyes — the deep purple bruising of splintered limbs.

He swayed to the thudding beat — his body whippet thin. His jeans clean — pale blue.

He was drunk.

If he got on the right bus, he would be home before 4 o'clock — before the kids came home from school.
He bowed elaborately, and stood aside to let a woman get on the bus in front of him — tarty bitch in her too-tight skirt and rickety heels — the fabric stretched — creasing on her heavy thighs.
He could think of all sorts of things he'd like to do to her.

He had a room in a blind rundown house, in a street of blind rundown houses near Harrow Road — with flaking plaster, and non-existent paint — the basement areas stuffed with rubbish — black plastic bags torn apart by cats.

He had to go downstairs to the basement to the toilet and stone sink he shared with Mrs O'Sullivan — slovenly in a shrunken wool dressing gown dribbled with food, over a soiled winceyette nightdress — or a shrunken wool cardigan dribbled with food, over a soiled, shrunken dark brown wool dress.

There was a single cold tap, and a temperamental gas water heater which spat boiling water and jets of steam.

The rest of the basement was uninhabitable and boarded up.

There were two kids in the room above — rude noisy kids…

One day he would deal with them. One day…

Across the hall Mrs O'Sullivan's TV jabbered — she, greedily watching the comings and goings from behind torn yellowed curtains — the uncombed tarnished hair bedraggled against her coarse, lined face.

She drank spirits — only spirits — beer was too common. It was unladylike to drink beer.

What did she know about being ladylike? Old hag. You could smell her breath across the hall.

She shouted abuse at Mrs Parsons — that dirty slut — leaving her rubbish unwrapped in split Safeway bags on the front step.

And those boys of hers — Insolent Little Bastards — and that's what they were — Bastards.

She had a new boyfriend — parked his van the other side of the street — A. E. Jones Builder and Decorator written on the side in smudged black letters.

Griffin hated them all. When he said 'Good evening' to Mrs O'Sullivan, he had his hands round her throat — shaking the foul breath from her — squeezing until the watery eyes popped from their sockets.

Mrs Parsons he would beat about the head with a 'blunt instrument' — smashing her stupid, leering face — knocking her false teeth down the stairs.

And the boys? He wasn't sure — maybe he would tie bricks to their legs and throw them in the canal.

He lay on the canvas camp bed, propped against the mildewed cushions, drinking lager from the can.

Last night's half-eaten fish and chips still on the table in the greasy white paper — the strong smell of vinegar settling uneasily amongst the accumulated smells which hung in the room — a thick invisible mass.

He would go down to Piccadilly — see a bit of life — mingle with the gawping tourists — the la-di-dah — the lost and hungry — the homeless — the kids prostituting themselves for a couple of quid.
Perhaps pick up a girl — a 'good' Catholic girl — from Southern shores.
They were always easy — open their legs to anybody for chips and a burger.
That is, if he could stand their smelly bodies and hairy armpits — the sickening noises they made...
Anyway, he had spent his giro on the new trainers. It was important to be smart.

He had got them cheap in a sports shop on the Edgware Road. They were having a closing down sale.
'Business,' said the man who served him. 'What business? Business is dead. Did you say a size 9?' He took the trainers out of the box.
'A real bargain — practically giving them away. How about a nice sweatshirt?'
He wore a striped shirt and knitted waistcoat. His hands were freckled, and he had a gold wedding ring. 'Do you want the box?'
He put the box in a carrier bag.
Griffin counted out the money carefully on the counter.
'Thank you, sir. Good morning, sir...' He came with him to the door of the shop. 'I think it's going to rain,' he said.

He was pleased the flowers in the window box two doors up had died. Defeated by the blanketing heat of the summer.
Stupid old cow! How could she expect to grow flowers in this polluted city of wheezing asthmatics?
She had hairs growing down her chin — and a bandaged leg — slopping up the street in broken slippers.
He would have to shoot her. He would not be able to touch her.
She was disgusting.

The old drunk with no legs, who sat at the Shaftesbury Avenue entrance to the tube — moaning and rocking — rocking and moaning — was not there.

Perhaps the heat had finished him off too — or the police had taken him away — at last...

Griffin had spat on him — wanting to kick him — to force him back against the railings — hearing his ribs crack — stopping his moaning and rocking for ever.

A burly man in a baseball cap was selling copies of *The Big Issue* outside the Globe Theatre.

'*Big Issue*, sir — *Big Issue*, madam — Think positive — Change your life — Think positive — Positive thinking — *Big Issue*, sir — *Big Issue*, madam...'

Contempt prickled Griffin's scalp. He wouldn't demean himself selling papers to these vermin.

He punched the boy — punched him hard in the stomach.

He had walked straight into him — arrogant — chewing gum — swaggering in the studded jacket.

He punched him in the face — seeing, with a jab of satisfaction, the blood spurt from his pocky nose.

He went on hitting him — hearing himself shouting — 'Fucking bastard!'... 'Fucking bastard!'

And then he was sick. The contents of five cans of lager spewing out — soaking his clothes and the boy lying on the pavement with his arms over his face, among the stinking debris — the cartons and squashed chips — cigarette ends — patches of grease and spit — the discarded filth of filthy people.

The policeman got him from behind in an armlock.

Griffin screamed abuse — struggling and vomiting.

They would take him in for the night — and he would be fined for disorderly conduct — and he wouldn't be able to pay the fine — and they would send round a nice lady with round glasses — or maybe a soft-spoken Indian lady with gold studs in her ears — and none of them would realise that he was waiting for the time, for the opportunity to take his revenge — to slice into the soft bellies — cutting into the soft flesh — severing veins and sinew — watching the surprise — the horror — as they choked on their own blood.

'Shut up you little sods,' he shouted up the stairs, as Mrs Parson's idiot bastard sons played their nightly war games on the floor over his room.

'Shut up you fucking little sods! I'll get you one day — One day I'll get you...'

Heartburn

As Alistair passed the file across the desk, their hands touched.
She didn't look up.
'I think you'll find everything there,' he said.
'Thanks, I'll go through it,' she said.
She pulled it towards her.

The touching had become more frequent lately — hands, arms, bodies...

She pretended not to notice, but took great care with her appearance. She always wore high heels to give her legs extra length, and avoided trousers which drew attention to her less than slender hips and thighs.
She wore short skirts and mannish tailored jackets with many Chanel gold chains.
Lately she used more perfume, extra-sheer stockings, and had her hair done more often at Toni & Guy.

There was no doubt he was very attractive.
She looked up now he had left her glass-walled office and watched him, standing in the outer office between the lap-topped desks, talking to Meredith.

He had a supremely casual way of wearing formal clothes.

Toby, though, was always strictly *formal* formal.

He walked away through the swing doors with an easy stride.

Toby was in Dusseldorf.
His secretary Julia came in with some papers for her to sign. She regarded Harriet with disdain. She didn't approve of women directors, particularly ones married to a fellow director.
She was unmarried, her short jackets unflattering to her heavy figure.

She presided over the office with menopausal bad temper.
She doted on Toby who played up to her dreadfully, bringing her
back expensive body sprays from his travels.

'Could you see to these as soon as possible *Mrs* Richardson,' she said,
emphasising the 'Mrs'.
'Thank you Julia,' said Harriet, glancing through them. 'I'll do them
now,' and unscrewed the cap of her gold fountain pen.

Toby phoned from the hotel lobby.
Harriet was still in the office.

The meeting had gone on and on, and now they insisted he should
join them for dinner. It was a frightful bore, but everything was
going so well, he couldn't really refuse.
He'd be back tomorrow. 'Sorry Angel... Miss you!'

He left the sound proof booth and made his way across the thick
dark red carpet to the Reception Desk. Sickly music leaked from the
hidden PA system.

He was filled with pleasurable anticipation.
What an unexpected bonus!
He took his key and waited for the lift.

The reception last night had been the usual dull affair. Everybody
talking business. Second rate white wine. Strongly flavoured peppery
canapés.

'This is Elsa,' said Karl. 'She heads our PR Team.'

She was stunning. Boyishly short black hair, white skin, intense
green eyes. She wore a black velvet suit covered in glittery stuff.
He grasped her hand, massaging it with his own, and murmured
flirtatious platitudes.
They were the same height.
As a young man he had worried about not being tall, but it had never
seemed to deter the women.

She looked boldly into his eyes, and asked which hotel he was staying at.

She seemed keen to divest him of his clothing whilst still in the taxi.

In his room there had been no need for coy preliminaries — drinks — persuasive sly unbuttoning...

She had walked naked into the shower, and said she must go, otherwise her boyfriend would worry.

She suggested they should meet tonight night for dinner. She would arrange to be free a little longer.

Toby couldn't believe his luck.
Of course he had brief alliances before whilst away on business trips, sometimes when he was *not* away on business trips... They usually took some engineering, and were frequently a disappointment.

Elsa was certainly not a disappointment.

As he got changed he flexed his stomach muscles. He would have to start going to the gym more regularly when he was home. He was getting flabby.

At least his hair wasn't thinning.

*   *   *

Harriet let herself into their modern Georgian town house in Springfield Road.

It was spotless. They had an Italian maid who came twice a week. She also did the ironing, leaving the neatly folded garments on the gleaming kitchen table.
The house was always spotless. She and Toby were both exceptionally tidy people. They didn't like clutter.

The success of their business was due to their orderliness and sense of purpose.

She poured herself a large gin and tonic. She would have had a sherry if Toby had been home.
She would have a bath, and another drink, find something to eat and watch TV.

She was getting out of the bath when the phone rang.
It was Alistair.
'Julia told me Toby won't be back until tomorrow,' he said. 'Why don't we have a drink?'

She felt a frisson of excitement. She should say No.
'What a good idea,' she said.

They agreed to meet in The Feathers in Covent Garden.
She made up her face carefully, and chose a dress of black-draped jersey, which clung a bit, but not too much. She didn't want to look over-dressed. She put on her long black Burberry.

She would go on the tube. She could get a taxi home, and she wouldn't have to worry about parking.

They had steak pie and chips. She had another large gin. Alistair drank whisky.

His flat was modern and stylish. Black furniture, chrome and glass. The bed quilted in navy and white, discreet dark-shaded lighting. They drank champagne.

She made a small effort to resist.

She and Toby had had a very physical relationship at the beginning of their marriage. They could hardly leave each other alone.
They had spent their fortnight's honeymoon almost entirely in bed, surfacing for the occasional flambéed dish in the dining room of the luxury hotel.

*　　*　　*

Elsa was wearing a satiny garment which moved with her body. She was as hungry for food as she had been for him the night before.

They had oysters and venison in a rather unpleasant sweet sauce, hot goats' cheese salad, nougat ice cream and a great deal of wine.

Afterwards in his room her hunger for him was unabated. They drank more wine. Toby felt decidedly indigestible. He was not used to so much activity on top of a rich heavy meal.

When she had gone — her boyfriend was expecting her — he took some Alka Seltzer, and poured the remaining wine down the basin.

*　　*　　*

Alistair said she was wonderful... captivating... beautiful... all that he wanted in a woman!

Harriet basked in the fierceness of his desire.

It was going to be a bit difficult when Toby was home. It would need some careful organisation. Other people seemed to manage to have affairs under their partner's noses. They would find a way...

It was Toby's birthday. They were going to the Inn on the Park for dinner.

They left work early.

Toby opened a bottle of Moët & Chandon and took a glass up to Harriet in the bath.
He fondled her automatically beneath the blanket of scented foam, and put the glass of champagne on a chair by the bath.
Turning down his shirt sleeves, he inserted the square gold cufflinks, and went downstairs to put on the Pavarotti CD that Harriet had given him for a birthday present.

The phone rang. It was Elsa.

He lowered his voice, clearing his throat. How absolutely wonderful! How the Hell had she got his home phone number, surely Julia hadn't given it to her? In London! Wonderful! Representing the German end whilst the contract was finalised. Wonderful! When could they meet? What about lunch tomorrow? She was staying at the Brunswick Hotel in Tavistock Square. Good! Wonderful! One o'clock tomorrow then!

What the Hell was he going to do now? She might even come to the house!

Toby ordered Canard à l'Orange.
Harriet had steak — very rare.
Toby watched her cut it deftly with the serrated steak knife. He was repelled by her hands. Stubby be-ringed fingers with short bright polished nails, as red as the blood which oozed from the steak.
Why on earth had he spent all that money buying those rings? The diamond was far too big.
He must have been out of his mind.
He chewed the duck glumly. It tasted of fishy marmalade.

Harriet wondered why Toby was so quiet. Surely he didn't know about her and Alistair.

They had only managed one delicious afternoon in the Brunswick Hotel, whilst Toby had a meeting with the Chairman Sir Ralph Cobb at his Club in Pall Mall — and two speedy sessions in the Records Office, ostensibly searching for missing files.
Spread-eagled against a filing cabinet, keeping a wary eye on the door was hardly conducive to passionate abandonment.

*   *   *

Toby was punctual.
He would be kind but firm. It had been wonderful, but 'just one of those things', etc., etc…

Elsa was at the bar, languidly sensuous.
He ordered her a large vodka, and himself a whisky.
His resolve was weakened by lust. The whisky burnt his throat. She swallowed the vodka and taking him by the hand, led him to the lift.

Harriet was annoyed to find that Toby had gone out. It was too late to contact Alistair. He had already gone to lunch.
They could have had a room at the Brunswick.

Disgruntled she went to the Open Sesame Wine Bar in Bedford Place, descending into the smoky gloom. She had a shrimp and avocado salad and a glass of rosé.
A bronzed Australian in blue serge came and sat at her table. He was openly trying to pick her up. Safe in the knowledge of her lover, she countered his suggestive remarks with a demure smile.

There was a reception to celebrate the signing of the German Contract.

Harriet noticed Elsa immediately.
It would have been difficult not to.

She was wearing a long-sleeved black chiffon blouse with nothing underneath.

Harriet was shocked, and annoyed — mostly annoyed.
She kept a careful eye on Toby, but he did not seem to be taking much notice, shaking hands politely, and after a few words, moving on.

When she looked again Alistair was talking to her, his dark head bent close to hers, his body subtly intimate.

Jealousy punched her in the stomach, making her flush.

Toby said he was sorry, he had promised to take Sir Ralph back to his Club and stay for a night cap.
'I'll try not to be too long,' he said, kissing her cheek, and squeezing

her shoulder lingeringly.

Harriet noticed Elsa had gone.
She sought out Alistair.
They took a taxi to his flat. His eagerness dispelling her jealousy.

*   *   *

They emerged from room 269.
Toby could still feel her body heavy against his.
He held her arm lightly as they waited for the lift.

There were a middle-aged American couple waiting, plastic macs and waterproof hats — she with an umbrella, he with camera and a large A to Z.

The lift stopped at the fourth floor.
Harriet and Alistair got in.

Harriet was feeling pleased with herself.
Alistair said he adored her.
He lay back in the sheets, smoking. He wanted her to get away for a weekend. Surely she could make some excuse. A dying relative, a sick friend, anything?
Harriet started to dress.
'We have to get back,' she said, smugly satisfied.
Alistair pulled her down and they rolled together across the kingsize bed.

He kissed her neck as they waited for the lift.

They stood face to face. The American couple obligingly moved to one side to give them more room.
At the third floor two men got in. One creased and balding, the other thin-lipped, petulant. 'I told him Giles would mess it up,' he was saying, pushing them closer together.
On the second floor a heavily veiled woman and a young girl in school uniform sidled her way in.

Nobody could move.

*   *   *

Toby and Harriet went away for the weekend to the Grand Hotel in Torquay to 'talk things over'.

They drank a lot, sitting in the over-furnished hotel suite, looking out on the drizzle-sodden gardens, dotted with dispirited palm trees.

There were tearful recriminations and vows of eternal fidelity.

They returned to London, outwardly subdued, each secretly anticipating the next meeting with their lovers.

Toby had another trip to Dusseldorf.

Elsa was still in London.

He returned in very good humour.
He was particularly solicitous and affectionate to Harriet, bringing her a large bottle of Rive Gauche perfume, and a box of Lindt liqueur chocolates from the Duty Free.

He had had a most successful trip.
This time a curvaceous blonde he had met at the airport.
He had helped her sort out her luggage, which had become jammed in the carousel.
He offered her a lift in the Company's chauffeur-driven BMW.

He had had to play the whole game with her.
Flattery — dinner — an expensive gold-linked bracelet — drinks — more drinks. More flattery to get her to his room. When she finally succumbed, he sank thankfully into her yielding flesh.

On subsequent visits she was always available and willing.

Elsa was still in London. Stimulating... tantalizing.

This way he had the best of both worlds. Compliant adoration, and dangerous excitement.

An excellent arrangement.

*   *   *

Harriet asked Alistair to lunch whilst Toby was in Dusseldorf. It was his third visit this month. He wouldn't be back until the evening.

She thought they could have a serious talk over lunch.
Something must be decided. They couldn't go on like this. The snatched rendezvous, long lunch hours at the Lonsdale Hotel in Marchmont Street. They had thought it wiser to steer clear of the Brunswick.
Should she leave Toby?
Should she ask him for a divorce?

Alistair refused to waste their precious time together in conversation. All the same something had to be done.

She set the table with a white lace cloth and made the dressing for the salad with virgin olive oil, rubbing the bowl with garlic. The salmon steaks she had bought ready cooked from Waitrose. She had two bottles of Chablis cooling in the fridge, and ice ready in a bowl for the gin and whisky.

They ended up spending the afternoon in the marital bed. The dirty dishes hurriedly left on the dining room table, small salmon bones congealed on the sides of the plates, the salad half eaten.

Alistair left just in time for her to clear everything up and change the sheets before Toby came home.
Alistair was reluctant to leave, he seemed very pleased and very loving.

Alistair stopped his car at the nearest telephone box.
He dialled the number of the Brunswick Hotel and asked for Elsa.

She had just come in from shopping. He could come right over. She had bought some lovely new things, she was sure he would approve.
They had the rest of the weekend.
'We'll have food sent up!' she said.

*   *   *

Harriet saw them first, and almost gasped aloud.
She and Toby were waiting for Sir Ralph and his wife Priscilla in the bar at the Dorchester. They were going to Boulestin's for dinner.

Harriet had decided to ask Toby for a divorce. The situation was ridiculous.
Toby found Harriet's close proximity distasteful. She had fat knees.
He longed for Elsa's scented limbs.

They came across the lounge, arm in arm, laughing.
Alistair in elegant dinner jacket. Elsa in a skimpy slip of silvery thread, concealing nothing.

They were so engrossed in each other they didn't notice Toby and Harriet at the bar in a state of stupefaction.

They merged together in the revolving doors... kissing... and disappeared into the night.

Charmed

1

'Get those Goddam birds out of the way for Chrissake!'

At last the sun was shining, and they were able to shoot the scene — under the leafy branches of the massive oak — in front of the white-pillared mansion.

The last rapturous embrace before the credits started to roll. The white birds fluttering up — up — over their heads into the clear blue sky.

They refused to fly — remaining stubbornly earthbound — scratching and squawking — fluffing up their feathers — pecking at the short blades of grass round Greg and Lara's feet.

'They're supposed to fly for Chrissake! Where's Bernard! Where's the fucking trainer — Bernard! Find the fucking trainer!'

Greg and Lara released each other — watching Bernard's long figure loping towards the stables.

One of the outhouses had been converted into a canteen. The catering company arriving every morning with loaded vans — supplying snacks, light meals, coffee, alcohol and cigarettes throughout the day.

'Cut!' shouted Christian. 'Cut! Break for lunch — Get rid of those Goddam birds!'

Lara was vegetarian — she ordered salad — no mayonnaise.
Greg ate steak and chips.
Christian drank whisky and ordered a steak sandwich. Rare, with mustard.

'Chris honey,' said Lara. 'Does Greg have to keep his hat on whilst we're kissing? How can I concentrate on being amorous with his shitty hat brim in my eye?'

'The Good Guy always keeps his hat on,' drawled Greg, lighting a cigarette.

'And he's wearing exactly the same shirt as when he went away two years ago. For Christ's sake, Christian, whose doing the wardrobe?'

'Those Goddam birds,' said Christian, ordering another whisky.
'You wanted the birds honey,' said Lara.
'Flying birds for Christ's sake,' said Christian. 'They're supposed to Goddam fly!'

'Look,' said Greg. 'It would be easier to kiss if I took my hat off...'
'No,' snapped Christian. 'You keep your Goddam hat on!'
'OK! OK!' said Greg. 'We'll practise, won't we honey — try it out 'til we get the right angle...'

Christian pretended not to hear — sawing at his steak sandwich with a serrated knife.

'Gentlemen always remove their hats in the presence of ladies,' said Lara.
'This is a Yank, honey,' said Christian. 'A Goddam Texan — He keeps his hat on.'

2

Lara had met Christian at one of Mercedes' parties in London. Everybody — but Everybody went to Mercedes' parties. She had been in an Oriental phase — dressed in a lime green sari trimmed with gold — gold necklaces and bangles — a red spot on her high, pale forehead — her hair hidden under the lime green silk.

Mercedes had natural red gold hair cut close to her scalp. A long pale face — a long pale neck. Her thin-lipped mouth a brilliant slash of puce — orange — cherry red — metallic silver — she liked dramatic colours.

In one of her black phases she dyed her hair jet black, wearing a hooded black cloak — her mouth the colour of dried blood. A vampire queen, swooping bat-like down the curved marble staircase.

The night Lara met Christian the house was full of tiger skins — burning sticks of incense choking the air with scented smoke — candles guttering in dimpled glass jars and lilies floating in the swimming pool. There were plates of withered canapés, God knows what they were, and bowls of wrinkled dried fruit — mercifully there was also a great deal of champagne.

Being called Mercedes put her under a certain obligation — a name to live up to. She did her best.

Exotically clad in jewelled turbans, native-woven, hand-dyed kaftans — satin pyjamas, a monk's robes with a heavy golden cross and open leather sandals…

She changed the decor of her house to suit her moods. Grecian, Empire, Minimalist — Red, White, Black.

Always in the front row of Yves St Laurent and Lucien Lacroix — dropping into Armani for a few shirts or slacks — the odd belt — dresses from Ralph Lauren.

Pint-sized bottles of Lancôme and Dior perfume in the spacious bathrooms — walled with mirrors and priceless paintings.

She had an impeccable Japanese manservant — Jonathan — who ran the house with silent, faultless expertise. Two Japanese maids and a homosexual English cook. Her own personal maid Monique, a grim, angular French woman with a tight grey bun and pins in her collar. She looked after everything which concerned Mercedes. She knew all her secrets.

When Mercedes impulsively threw a few things in a bag and headed for the airport — Monique would be on the next plane with the hand-made luggage beautifully packed — Mercedes' jewel case attached to her wrist by a padlocked gold chain. She spoke no English, but understood it perfectly.

3

Christian had pretty well kidnapped her. She had been with Rodney Clarke — head of Sunlight Studios. She was not madly enthusiastic — his lovemaking was noisy — he snorted a lot, and his hair made grease marks on the pillows. She would find her mind wandering. Still, he had got her her first big film role in 'The Silver Forest', and he could be useful. He kneaded her bare shoulder as he talked to a short man with red hair and a kilt, who looked like something off a tin of shortbread.

Christian had eased her on to the dance floor — dropping his cigarette into an abandoned cocktail.
The band in white tuxedoes, partially hidden by tropical greenery, were playing 'Moonglow'.

'Jesus,' he said. 'You're the best thing I've seen since I arrived in this Goddam country.'

Of course she knew who he was — everybody knew who he was. His latest film 'The Chinese Madonna' had been a tremendous hit.

'Let's get out of here!' he said. 'That's a corny line — but Jesus this place stinks — and honey, I'd sure like to get to know you better...'

Christian had wanted her to move in with him in the mews house he had rented off Montpelier Square, but she had said no. The living room was tiny, and Christian was constantly on the phone — sometimes on two phones at once. The kitchen was no bigger than a ship's galley.

She was not prepared to play the submissive hostess — producing tasty snacks at all hours for the hordes of sycophants who were always dropping in, 'Just for a cup of tea — Just a teeny whisky, darling! — A sandwich would be wonderful, sweetie!...'

She was glad to escape to her own flat for a little peace and quiet.

Christian was ardent and demanding. He adored her. She was used to the adoration of small men, bending down so that they could kiss her.

He had the single beds removed from the coyly-draped bedroom, ordering a kingsize from Harrods, which reduced the floor space to a small Afghan rug to put their slippers on.

He was very dynamic.

Dynamism was very tiring.

He was always firing questions at her about her feelings for Greg. Aggressive in the short black dressing gown embroidered with gold boxing gloves — not waiting for her answers.

Did she find Greg attractive? He was supposed to be the sexiest star around. Did she find him sexy? What was it like when he kissed her?

Lara, yawning, struggling to keep her eyes open, was tempted to say she found Greg irresistible.

Most of the time she was just trying to avoid the brim of his hat.

'Come to bed, honey,' she said.

'What do you want with that little shit?' Rodney had said angrily on the phone. He left a lot of messages on her answermachine. 'He's just a little shit!'
Rodney was a bore — BORING in capital letters. She did not respond to his calls.

'Come to bed, honey,' she said again. 'You're the sexiest man I know — but you're wasted over there...' and she pulled the satin nightdress off over her head and threw it down — a silky white mound on the Afghan rug.

4

Lara's mother chewed gum instead of smoking — at least — she chewed gum between cigarettes.

She was short, and wore very high heels to increase her height — teetering down the uneven path in her short tight skirt and short fake fur jacket — to catch the bus to work.

She wore the thick orangy-pink pancake makeup which had been fashionable when she was young — her eyebrows plucked and heavily pencilled — black shoulder-length wavy hair.

She had a job on the checkout at the big supermarket on the London Road — sitting all day at the till in her pink overall piped with grey — name badge pinned to her breast pocket — 'Mrs Burns'.

She viewed Lara's increasing growth with alarm.

'Heaven help us, Lara!' she would say, clicking her tongue against her teeth. 'When are you going to stop growing...?'

They lived in an ugly semi-detached bungalow in a street of ugly semi-detached bungalows and narrow houses with flat roofs. The front garden — a small patch of piebald weedy grass — was strewn with toffee papers and trampled beer cans, deposited by passersby. Somebody had ridden their bike into the gatepost — preventing the gate from shutting.

When she was small, Lara would sit at her bedroom window tracing patterns with her fingers in the condensation.

The whole bungalow was very damp and shabby — last year's calendar of Alpine scenes and a barometer which didn't work, hanging in the hall.

Her father was a long distance lorry driver.

As a kid she would lie in her bed and think about him — thundering across Europe in his massive lorry — the large kind hands guiding it through mysterious foreign cities — Marseilles, Trieste, Istanbul…

He would bring her back slabs of tough, chewy nougat, and celluloid dolls in national dress — their clothes glued to their bodies — cheap necklaces of glass beads — and once a box made of shells.

Lara really liked her father.
A big man, with a big laugh — swinging her up in his arms — sitting her on his shoulders.

'For Goodness sake, Lionel!' her mother would say. 'Put the child down!'

But before they got used to his being there, he was off on the road again — high in the lighted cab — a packet of custard creams and a flask of tea beside him on the worn, shiny seat.

There was always just enough money. They never went short of anything. Bills were always paid, her mother went regularly to the hairdresser. There was enough for a tennis racket, and the short white pleated skirt. The small front room was dominated by a 23-inch TV, a mock leather three-piece suite, and a glass-fronted cocktail cabinet.

Her mother hated cooking. They lived on junk food — Kentucky Fried Chicken, fish and chips, burgers, TV meals in foil trays rimmed with hardened gravy, chips and chips and lots of ketchup, biscuits and buns and lots of cereals — Cornflakes, Rice Crispies, Frosties, Coco Pops — Lara ate hers swimming in milk with a thick coating of sugar.

Lara was fourteen when her mother left home. She was already five foot nine — willowy and blonde.

She came home from school one day to find a note propped against the teapot on the kitchen table — written on a sheet of lined paper torn from the ringed pad her mother used for shopping lists.

'I have gone to start a new life with Norman — will send address when we are settled. Love, Mum. P.S. Don't forget to lock up when you go out.'

The teapot hadn't been emptied.

5

'I say,' said Cassandra. She stood in the doorway — immaculate — the fine blonde hair held in place with a black velvet headband. She wore a black velvet suit with a long jacket and short skirt, and a white fluffy blouse.

Lara's mother had had a black velvet suit and white frilly blouse, but she had just looked cheap and common and tarty. How was it that Cassandra looked so elegant and classy?

'I'm frightfully sorry to butt in — but Mercedes — well — she seems to be floating in the pool...'

Mercedes' white taffeta coat floated — a swollen ghost — arms outspread on the azure water — the fountain sprinkling feathered drops — diamond chips on the still, glassy surface. Somewhere a trumpet sobbed 'What Are You Doing The Rest Of Your Life...'.

Cassandra made a sort of choking sound — clapping her hand to her mouth, and rushed away — her heels clattering on the white marble floor.

Lara wished she hadn't had so much to drink — the edge of the pool bent and swayed. She sat down abruptly on a white-cushioned cane lounger.

They had all had too much to drink — sitting around in Mercedes' white drawing room, lit by white glass pyramids and white china-petalled flowers drooping on steel stands. Two white rose trees in tubs by the French windows. There were tables covered with Lalique glass bowls with birds and girls throwing balls.

Jonathan had wheeled in a glass trolley of bottles and crystal glasses, and crystal bowls of ice and lemons, and a silver tray of hot savouries — miniature vol-au-vents, and star-shaped morsels of flaky pastry filled with fresh salmon.

'Bring some more fruit, will you Jonathan?' said Mercedes. 'Oranges, and pineapple, and strawberries — if we have any. Mr Zimmerman is making cocktails.'

Christian was determined to create a new cocktail — something nobody had had before — whisky, benedictine and orange — Pernod, brandy and lemon — rum and gin, lemon and sliced pineapple — vodka and strawberries. They tasted them all.

Greg was too long for the white chaise longue. His feet dangled over the end. He wore a white suit, his hair thick and brown and curly. He lay with his eyes closed, lazily accepting the drinks Christian handed him.

Bernard was too tall for the curved perspex chairs — his knees nut-crackered to his chin — his thin face worried — nervously gulping down drinks — austere in his black dinner jacket.

Mercedes was too tall for the white leather footstool she had chosen to sit on. She wore white silk trousers and the white taffeta coat — smoking gold cigarettes in an ivory holder.
Lara reclined in a vast white armchair. She was wearing blue — a deep shade of lavender — long and fitting, fastened on one shoulder with dark blue silk roses.

Christian insisted she let her thick golden hair hang loose on her shoulders. She had wanted to put it up.

'Jesus, you're gorgeous honey,' he had said. 'Why do we have to go out? We could have much more fun here...'

Lara had kissed him on the forehead and straightened his black bow tie. His ties were always crooked.

He was bristlingly aggressive among this bevy of very tall people — mixing and shaking — smoking small cigars and dropping ash down his spotless white pleated shirt front. He looked good. He always looked good in his dinner jacket.

'White is purity,' said Mercedes. 'Purity is white — white is cleansing,' she giggled. 'Soap powder is cleansing — soap powder is white — soap powder is pure...' She tried to get up, falling forward on her knees — knocking the table, a thick slab of perspex with trapped air bubbles and twisted steel legs.

Greg swung his long legs off the chaise longue and helped her up.

'Let's go look at the moon Ma'am,' he said, putting his arm across her shoulders. 'That's mighty pure...'

*   *   *

Bernard took off his jacket and glasses and dived into the pool, grabbing the ballooning coat and dragging it to the side.

'She's not there,' he spluttered. 'There's nobody in the pool...'
'No Body in the Pool,' said Christian. 'What a title for a film...' and he chuckled quietly.

The distant trumpet started to rumba.
Rhythmically, in slow motion they helped the sodden Bernard out of the pool, leaving the coat to float away, empty white sleeves outstretched.

Christian kissed her — he smelt of alcohol and cigars.

'It's OK honey,' he said. 'False alarm — she's probably fucking Greg in the sun parlour — or should I say moon parlour...'

6

'I should have known,' said her father. He spooned sugar into his tea — the spoon insignificant in his large hands.

'I should have known things weren't right...'

Lara didn't speak. Her mother had always been down the pub when her father was away. Tottering home with whoever wanted to escort her — giggling and falling against the telephone table — knocking over the vase of dusty dried flowers.

'What are we going to do about you, Princess?'

He had brought her a plate with a raised pattern of purple grapes, and a mug with a picture of the Vienna Opera House.

'Perhaps you should go and stay with your Aunt Nell...'

He spooned more sugar into his tea.

Lara said no. She didn't get on with Aunt Nell. Aunt Nell didn't like her.

She was working for her GCSEs. She was going to go to College — he wanted her to go to College didn't he?

She had told everyone that Mum had gone to look after her sister who was ill. She was perfectly alright on her own. They didn't want anyone nosing around asking questions — they might try and put her into 'care'.

'Your Mum doesn't have a sister,' said her father. He stirred the tea.

'What was he like … this bloke?'
'He was a creep,' said Lara.

She had known there was something up when her mother brought him to tea. She never brought anybody home to tea — not even her friend Mavis.

She had bought scones, and an iced fruit cake.

Lara had disliked Norman on sight. She didn't like the way he looked at her. Stripping her with knowing eyes, smiling a knowing smile. Ugh!

She had told Myra on the way to school.

Myra said all men were creeps. Her mother had an endless stream of boyfriends from the dim and loutish to the downright repellent.

'What about your Dad?' she said.
'I don't know,' said Lara. 'She asked him to tea…'

'A smarmy creep,' she said, wishing she could think of something comforting to say.
'Well I suppose we'll just have to make the best of it,' he said. 'Sure you're alright?'

Lara was quite sure. She was used to looking after herself. She'd just got to be careful with the neighbours. Didn't want them getting suspicious.

She was glad her mother had gone. She had hated Norman skulking around — didn't like seeing her mother emerging dishevelled from the lounge or later, glimpsing Norman, naked in her mother's bed.

She locked her bedroom door and closed the curtains, pretending to do her homework so she could avoid seeing him.

'I'm sure we're going to be great friends,' he had said, whilst her mother fetched the tea — and he reached out a bony hand and squeezed her knee, leaving fingers resting against her leg. She was always careful to keep out of his way.

Myra had had trouble with several of her mother's lovers — once having to take refuge in the 'roof space' — it was not high enough to be a proper loft — crouching on the rafters, scared of putting her foot through the bedroom ceiling..

'Hours,' she said. 'I was up there for hours. Mum was late coming home...'

'I'll be fine,' she said. 'You don't have to worry. I'll be just fine...'

7

She was to fall from her horse — lying inert as Greg galloped towards her — leaping from his foaming mount to scoop her in his arms, and carry her into the house — laying her on a convenient sofa — murmuring endearments, and then, as she regained consciousness, they had their first passionate kiss.

'What do you need a hard hat for, Dotty? Your head's hard enough — solid wood...'
'Riding horses doesn't do anything for bandy legs, Dotty!'

Dotty was square and tough, and could spit her chewing gum straight across the room. She won a jar of sweets in a raffle at a Point to Point, and brought them to school to share out — firing them round the room for the others to catch.

Christian insisted she had a woman instructor. He could not bear her to be handled by a man. They also had to find a large, docile horse.
Cassandra was despatched to find both, returning with Tabitha Stiles, and a calm chestnut mare.

Tabitha, an incredibly well brought up girl with ginger hair, no eyebrows and a pretty freckled nose, was quite famous as a show jumper.

'Gosh!' she said. 'This is all terrifically exciting. Gosh, Miss Burns! You look absolutely marvellous!'

Lara had to learn how to fall off, as well as stay on. Of course she would not really fall, Christian would cut it to look as if she had fallen. Tabitha was very patient, coaxing her, as if she were a horse.

This scene was to be shot in the rain — Greg squelching and sliding in the mud in his highly polished riding boots as he rushed to lift her up.

'For Christ's sake, Christian!' he said. 'She's 6ft tall!'
'5ft 11,' said Lara.
'Well, whatever. How the Hell can I carry her all the way into the house? I can't even stand up.'

Greg was a fine horseman. Christian wasn't bad either. They would canter off with Cassandra over the fields whilst Lara was led round and round the yard on a leading rein, with Tabitha making encouraging noises.

'That's the idea. That's better. Gosh, Miss Burns, you look absolutely marvellous. Just relax. Don't clutch the reins so tightly. Good girl!'

Lara almost expected to be given a sugar lump.

8

'Always make the best of yourselves,' said Miss Leigh.

She stood at the front of the class — her face flushed a deep menopausal red.
She wore her too tight two-piece in unbecoming turquoise. The

jacket had three-quarter length sleeves with which she wore a long-sleeved white acetate blouse, making the jacket look as if it had shrunk. The skirt cut across the middle of her fleshy knees. She wore brown stockings and black court shoes.

Lara couldn't believe anyone could wear anything so ghastly — could actually choose anything so ghastly — could go into a shop and buy anything so ghastly.

'Never undervalue yourselves — and don't let anybody else undervalue you.'

It was their last morning at school before going on study leave for their GCSEs. For once nobody sniggered. There was no whispering, shuffling of books, scraping of chair legs. Even the slag Becky stopped chewing gum.

Miss Leigh was a 'good sort' really, despite the lengthy diatribes on their future conduct and her terrible clothes. At least she treated them like human beings, and not as an ineducable riffraff like most of the other teachers.

'Where is your homework, Carmen?'
'How many times do I have to tell you, nail varnish is not to be worn in school...'
'Since when was *pink* part of the school uniform?'
'The buses were *not* on strike yesterday, Susan.'
'Food is to be eaten in the dining room — not during a Maths test...'

Cooper sat slumped in a chair by the desk — staring at the floor, exasperation visible in her tightly clasped hands and swinging foot.

Cooper had short dark hair — the greasy sort that goes with bad skin. This she concealed under a thick layer of yellowing makeup, dried into a stiff mask mapped with tiny cracks like a dried-up river bed. She wore a 'mock' suede jacket with knitted sleeves and brown twill trousers with a plastic belt. She considered Miss Leigh's idealistic ramblings irrelevant and nonsensical. Most of these girls would do nothing at all — didn't want to do anything at all — aspiring no higher than a job at one of the big supermarkets, or maybe something secretarial at a building society — some already in line to swell the ranks of single parenthood. She hoped that Lara and Myra would do well, perhaps even get to university. They were both clever.

It was not 'done' to be clever. Cleverness was treated with hostility and suspicion, with sneers and jeers — tweaking and poking in the dinner queue, threats and jostling in the corridors and playground. It had to be hidden, like Cooper's bad skin — disguised beneath a layer of contemptuous disdain for anything academic, for the whole concept of 'education'.

Cooper was well aware of this. She returned their exercise books closed, with caustic remarks about their punctuality and appearance, writing comments in the margins in her small neat hand — 'Well thought out.' 'Excellent.' 'Lucid and imaginative.'

Lara was going to leave home after the exams. She would do as well as she could, so that at least she would have decent grades if she wanted to do something later on. She had told Myra.

'What about college?' said Myra.
'I'm not going,' said Lara. 'I'm going to London. I've been saving up. I can't stay here when Dad brings that bloody woman home...'

Her father had brought Grace to the house at Christmas. He had met her in Amsterdam. They had both been on a trip to the bulb fields. She had been on holiday, and he had had a day to kill waiting for his next load — there had been a problem with the papers. They had wandered together through the tulips, and he had visited her afterwards in Birmingham, where she had a flat.

She was a short plump woman — clattering with jewellery, chains and rings and bangles — cheaply scented — vulgarly dressed in jersey suits with frilled and flounced blouses — her hair an unbelievable blonde. She had sat on Lara's father's lap cooing and giggling — her eyes coldly appraising — evaluating. They circled each other in mutual dislike, whilst her father, innocently unaware, chuckled about his 'two' girls, and how good everything was going to be. She was going to sell her flat and move down there with them.

'It might not be that bad,' said Myra.
'I'm not staying to find out,' said Lara.
'What will you do in London?'
'I'll get a job,' said Lara.
Now Myra was pregnant. They sat on Lara's bed and smoked. Myra's face was puffed and blotchy from crying.

'Go to the doctor before it's too late,' said Lara. 'I'll come with you and wait outside…'
'I can't,' said Myra. 'What if he tells Mum…?'
'Why should he tell your Mum? You're sixteen — he's not going to bother to tell your Mum. Anyway, there's patient confidentiality and all that stuff…'
'I'm scared,' said Myra. 'I'm just terribly scared. I don't think I can go through with it.'

Lara felt a mixture of anger, pity and disgust boil up inside her, spilling over like the damson jam they had made in Home Economics — 'Minnie' had a glut of damsons in her garden. It had erupted suddenly, a dark purple mass bubbling down the sides of the stainless steel pan and the white sides of the cooker.

How could Myra have done 'that' with Lenny Jones? Weasel-faced Lenny? He had tried it on with all the girls — coarse, obscene, physically urgent — a repellent creature. He had waylaid her on the way to the post office — pushing her against the wall beside the launderette — grabbing the front of her blouse — squeezing. She had told him to 'Piss off — slime ball'. How could Myra have let him do 'that'?

'I'll come with you to the doctor,' she repeated. 'You've got to do something. You've got to do something before the exams…'
'I can't take the exams,' said Myra, starting to cry again, twisting the

fringe of Lara's faded candlewick bedspread, the blue stained with darker patches where she had spilt ink.

'What's the point? I shan't be able to go to college. You're not going to college…'

'That's different,' said Lara. 'You've got to go to college if you can. You have to. Whatever happens, baby or no baby, you have to do well in the exams. If you go to the doctor now it'll all be over before the exams.'

'He might make me keep it,' said Myra.

'If that happens, you mustn't tell anybody until after the exams. Your Mum will never notice. You can come here every day and work with me. It's important, for God's sake. You don't want to end up like your Mum — or my Mum — or that stupid Sandra with her five snivelling kids…'

9

They sat in a disconsolate group — crowded in Christian's tiny lounge. The chairs stiff and uncomfortable. The sofa, hardly big enough for two, upholstered in brocade with scratchy piping. There were narrow French windows leading to a small paved garden, with miniature plants, a magnolia tree with drooping brown-edged flowers, and a feeble fountain dribbling water into a stagnant marble basin.

Christian had unplugged the phone.

They were watching videos Cassandra had made of possible locations. She had been to Norfolk and Suffolk and a bit of Lincolnshire. Lara and Christian sat on the sofa — Greg, Bernard and Cassandra on the stiff chairs.

Christian had ordered a crate of Burgundy from a prestigious firm in the City, recommended by Mercedes.

'Wonderful wine, darling,' she had said. 'Absolute nectar. You simply have to try it. Tell Binky Hatton I sent you. He's a real sweetie…'

They had drunk quite a lot of it already. It was a heavy wine with a metallic taste.

Christian had sent out for pizza — cheese and tomato, with plenty of black olives. The coffee table between them was cluttered with half-empty glasses and paper plates gummed with tomato and piled with discarded pizza crust.

Christian rewound the video — the images hurrying backwards — walls and windows, trees and sheds, figures jerkily reversing across yards, down drives, into doorways. He jabbed the 'Pause' button and held the frame, and there was a groaning chorus of 'Nos'. Cassandra's upper-class voice commentating.

'Great stables, but the house is simply awful. This was alright from the back, but absolutely too many rhododendrons in the front — can't even see the door. This is Talgarth Manor. Super place. It has a moat, but no stables. This had plenty of stables, but the house is too terribly twee…'

Greg said 'For Christ's sake, Christian, my legs have gone numb, my brain has gone numb. None of these are any bloody good.'

10

They went to see 'Minnie'.

In between bouts in the Home Economics kitchen, teaching the girls to weigh flour and currants, make rissoles with left-over scraps and solid sponge cakes, whilst the less attentive heated cups of coffee in the newly acquired microwave, she acted as Welfare Officer — occupying a minute office next to the Staff Cloakroom, every morning between ten and twelve, except Wednesdays, when she took the 2nd year for Modern History.

'It'll be OK,' said Lara. 'Just cry a lot. She's quite decent really.'

She waited in the corridor, taking an unaccustomed serious interest in the Notice Boards.

There were a lot of 'Lost' items — new plimsolls, size 6 and a half, a lunch box containing a cheese sandwich and a KitKat, an Arsenal scarf, a copy of 'Riders' by Jilly Cooper — somebody had scribbled 'Who's riding who?' underneath in red ink.
There were several things for sale —
a navy v-necked sweater, slightly worn, 38 bust,
two black and white kittens,
a French dictionary,
a ten by twelve photograph of Prince,
a pair of calf-length boots size 5, and a leather-look jacket size 14.
There was an announcement in green felt tip that the Netball Team to play St Agnes on Saturday would be picked this afternoon.

Nobody would go. Nobody wanted to play netball on Saturdays. Nobody wanted to play St Agnes at anything.

'They're all slags,' said Carmen. 'They'll do it with anybody…'

They had grey uniforms and red ties, and hats with striped hatbands. They got good exam results and had an orchestra which played at functions in the town hall. They had a hockey team, a netball team, a tennis team. They took cups in the swimming gala and put on performances of 'My Fair Lady' and 'Little Women'.
They all loathed the girls at St Agnes'.

'Minnie' arranged for Myra to go into Bournewater General for a termination. She had been flustered, but sympathetic.

Everybody knew what sort of woman Myra's mother was — what could you expect with a mother like that? The girl was bright. She deserved a chance.

She gave Myra a little chat — about respecting oneself, of not getting 'carried away,' and the absolute necessity of taking precautions if the situation got — er — out of hand.

Lara went with her to the hospital. She was to stay in overnight —
her few things in an Asda carrier bag.

She had left a note for her mother to say she was staying with Lara.

They had to wait a long time for the bus. Myra was shivering.
Lara took her arm. 'It'll be OK,' she said.

The nurse told Myra to get into bed — drawing the curtains with a
disapproving swish.

There were four women in the ward — all with newborn babies.
One with an unsuitably revealing nightdress complained about
her stitches — a younger one with lank dark hair, her face red and
swollen from crying, said Sister had told her they would have to give
the baby supplementary feeds as she wasn't producing enough milk,
and he was losing weight.

'I've got enough to feed an army,' boasted a fat woman in the corner
bed. She wore a hand-knitted coral pink cardigan with large buttons.
'I expect they'll syphon some off for the premature — poor little
mites.' She had a thick mouth, wet with saliva.

'I wouldn't want a boy,' said the woman in the bed next to Myra's.
She wore a long-sleeved wincyette nightdress, her mouth a mauvish
circle. She was knitting with pink plastic needles.
'Too much trouble. Of course my husband wanted a boy. They
always want boys. I told him — You want a boy, you find another
woman. I've done my duty...' she smiled smugly.

Lara was filled with nausea and disgust. She found it impossible to
imagine any of these women participating in the activity necessary
to produce babies. The fat woman leaned forward.
'So what are you here for dear?' she said, addressing Myra, adjusting
her heavy bosom beneath the cardigan.
'She's having a gynaecological investigation,' said Lara. 'Under
anaesthetic.'

She went down to the shop on the ground floor, and bought Myra *Marie Claire* and *Cosmopolitan* and a large bar of milk chocolate.

She'd need something to take her mind off things — especially with that obscene, fecund quartet...

11

Christian had been on the phone half the night.

'No violins, Chris buddy,' said Zack Muller. 'I don't do violins — no schmaltzy crap.'
'OK, OK!' said Chris. 'No violins. But romantic, OK?'

He spoke to Gabrielle Stone. Gabrielle was difficult. She was always difficult, known for her deliberately orchestrated tantrums, unpunctuality and generally unpleasant behaviour. She also tended to drink too much.
She had to be cajoled and flattered.

Greg had said 'Shit, Chris!'

His previous encounters with Gabrielle had been less than successful. She had accused him of smothering her in the love scenes, of almost fracturing her collar bone, burning her arm with his cigarette and crushing her foot when they were doing a dance sequence.

The thought of weeks in the desert staying in remote motels with faulty air-conditioning, nylon sheets and warm beer, with Gabrielle complaining, getting offensively drunk and difficult, was less than enticing.

Christian insisted she was the only one for the part — a sultry, sexy femme fatale.
'It's perfect for you, honey,' he said. 'You'll knock 'em over when you breathe...'
She said she would have to discuss it with Bud.

'I just don't know, Chris honey. I have to think about my career. Who is this English girl? I don't want any fuss over my billing...'

They borrowed Mercedes' white Bentley. They were going to look for locations in Derbyshire.
Mercedes said Christian had to see Chatsworth.
'It's absolutely divine, darling. Little temples, waterfalls — all that sort of thing...'

Mercedes had a white Bentley, a black Bentley, a silver Lagonda and a red Peugeot 205. Her chauffeur, a solid, wiry-haired Scotsman, was used to being summoned at any time of the day or night. He had probably driven more miles than Lara's father in his lorry — through wasteland and vineyard — in the shining shadow of mountains and reflecting lakes, arid plains, sudden snow.

He was expert at negotiating Customs, ferries and border crossings — going on frequent trips to Heathrow and Harrods to fetch groceries. They made up a special muesli for Mercedes and boxes of fish in packed ice — whole turbot and halibut, salmon and prawns. Mercedes was very fond of fish.

She was taking Greg off for a Country House weekend, at Timothy and Lavinia's place in Gloucestershire — a turreted monstrosity with a trout lake and crumbling gazebo.

She took him to Burberrys in the Haymarket to buy heavy sweaters and a raincoat.
'It's a frightfully cold house,' she said. 'Tepid water and draughts — groaning with antiquities and aged retainers who can barely stand. Wonderful English breakfast — kedgeree, kippers, devilled kidneys. You'll adore it. We might even get some tennis if it doesn't rain.'

She rang Harrods and ordered two pairs of their warmest pyjamas. It was a long walk to the bathrooms.

She had sent Monique on ahead, laden with rugs and pillows, to make sure the fires were lit in their rooms.

'Tim and Vinnie are sweeties,' she said. 'But the British aristocracy have no idea about comfort. Bed socks and bread and jam in the Nursery, and dreadful hard bolsters which give you a crick in the neck...'

Christian said they could have lunch in Oxford. He had never been to Oxford. Lara had never been to Oxford either. Bernard was a Cambridge man. Cassandra was just well connected — most of her circle had been to one or the other.

They ate in a beamed pub. Christian insisted on lunch in a beamed pub. The beams were black and worm-eaten.

They had steak and kidney pie in individual brown earthenware dishes — the pastry a thin cardboard, covering stringy steak and hard wedges of kidney in a glutinous gravy. Lara had macaroni cheese, stuck together in a solid block.

Christian had several whiskies and they had a bottle of passable red wine. The waiters, who could have been students, wore red waistcoats and striped shirts. They sniggered together behind the bar, and had to be asked several times for mustard. Christian smoked between mouthfuls. He said Gabrielle would probably want all kinds of impossible conditions written into her contract, like demanding that the temperature in the desert didn't exceed 70 degrees.

Lara said, 'Don't worry honey, you can handle her. You're so good at handling people.'
Bernard cleared his throat and sipped his wine. He had not slept much either, had also been on the phone to LA, talking to the head of the American production team. There were so many arrangements to be made.

Cassandra poked the remains of her steak and kidney under the beige pastry at the side of the plate. She was just tired — hoping they would find a suitable location — somewhere, that everybody approved of.

They had coffee, which was a mistake. Christian said English coffee was shit — where the Hell did they get it from — scraping the bottom of birdcages?

Lara sat in the back of the Bentley with Cassandra.
It was very comfortable.
Bernard drove. Christian smoked a lot, and kept a running commentary on the scenery — the difficulties of convincing the backers to let him have more money, the necessity of working with fucking prima donnas like Gabrielle because they had to have a fucking star. There would be trouble. There was bound to be trouble...

It had been raining and the trees and hedges hung, faded and dripping — grim cottages squatting at the edge of waterlogged fields.

Cassandra was asleep. Lara closed her eyes and stopped listening to Christian.

12

Rodney had seen her picture in Harpers and phoned to ask her to lunch. They were casting 'The Silver Forest', he thought she would be absolutely ideal for one of the parts.

They met in La Plume d'Or in Greek Street.
A discreet restaurant where Rodney had his own table and called the head waiter Charles, and the wine waiter Thierry.
He ordered champagne and said the veal was always excellent.
Lara said she was a vegetarian, and chose Spinach Florentine.
Rodney wore a red silk cravat, a fine tweed hacking jacket and a gold signet ring.

He was very smooth — very plausible — very well mannered.
He didn't seem to mind that she had no acting experience.
'Learn as you go,' he said affably and raised his glass to her. 'I shall

take great pleasure in guiding you — showing you the ropes, as they say…'

They went to Scotland first and stood about in damp woods, getting wet pine needles down her back, and then, unaccountably, to Greece, to wander scantily clad on the white sand.

She did not have many lines to learn. She was mostly required to lean against things, lounge beside things and waft about in the dusk in flimsy dresses with flowing hair.

'You're an enigma, darling,' said Rodney. 'A mystery — driving Craig wild…' He let his arm lie heavy on her shoulders, squeezing gently, his hand straying downwards as he bent to kiss her cheek. 'Like you're driving me, darling.'

Craig hummed 'You're Driving Me Crazy', and put his yachting cap on back to front.

He was very good looking in an unrealistic sort of way — clean cut, bronzed, blue-eyed. The ultimate advertisement for anything.

They got on well. He had a great sense of fun and giggled a lot. Lara had never met a man who giggled before — shaking with mirth at the most enigmatic moments, dissolving into helpless laughter when Robyn, Lara's screen rival, missed her footing as she imperiously descended the steps to the pool in a figure-hugging white swimsuit and disappeared into a bed of rhododendrons, emerging scratched and swearing, her hair full of twigs.

Lara rejected Rodney's advances for a while. She didn't really fancy him but he was very persistent, besieging her with flowers, little notes and breathless, beseeching phone calls.
His room was on the floor below.

He was OK and treated her very well. After all he had given her this part, and might find her others. He introduced her to a lot of people including Mercedes. They became good friends. She was always invited to Mercedes' parties and spent Easter with her in Italy at her villa in the Tuscan hills — which was amazing — and a week in Paris choosing clothes — which was also amazing.

By then she had her own flat in Hampstead, and could always tell Rodney she was busy or tired if she didn't want to see him. He was unremittingly eager and possessive.

'I am weak with longing for you,' he would say, and she would visualise him in his business-like flat, with the brass-studded leather chairs, and the leather-topped desk with the silver inkstand and golf trophies.

Rodney in his silk pyjamas, begging her to come to him.
'For God's sake, have pity on me, you darling girl...'

Lara didn't like being called a 'darling girl', but she tried not to take any notice. She didn't like Rodney pleading either, or panting and groaning. Unmoved, she felt awkward and embarrassed.

The film had been a great success. Craig had escorted her to the premiere which had not pleased Rodney.
'Good publicity, old man!' said Craig.
Their picture was on the front of all the tabloids.
'Has Craig Scott found True Romance at last?'
'The new woman in Craig Scott's life...'
'Craig Scott with the beautiful newcomer Lara Burns. "We're just good friends," said Craig, holding the lovely Lara's hand...'
Rodney was furious, but had to pretend he was pleased, after all it was, as Craig said, wonderful publicity.

13

Christian said 'Stop the car! This is it! Do you believe it? Just look at that! Wake up, honey — we've found it!'

They stopped in front of an open white gate and sweeping drive. On a slight mound, the house, square and pillared, overlooked sloping fields, and a sufficient number of large oak trees — not too many — just enough. Behind the house there were stables — there was even a horse in the paddock.

It was perfect.

Christian and Bernard got out of the car and leant on the fence.

Cassandra put on her sheepskin jacket and got the video camera out of the boot.

Lara opened the door. 'Great!' she said. 'Great!'

The macaroni cheese had given her indigestion. She hoped she had some Milk of Magnesia tablets in her bag. She got out gingerly — the lane was awash with mud. Christian hugged her.
'Gee, honey, isn't it great! Would you believe it, it's just great! No hitches Cass — offer them whatever you like — give them whatever they want.'

14

'How's your Auntie then, dear?'

Mrs Harvey leant on the fence — she wore a grubby white anorak over a pink acrylic jumper. She did not wear a bra, the front of her jumper lumpy and uneven. She must have been waiting for Lara to put out the rubbish. It was Thursday. The dustmen came on Thursdays.
Lara looked suitably serious.
'Not good at all I'm afraid,' she said. 'She had to have pints of blood...'
'Dear, dear!' said Mrs Harvey, perking up in anticipation, sensing terminal illness — the tubes and paraphernalia associated with ebbing life.

She reminded Lara of the crows she and Myra had seen when they were walking in the park — cawing gleefully — black wings outspread over the limp furry body of a dead rabbit. Myra had chased them with a stick. She had wanted to bury the rabbit, but Lara had told her not to touch it — she might catch something. They had covered it with leaves.

'Well, dear,' said Mrs Harvey, 'you just let me know if I can do anything to help. After all, what are neighbours for? It's a good thing you're such a sensible girl...'

Of course she didn't really think that. Stuck up little madam — too good-looking for her own good. She didn't like the look of that friend of hers either — she had dyed hair! Dyed hair at that age!

'Thanks Mrs Harvey,' said Lara sweetly. Nosy old bag!

15

It was easy leaving home. She waited until Mrs Harvey had gone shopping — trundling her tartan shopping trolley — feet spread in her two-tone slip-ons with manmade uppers and a camel-coloured jacket with an oily stain on the back.

She went into the little cupboard in the corner of the hall, switched off the gas and the electricity, picked up her bag and left.

She had written to her father c/o Grace in Birmingham, telling him what she was going to do.
'Don't worry, I'll be fine.'
She tipped her drawers out on the bed. Small mounds of fluff and hair slides, cough sweets adhering to hairbands and bits of cheap jewellery, half-used nail varnish, a torn packet of cotton wool, tights, assorted socks, underwear, jumpers, blouses, pyjamas.

'What about your ornaments?' said Myra.

There were a few things on the bookshelf over the bed — mostly stuff her father had brought her. A wooden windmill, a fir tree candle, a jar of Turkish Delight drained of all colour, a hideous glass elephant Grace had given her for Christmas, a picture of a fish with large teeth. There were a few books — an illustrated copy of Hans Anderson's fairy stories, *A Passenger to Frankfurt* by Agatha Christie, *Kings and Queens of England, First Year French, Jamaica Inn.*

'Have what you like,' said Lara. 'I shall just take one bag. I don't want lots of stuff.'
'What about your anorak?' said Myra. 'And this navy sweat shirt?'
'I don't want them,' said Lara.
'You have to have a coat,' said Myra.
'I'll get a jacket. I hate that anorak. Jackets are smart. I'll get a jacket in London...'

They didn't talk about the abortion.
Lara had fetched Myra from hospital.
They had gone to the Wimpy Bar and ate burgers and chips.
Myra had a chocolate milk shake.

'Thank God that's over,' she said. 'It was bloody awful.'

She came back home with Lara for a couple of days.
Lara phoned her mother to say Myra was staying with her.
'We're studying,' she said.
'OK, dear,' she said. 'Thanks...'
Her current boyfriend was unemployed — spending the day on the sofa watching TV with a six-pack.

Lara threw more clothes on the bed.
'Don't you want these striped pants?' said Myra.
'I don't want anything,' said Lara.

Myra wanted her to go dancing at a local club. They had rock bands every weekend, but Lara had said 'No, thanks...'

She didn't have time for the 'local talent' — an uninteresting, randy bunch, with a few 'single' gropers on the lookout for a quick shag.

'It'd be fun,' said Myra.
'Well, watch yourself,' said Lara. 'Remember Minnie's words of wisdom.'

Myra pulled on a green poloneck. 'Can I have this?' she said. 'Where are you going to live?'
'You can have what you like,' said Lara. 'I'll find somewhere.'

16

The film was to have been called 'A Flight of Doves', but since the debacle with the birds, Christian said it had to be changed.

Cassandra had found them a house to rent in Little Clavering — beamed and 'quaint', furnished with dark furniture and frilly damp chintz. The radiators clanked and rattled, giving off little warmth — dimly lit with low wattage bulbs hanging from brown furry wires — the beds slung low like hammocks.

Apart from Christian, they all had to duck to avoid cracking their heads on the beams.

There was a brass coal skuttle, horse brasses and brass candlesticks above the fireplace, which had an electric log fire with a revolving light which cast red shadows on the back of the chimney.

The house was chilly — smelling of damp soot and Brasso.
The rest of the cast and crew were housed round about, in pubs and rented cottages.

Christian was not happy. He couldn't stand the gasping water pipes and slow-filling lavatory cistern, the icy bedrooms and creaking floor boards.

They sat on wooden 'farmhouse' chairs with round slippy cushions at the dark oak table, which snagged sweaters and tights, trying to think of a new title.

Cassandra suggested 'White Gates'.

'Oh, no!' said Lara. 'Sounds like Enid Blyton...'

'What about "The White Fence"?' said Bernard. He had caught cold chasing about in the rain, and was shivery and feverish.

He stifled a sneeze.

Cassandra had engaged a cook-housekeeper from an Agency in Derby — a stringy woman with jutting hip bones — a good, plain cook.

Cassandra said that would be fine. They would not be requiring anything elaborate.

'Miss Burns is a vegetarian,' she said.

'I don't hold with fads,' said Mrs Tims. 'I'll do extra potatoes...'

Cassandra said that was fine. They would probably eat out most of the time.

It was too late now to go anywhere to eat. There was only the pub. Heaven forbid! Greasy cold sausages and pickle, crisps and nuts for Lara.

Mrs Tims said it was 'very late', she was just going to bed — reluctantly agreeing to 'do a few sandwiches' — cheese — cut in quarters.

Bernard helped himself from the glass plate — he had hardly eaten anything all day. The mustard was too hot, it made him cough. "Under the White Hat",' drawled Greg. 'Isn't there any whisky?'

Cassandra giggled. Lara snorted and choked on a bit of crust.

'For fuck's sake,' said Christian, 'it's going to be called "The Green Leaves of Summer"...'

'That's a song, honey,' said Lara. 'You can't call it a song...'

'You're thinking of "Little Green Apples",' said Bernard. He sneezed.

'For fuck's sake!' said Christian. 'Let's get out of this Goddam place…'
'No tea, thank you Mrs Tims,' said Cassandra, as Mrs Tims appeared in the doorway with a tray. 'Could you bring some ice?'
Mrs Tims sniffed. She sniffed a lot.

'For Chrissake,' Christian shouted at Cassandra, as Mrs Tims withdrew, banging the door behind her. 'This Goddam place isn't big enough for Snow White and the Seven fucking Dwarfs. I didn't ask you to find a Goddam pixie hut. There's nowhere to fucking sit, and we're all Goddam frozen…'
'Calm down, honey,' said Lara.

Christian refused to be pacified.

Bernard was sent to get the car out of the garage — splashing through the puddles in the pitted gravel — struggling with the garage doors, warped with years of rain.

They bundled a few things into overnight bags, and drove away to find a hotel — preferably a five-star hotel in Derby.

17

It had not been difficult to find a room, or a job.

She made for South Kensington.

Once they had come to the National History Museum from school — on a coach.
They traipsed apathetically behind Cooper, miserably laden with raincoat, ring files and bulging hold-all.

'You'd think we were going on a jungle trek,' said Carmen. 'All she needs is a bedroll and a billy can…'

Andrea Hunter's mother, trendy in M&S jeans and check shirt, had come along to 'help'. Like Andrea, however, she was quite hopeless. She did not know what she was supposed to do, and got lost among the fossil cabinets, attaching herself to a group of girls from another school.

It was easy to sneak off.

'I'm not spending all bloody day looking at old bones,' Carmen had said, taking off her blazer and stuffing it into her Top Shop carrier bag with her tin of Coke, Mars bar and exercise book. 'I'm going up to Hyde Park to find some "live" ones...'

She departed with Susan, returning innocently in time to join the line waiting to board the coach.

'Lovely, wasn't it, Mrs Hunter?' said Carmen. 'Ever so interesting...'

She found a room near Gloucester Road.

She had wandered around the side streets looking at the notice boards in newsagents' windows.

Typing undertaken — reasonable rates.
Wanted — reliable lady for ironing etc.
Dining table and six chairs — good condition — £50 or n/o.
Lady's bicycle — needs new tyres.
Home help urgently required — must have references.
Trained chiropodist will visit you in your home.

The street was shady — the houses comfortably dilapidated. The room was at the top — one flight down to the shared bathroom and kitchen.
The hall was full of plants and wooden carvings, and a full length portrait of a lady with carrot-red hair, wearing a long brown coat, holding a bunch of flowers.

Carolyn Masterson wore a long black skirt patterned with purple and yellow smudges — a denim shirt and plastic flip flops.

'No men,' she said, eyeing Lara suspiciously. 'Do you have a boyfriend? Good,' as Lara started to say no. 'No cooking curry — it smells the house out. Always remember to shut the street door, and don't put "things" down the loo...'

The room was uncomfortable. The bed was uncomfortable. The chair was uncomfortable. The table wobbled. The curtains came down every time they were opened or closed.

She had to go out to buy some sheets and towels. There were blankets and pillows — unsavoury with mysterious stains. There were various bits of chipped china and bent cutlery in the kitchen. She only needed a plate and a mug.
She was not intending to do any cooking.

There was a student at the Royal College of Art on the floor below, in the room next to the kitchen. Heavily made up with black and silver, red and green streaks in her hair. She was very quiet — practically speechless — a black wraith slithering in and out — leaving the cooker brown and sticky from boiled-over milk.

Lara found a job in the Burger Palace in Gloucester Road. She worked there with Shirley and Annette.
They wore red nylon overalls with yellow initials on the pockets, and jaunty yellow hats with red initials.

'They stink,' said Shirley. 'Nylon stinks.'

Annette got flustered, especially when they were busy.

'Let them wait,' said Shirley. 'If they knew what went into the burgers they wouldn't be in such a hurry.'

They were both hoping to 'make it' in show business. To get into TV or films — to do a show.

Annette was strictly 'legit,' attending auditions for forthcoming plays and serious TV dramas.

Shirley sang and danced a bit. She was prepared to do anything. 'Versatility is the thing,' she said. 'I'd stand on my head with no clothes on, or pretend to be an orange, so long as they paid me.'

They were both 'resting'.
They were always 'resting'.

Shirley had a bed sit in Latimer Road, behind Portobello Road.
The house was in a state of disrepair.
The broken chain on the toilet cistern had a piece of string attached to it — the fridge door secured with a loop of wire.
The sashes on the windows were broken, the window wedged with wads of paper.

Shirley said it was disgusting, but she couldn't afford anything better.

Annette had a room in Victoria. It wasn't as bad as Shirley's, but it was very small.
She had to do her cooking on a single gas ring on the floor, and there was only hot water first thing in the morning.
They decided to share a flat together, and found one that was reasonably decent near High Street Kensington.

Annette was hoping to get engaged. Her boyfriend was studying to be an engineer. He was at Aberdeen University so he wasn't around much.

It was a lengthy and expensive journey from Aberdeen to London.
Sometimes Annette would go up on the night coach, but she had to find someone to cover for her at the Burger Bar, as they only had one day off.
Sometimes he would come down on the night coach, and sleep all day on the sofa.

They would go for a walk round the streets, and get some fish and chips, and quarrel about nothing in particular, and after he was gone Annette would have a quiet cry and say she wished they could get married straight away — she had seen a lovely dress in a shop in Oxford Street — with long sleeves and lots of buttons.

Shirley's boyfriend Seth had a group. An unsavoury lot in ragged black jeans and black T shirts with controversial and obscene slogans. They wore a lot of silver jewellery — chains and rings — bracelets and earrings. They were not very clean.

When they performed, they wore black shirts open to the waist, revealing various quantities of body hair. Seth was very hairy, his silver chains tending to get caught up, making his chest look like a hairy mat threaded with silver.

He was a vegan, living on special biscuits, dates, neat vodka and sweet black coffee.

He sat about in the poky sitting room, legs and arms spread over the shabby armchairs.

Shirley and Annette had added their few belongings to the drab furnishings. Annette had several vases and china figures of horses and dogs — beige velour cushions and a cane chair. Shirley had a white desk lamp and two scratched tin wastepaper baskets painted with flowers. They both had assorted mugs and odd pieces of china and cutlery. Annette had a non-stick frying pan.

Lara had only her bag of clothes, and the sheets and towels.

Seth's group, The Wailing Wall, had a regular gig every Thursday, in a pub in Vauxhall. The group was pretty terrible. Seth's singing was pretty terrible. Shirley also sang with them. Her singing was pretty terrible too.
The drummer made a great deal of noise.
They all made a great deal of noise.

Lara went with them every Thursday — sitting at a corner table — trying to be inconspicuous — her hair scraped back, in jeans and denim jacket — ready with a cutting 'Get lost!' or 'Piss off!' to the men who tried to pick her up. 'No thanks' and 'I'm with a friend' to the politer ones.

Mark put his hands flat on the table and looked at her.
'Mind if I sit here?' he said.
He was a friend of Seth's — a photographer. He had come to take some pictures of the group in action.

He sat down — straddling the chair, offering her a cigarette.
'I could do a lot for you, doll,' he said.
'Oh, really?' she said, resisting the impulse to push him in the face.
'Yeah, really — you'd be a great model.'
'Leave it out,' said Lara. 'What do you take me for?'
'No, no, doll!' he said. 'I mean the real thing — catwalk stuff, trailing furs, the cover of Vogue, TV adds...'
'Look!' she said. 'Don't take me for a pushover...'
'I'm serious, doll,' he said. 'Come down to my studio and I'll take some pictures. If you don't have any work within six months you don't have to pay me.'
She hesitated. 'Straight up?' she said.
'Straight up,' he said. 'Bring a couple of decent outfits...'

18

'Tell the old Dame to get the Hell out of here,' shouted Christian.
'That's the Duchess, Mr Zimmerman, Sir.' The continuity girl flustered, clutched her clipboard.

The Duchess wandered across the lawn in front of the house — bending to pluck weeds from the newly mown grass. She wore a brown waterproof jacket with a corduroy collar, and an old squashed Trilby.

A white picket fence had been erected against which Greg and Lara embraced — her face obscured by the brim of his white Stetson.

'Goddam it! I don't care if she's the Queen of Sheba,' shouted

Christian. 'Tell her to get the Hell out of here. We've waited long enough for the rain to stop for Chrissake...'
They spent a lot of time cooped up in Christian's specially equipped trailer — which Cassandra disparagingly referred to as 'The Caravan' — waiting for the rain to stop.

Greg and Christian played endless card games, whilst Christian simultaneously chain-smoked, talked on the phone and sent Bernard on fruitless, time-consuming errands.

Lara didn't play cards — she disliked card games. She and Cassandra watched TV, Lara curled up in an easy chair, smoking and drinking black coffee, Cassandra sitting neatly with hands folded and ankles crossed.

They watched game shows and flecked black and white movies, with paste-board towns and plywood jungles, the back projection speeded up, stiff pines and sharp mountains rushing past. Saccharine-sweet soaps, action packed with 'Real Life' drama, tackling head-on Death, Birth, Murder, Rape, Fraud, Deceit, Divorce, Animal Rights, Kleptomania, Anorexia — no subject was too demanding to be broached or solved in the thirty-minute slots.

A real 'Real Life' audience answering questions and commenting on their Personal Problems, hosted by sanctimonious presenters with careful hair and careful smiles, and visiting experts — the men bearded and untidy, or snappily dressed with tight button-down collars, the women sensibly suited, or haphazardly attired in garish blouses, with wild hair and glasses hanging on coloured chains.

'So how did you feel — er — Mrs — er — Jones, when your husband hit you with a crow bar...?'
'I should say Mr — er — Brown, that consuming two bottles of whisky a day, does — er —almost certainly, constitute a drink problem... Yes, it is a shame you burnt down the garden shed...'

The secretary, Annabel, sat in a little field office at one end of the trailer — sending faxes, fielding awkward phone calls, polishing her nails, sucking peppermints, providing coffee and emptying ash trays.

Christian, having sent Bernard to look for something, or somebody, would send Annabel to find him — putting on her red vinyl raincoat and pixie boots she would disappear into the rain under a black umbrella with a spoke missing.

Christian muttered morosely 'Goddam England — Goddam green and pleasant and fucking wet...'
'Spades are trumps, Chris,' said Greg. 'You shouldn't play your ace.'
'Shit...' said Christian.

Now the sun was shining and the Duchess walked across her parkland. She carried a shooting stick and a pair of shears.

'Now there are no Goddam birds, we've got the Goddam Duchess!' Christian threw his arms in the air. 'Bernard!! Where the fucking Hell is Bernard? Go and tell the old Dame to get the Hell out of here. Scram. Make it fast!'

19

Mark picked through the pile of clothes, holding up a washed-out dress with short puffed sleeves and a buttoned front, a flowered mini skirt, some black leggings, and a black polo shirt.

She hadn't bought any clothes since her mother had gone — saving as much as she could from the money her father gave her, for when she left home. She had a very satisfactory amount in her Post Office Savings Account.

'Jesus, doll!' he said. 'Where did you get these crummy clothes? What the Hell are we supposed to do with these?' He looked at her and grinned. 'Of course we could just forget the clothes, and do a centrefold for Playboy!'

Lara liked him. She liked the way he looked straight at her. He had nice strong hands, and pleasantly tanned arms. She liked his denim shirt, and the way he screwed up his face to avoid the smoke from his cigarette.

'I don't have any money to waste on clothes,' she said.

'You soon will have, doll!' he said. 'The Good Life is just around the corner. Believe me, sweetheart! You'll soon have so many clothes you won't know what to wear...'

They went to a building site, and he posed her among nettles and sticky weed, rusty tins and broken bricks, wearing the outgrown faded button-fronted dress.

The pictures were sensational. Lara couldn't believe it was really her — this beautiful, long-limbed girl couldn't possibly be her...

Mark laughed at her astonishment. 'What did I tell you?' he said. 'A stunner. A complete stunner!' and he kissed her.

He sent her to see Eve in her tiny office above Shaftesbury Avenue — Eve ran one of the top agencies, called simply, Eve's.

The building was drab with a wide stone staircase and clanging lift cage.
The walls were obscured with photographs of beautiful people — scowling, smiling, solemn, seductive — in various postures, formally clothed, casually clothed, headshots with lustrous hair and perfect teeth.
Eve had a huge desk, which took up most of the floor space, covered in folders and files and telephones.

She had a shiny cap of black hair combed forward over her ears. She had glasses with upswept, jewelled frames, which she wore on the end of her large, hooked nose. She was incredibly thin. She wore tight black knee-length skirts and fitting jackets of black and white check, or black wool with grosgrain lapels. Sometimes she wore large flashy rings on every finger — her long vermilion nails scratching the desk top as she sorted through her papers. When she got up she looked like a black wading bird whose stick-like legs in their pale sheer stockings might snap at any moment.

Her assistant, Pamela, worked at a smaller desk in the corner, piled with train and plane timetables, worksheets, a typewriter and telephones.
She was a jolly, well-bred, pretty girl. Too short and plump to be a model, she basked in the glamour of the people who came in and out of the office. She was inclined to gush, her conversation punctuated with exclamation marks. Honestly! Wonderful! Terrific! Gosh! Darling! Fabulous! Angel!

The telephones rang incessantly.

Eve took Lara on without hesitation. She glanced through the photographs, took off the jewelled glasses and, leaning back in her chair, looked at her appraisingly.
'Think tall, child,' she said. 'Stand tall. Be proud to be tall, delighted to be tall. Straighten up!'
She paused to answer the phone.
'No, darling, I'm afraid not. Pamela was going to phone you. Anyhow, Chesterfords want to have a look at you for Moses Peanuts. I'll get back to you... Pam, darling, send Iris's details over to Chesterfords will you. I think she's too short...'

She gave Lara an advance to buy some clothes. 'Go to Henrietta's Place — South Molton Street — perhaps Bond Street,' she said. 'Don't mess about in Oxford Street — and no chain stores.'

20

Lara moved in with Mark in his flat above the studio.

He had navy blue sheets and towels, butcher-striped curtains and quilt. The kitchen bristled with stainless steel gadgets — mixer, juice

extractor, coffee grinder, sandwich griller, electric carving knife, microwave. There was a halogen hob, and a self-timing oven on the wall.
The bathroom suite was navy blue with white tiles.

The phone never stopped ringing.

She licked icecreams and bit chocolate with closed eyes, caressed wrappers of biscuits, the stoppers of bottles and the stems of glasses. She stood on windtorn rocks in strapless taffeta, soaked with spray, climbed ladders in slippery satin and elbow-length gloves, wandered through fields in long tartan skirts and long cashmere cardigans, drove cars in thigh-high mini-skirts, and strode the beach in knee-length shorts and flapping sarong skirts.

And then she got her first Paris Couture show.

When she returned exalted by her success, she found Mark had got himself another girl — a sumptuous, drawling redhead.
'Sorry, kiddo,' he said. 'Just one of those things. No hard feelings?'
She declined to shake hands.

'C'est la vie!' said Eve. 'All men are complete bastards, darling... Complete bastards!'

21

They were to shoot the scene where she quarrelled with Greg. She had just found out about his American girlfriend. The lighting people were measuring the floor.
She had to come down the stairs and stop, one hand on the banisters.
Christian said she was loping.
'Don't lope, honey — you're angry, upset, you feel betrayed. Bernard! I told you to get rid of that Goddam picture. Where's the portrait of her father? We need the portrait of her father behind her when she stops. And the dress, for Chrissake. Who chose that fucking dress? She's not being presented at Court...'

'You okayed the dress, honey,' said Lara.
'For the hunt ball — for the hunt ball, for Chrissake!'

22

She had phoned Myra several times — she was not much good at writing letters — but she was never there.

Her mother said, 'Sorry, dear. She's not here. Yes, dear, I'll tell her you called.'
Once a man — belligerent. 'Watch'a want? No she bleeding well isn't...'

She sent postcards when she was on location in Paris, Rome, Copenhagen, on a swimsuit shoot in the Seychelles. There was no response.

'She's probably got a bloke,' said Shirley, sitting cross-legged on Lara's carpet eating crisps. 'Blokes are very monopolising — especially at the beginning.'

Lara was concerned that she had got herself a lousy bloke.
She had not listened to Ma Leigh exhorting them to value themselves.
Myra didn't value herself. That was the trouble.

'Some girls fall for lousy blokes,' said Shirley. 'It's sort of more exciting — unpredictable. What about you and this Christian? He's just incredible...'

Lara was evasive. She didn't wish to discuss her feelings for Christian with anyone. She wasn't sure what they were, and it was unwise — very unwise — to become too committed. She might start thinking his passion for her was real — 'true love' and all that crap. She was under no illusions, the affair would finish with the film. Christian would go back to LA, and that would be that. She was not a fool.

Shirley got up, brushing crumbs off her leggings, and wandered round the room looking at things.

'You've got some really nice stuff,' she said. 'What a fabulous bottle of perfume…'
The bottle of spiralled glass had a sharp, spiky stopper.
Lara had done a promotion for Lalages' new perfume 'Danger' — pronounced as in French. They had presented her with a complimentary bottle.
'Take it if you like,' she said. 'Knock 'em for six in Stockholm.'

Shirley was going with Seth and the group on a tour of Scandinavia.
Bye, bye Burger Bar!
'Are you sure?' she said. 'That's great. Thanks…'

Annette had decided to go up to Aberdeen to be near Colin. It seemed pointless being so far away from each other. It might even be easier to get a break in Scotland.
There was certainly nothing happening in London.
Colin liked to go hill climbing in his spare time, and they could do that together.

Neither had been able to come to the premiere of 'The Silver Forest'. She had sent Myra and Grace and her father tickets, but nobody came. Myra didn't reply, which was worrying. Grace wrote a note in her childish handwriting saying that Lionel would be in Germany, and she didn't fancy coming on her own.

Sometimes Lara wondered what her mother thought when she saw pictures of her daughter on magazine covers, and on TV.
Perhaps she didn't recognise her.
She had heard nothing from her, apart from a Christmas card in the shape of Santa Claus carrying a sack — a cheap, ugly card — the first Christmas after she left.
There had been no communication whatsoever, no address, nothing.

It was lucky she didn't mind. Some people would have minded, but she didn't. She had never felt close to her mother. She thought her an ignorant fool. She deserved Norman.

23

Christian put his arms around her — he hugged her a lot — rushing up to her and hugging her — whenever and wherever they met, even in Heinz Erikson's office overlooking Park Lane.

He shook her limply by the hand — he had very pale blue eyes and a creased linen suit.
'So this is the lovely Lara. You sure are a lucky guy, Chris!'
And Lara had smiled and thought he was a little shit, and they went for a drink in the Dorchester, with Christian holding her hand.

Heinz Erikson was a financier. He had put money up for the film.
'Well,' he said. 'You've certainly got yourself a beautiful leading lady, Chris...' and he managed to brush her bare arm with his hand. 'With Greg and Gabrielle as well, it should certainly be a hit...'

She had to refuse to sell the estate to Greg, and quarrel with him about Gabrielle, so that he went off in a huff — only to pine for her so much he had to come back, to find her living in impoverished circumstances having lost everything paying off her dead father's debts. They fall into each other's arms — etc., etc....

'Great story,' said Heinz. 'Nothing like a romance where they all live happily ever after.' He had moved his chair closer so that his leg could touch hers.

She was hemmed in. Christian was too busy talking to notice, otherwise he probably would have given Heinz a black eye.
She excused herself, and went to the ladies' room, moving into the chair the other side of Christian when she returned — avoiding Heinz's gaze.

He did phone her, but she wasn't there. He left a message on the answering machine. 'Perhaps we could have lunch?' and later 'I feel we should talk about the film...'

24

Christian wanted to shoot the last scene again — on a lake — with swans. They would float away across the water in each other's arms — the swans sailing serenely behind them.

They were sitting in the lounge of the Hillview Hotel outside Derby. They had ended up here after escaping the chill gloom of the house in Little Clavering. Cassandra had been left to argue with the estate agents, and to pay off Mrs Tims. The lounge was furnished in green leather — the carpet maroon and cream — the tables stained dark 'rustic' brown.

Christian said Cassandra must find a suitable lake — with weeping willows and reeds for the swans to swim among.
'It must have a vista,' he said. 'A drifting skyline — with trees…'

Cassandra said swans could be frightfully nasty, and it would be practically impossible — well, actually — absolutely impossible, to ensure they would behave as planned.

Greg wanted to know if Christian had ever made love in a rowing boat.

Bernard said it would complicate the shooting — mess up the schedule — add to the budget. 'Mega expense,' he said, wincing slightly at the unaccustomed phrase.

Christian said if he wanted a fucking lake, he would have a fucking lake, and if he wanted fucking swans, he would have fucking swans.

Lara said 'Calm down, honey,' which she seemed to be saying more and more lately. 'But I think Greg is right. Making love in a boat is a potential disaster area — the oars may float away — we may fall in — it will be horrendously uncomfortable!'

'I am not arranging the film around your comfort, honey,' said

Christian. 'If I want you to make love under water, you would have to make love under water — or on a bed of broken glass — or anywhere I fucking well want you to.'

Lara's father had attempted to make a fish pond on one of his rare holidays.
He dug a large ragged hole in the middle of the small, scruffy back garden — piling the earth in an unsightly heap by Mrs Harvey's fence. She was not pleased, either with the earth, or the prospect of a pond.

'Smelly things — ponds,' she said, leaning on the fence which swayed alarmingly — the central posts were rotten. 'Unhygienic. Stagnant water breeds mosquitoes — my Ron's mother had a pond. Swarming with mosquitoes. We came back from visits bitten all over. Ron's legs used to swell up. The fish died. She was always buying new fish — they all died.'

Mr Harvey had tried to put in his own double glazing — the windows had fallen out one by one, shattering on his homemade patio which sloped towards the house. When it rained the water ran in little streams under the ill-fitting patio door.

Lara got covered in mud helping her father with the digging. Her mother said 'For God's sake, Lionel! The child's socks are ruined — and what are you going to do with all that earth?'
Her father said he would make a lovely rock garden — he'd go to the DIY store and get some rocks...
'They don't sell rocks in the DIY,' said her mother.

He lined the pond with plastic sheeting and they filled it with water with a garden hose he had borrowed from Sandy the builder, who lived opposite.

It leaked. Returning to admire it later, all the water had disappeared.

Sandy came, and stood shaking his head. 'You need a proper foundation — a proper lining — concrete...'

It was no use. They had to fill it in.

'Pity Ron's not here,' said Mrs Harvey. 'He could have given you some advice.'
Her father bought her two goldfish in a round glass bowl to make up for the failure of the pond. She called them Gog and Magog. They died.

'OK — OK, honey,' she said. 'Greg and I are happy to make love anywhere you say — aren't we Greg?'

'Sure,' said Greg. 'With or without my hat on...'

Christian said the coffee was shit, and would they shut up about Greg's hat for Chrissake.

25

Greg came towards her to take her in his arms. She put her hands on his chest, and pushed him away.

'Hey!' he said. 'What's with you, honey?'
'You don't really care about me,' she said. 'You just want to sweet talk me into selling you the estate.'

Chris said 'Cut — we want to come in close up here. Honey, look down when you start speaking, and then look him straight in the eye as you say 'You just want to sweet talk me — blah, blah — and then into the clinch. Melt, honey — melt.'

The conservatory stretched the length of the ball room — swathed and twined with greenery — fountains spouting water from shells and stone fishes — doors opening from the ballroom where the extras waltzed and fox-trotted in their glamorous hired clothes.

Christian had wanted a ballroom with a domed glass roof — not a hall with a high ceiling. A domed glass roof — conservatory doors and rooms for trees — those trees with a lot of small green leaves. 'Eucalyptus?' said Cassandra — making notes. 'Pampas grass — magnolia —'

'Lemons,' said Christian. 'Let's have some lemons...'

Mercedes said Teddy and Lavinia had a ballroom with a glass dome — well it had been a ballroom — some of the glass was broken and there was ivy growing on the dome. It was laden with dusty spiders' webs. There were probably birds' nests — there were bird droppings on the floor, but it would be super if it were cleaned up.

It had been transformed.

Teddy and Lavinia were thrilled.

'I say!' said Teddy. 'Christian, old man, it's absolutely marvellous...'

'Super, Christian darling,' said Lavinia. 'Now we'll be able to have absolutely super parties again...'

Mercedes clashed with Annie Kovacs, who was in charge of wardrobe.

Annie Kovacs was famous — responsible for dressing many major films — nominated for an Oscar for her costumes for 'The Higher They Climb'.

She wore dungarees and smoked black cheroots.

This was her first time in England. She hated it.

'For Chrissake, Christian,' she said. 'What do you want to film in this crumby place for? Everybody's real weird — it never stops raining — everything is damp — they've never heard of ice — Jesus!'

Mercedes said she knew nothing about Hunt Balls. The only men who *might* wear white gloves were footmen or waiters, and there would only be a few kilts. This was a Hunt Ball in Derbyshire, not a gathering of the Clans in the Highlands — and Lara couldn't possibly wear that ridiculous dress — a waisted crinoline with a bow at the back!

'This isn't a cotton plantation!' she said. 'The woman is a complete fool...'

Annie Kovacs spat out an olive, and told her to piss off.

Bernard was called to mediate.

An uneasy compromise was reached. Mercedes would *advise* on the clothes and matters of etiquette for the Hunt Ball, and then she was to 'piss off'.

Mercedes helped Lara with her dancing.

Lara's knowledge of ballroom dancing was scrappy. She just moved around in time to the music.

Mercedes clapped her hand firmly on her waist and whirled her expertly round, showing her basic steps.
'One has to be able to waltz,' she said. 'And do a decent quick-step. The great thing is to be rhythmical. Nobody will see much of your feet under your long skirt — just be rhythmical...'

26

It was three o'clock in the morning when Christian phoned. Lara struggled from sleep — groping for the receiver.
'Where the Hell have you been?' His voice exploded in her ear. 'What the Hell are you doing?'
'I was asleep, honey,' she said. 'It's three o'clock in the morning. I'm in Paris. In Paris it's three o'clock in the morning.'
'I phoned two hours ago — then it was one o'clock in the morning — so where the Hell were you?'
'I was at a reception. Jean Paul gave a reception...'

He had let them have dresses from the collection — his three favourite models.

Tomorrow they would be gliding the catwalk in Xavier Rigaud's clothes.

Lara always tried to be in Paris for the spring and autumn collections — to work for Jean Paul and Xavier. They had given her her first chance — gauche and inexperienced, they had redesigned her into a star.

She enjoyed the hysterical confusion — the temperaments and tears — the bitchiness — the near disasters. The thrill of being part of the hype — the excitement, the adulation. The expensive and famous clapping and cheering — standing on their little gilt chairs for a better view...

Christian had wanted her to go to the States with him, whilst they filmed the American section of the movie — Greg and the fiery Gabrielle, battling it out on Greg's Ranch — but Lara had to go to Paris.

'I have a contract,' she said. 'You know I have a contract. Besides, I'd just be in the way...'
'You'd be there,' said Christian. 'I like you to be there...'

Christian hated travelling, even though Bernard dealt with everything. He had only to get on the plane.
'What's the fucking hold-up?' Every time they hit a red light — his body stiff, clutching her hand in a fierce grasp.
'Relax, honey,' she said. 'You've got stacks of time.'

He embraced her as if this was their final farewell — groaning with misery.
'Why aren't you coming with me?' he said. 'You could still change your mind...'
'Everything will be fine, honey,' she said. 'As soon as I've finished in Paris I'll come and join you.'
'I want you to come now,' he said.
'I think we should go, Chris,' said Bernard. 'They're calling our flight.'

27

'How're things going, honey?' she said. For God's sake she had to get some sleep.

It was rumoured that Xavier's collection was to have a circus theme. Baggy trousers and silk ruffs — jewelled catsuits — top hats and plumed head-dresses — outsized tailcoats and diamante bow ties. The showroom hung with gilded trapezes — the cat walk sprinkled with sawdust.

Tansy said she hoped Xavier would not expect them to swing about on trapezes — or jump through hoops. She wasn't swinging from any bloody trapezes, or jumping through any bloody hoops.

'He said he had thought of having an elephant, but they're too heavy! He's crazy! He's got these God-awful boots that go over the knee — it's like that game you play as kids — drawing a head, and folding it over, and somebody else drawing the body. Clowns' heads, ringmasters' bodies with highwaymen's boots. Shit! He's barmy!'

Alicia said 'Forget it, honey. We just say "No hoops, Xavier darling" — that's what we say "No fucking hoops, No bareback riding. No feeding buns to elephants…"'

*   *   *

'That bitch Gabriella — she's driving everybody mad.'

Christian's voice demanded her attention. 'Are you listening?' There was a pause. 'Are you alone? Are you fucking well alone?'

'Of course I'm alone, honey,' she said. As if she would say if she wasn't.

Gabrielle was always late on set — she didn't know her lines — she fussed about getting dust in her hair — the heat melting her makeup — the food upsetting her stomach — wanted all the close-ups re-shot, *and* was followed about by a poncy poof called Gerald. *Gerald!* 'Shit honey, what a name — with a fan and a perfume spray! Air freshener for fuck's sake. Air freshener on a ranch! Who needs air freshener on a ranch...?'

'How's Greg?' asked Lara.

The room was full of flowers. They covered all available surfaces. There were vases standing on the thick eau-de-nil carpet — masses of lilac and lilies — roses — gladioli — bowls of sweet peas — large daisies — small daisies — carnations and carnations and carnations — pink and white, red and yellow — flowers she didn't know the name of.

She got out of bed, trailing the telephone wire, and bent to peer at one of the cards attached to a tall vase of delphiniums in every shade of blue — 'You are the most beautiful girl in the world, and I adore you. A bientot! Stefan.' — Who the Hell was Stefan?

'Look, honey,' said Christian, 'I'm dying here without you. Get on a plane...'

There had been messages on the answering machine. Eve, exasperated — phones ringing in the background — Pamela's soothing liquid voice — a police siren. 'Darling! I've had Rodney moaning on! Very peeved you have not been in touch. Very peeved you are in Paris. Cy Tyburn is in London until next Thursday. He wants to meet you a propos of your having a lead role in his new film 'Dream On Baby, Dream On!'. Rodney is setting it up. Should start shooting in the autumn. I said he would have to speak to you, so you'll probably have him whinging on at you shortly. Sorry, luv. Get back to me when you can. Ciao!'

Tabitha breathy and nervous. 'Er — hello Miss Burns — it's Tabitha. I — er — Mr Zimmerman wanted — er said he would like you to continue your riding lessons during the break in shooting. Perhaps you could let me know when it might be convenient. Sorry to bother you — only — er — Mr Zimmerman was very insistent.'

She could see Christian pacing the sun-drenched room — the trees casting long shadows on the terrace overlooking the beach — the sea shimmering crystal — trying to hold on to her — to order her life. Of course he was not in Malibu, he was in Texas. At least Gabrielle could ride a horse — very well in fact — so that was something…

'I'll call you, honey,' she said. 'When I'm finished here I'll call you…'

And Rodney! 'Lara, darling! I had no idea you were in Paris. Cy Tyburn's in London to discuss his new film. There's a wonderful part for you — just perfect — perhaps you could find time in your incredibly busy schedule to call me back…'

'For fuck's sake, honey — I need you here…'
'OK, honey,' she said. 'OK. I'll call you as soon as I've finished…'
'I want you here now, for Christ's sake…'
'I have to get some sleep, honey,' said Lara. She curled her toes in the luxurious carpet and got back into bed. 'I have to be at Xavier's at 8.30.'
'You don't have to do these fucking shows…'
'I want to, honey,' she said. 'I enjoy doing them…'

28

Christian said 'Why didn't you tell me for Chrissake? That bastard Rodney…'
He hated Rodney with a fierce, green hatred — trying not to see him making love to Lara. He stood with his back to her, looking out into the dismal garden. It was raining.

'Goddam rain!' he said. 'I thought you were coming back with me to the States.'

Lara said 'I didn't like to tell you on the phone, honey — you were having so many problems...'

She had had a most successful meeting with Rodney and Cy Tyburn. They had flown to Paris to see her.

They had lunched on the Bateau Mouche — asparagus, salmon mousse, meringues, champagne.

She had agreed to take the part in Cy's new film — it sounded really exciting. It was scheduled to start shooting in September. Christian's film, still unnamed, should be finished well before then.

The contracts were being drawn up. Rodney was keen to accompany her back to her hotel.

'Siesta time, darling,' he said, leaning against her in the taxi. She said she had to meet Xavier, which was not really true, he had just asked her to drop in anytime.

She missed Christian. She was going to phone and tell him about the film, but decided it wasn't a very good idea.

Gabriella and Greg had had a fearful row. Gabriella had pulled his hair, and he had pinned her arms behind her back and called her a drunken bitch.

'Poor baby,' she had said when he had called the night before.

She had just got back from a party at the Comtesse Lebrun's house overlooking the Bois de Boulogne. A really swanky party — a really swanky house. Glittering chandeliers dripped diamond light from ornately moulded ceilings — everything gilt and sky blue velvet — marble urns filled with blue flowers — a palm tree decorated with fairy lights. Some of the women wore tiaras.

Parties in Paris were much more formal than in London, but beneath the polite and gracious exterior there was a seediness, a decadence which made her feel uneasy. There were some very young girls and hollow-cheeked pale young men, hard-eyed men with square nails and cold-eyed older women who wore no underwear. There were also the well-coiffed and corseted — frilly shirt fronts, smelling of expensive cologne, bending to kiss her hand — to compliment her on her beauty.

She wished she was in London with Chris at one of Mercedes' parties. They were always fun — lavish — exotic — swinging — sometimes a bit weird, but always fun.
Here the men held her too close when they danced, trying to nuzzle her neck — fingers straying under her armpit — down the back of her dress — rubbing against her in an unpleasantly intimate way. She had been glad to escape — refusing all offers to escort her to her hotel.

She sat on the bed — kicking off her shoes — pleased to hear Chris's voice.

They had had to abandon shooting for the day.
Greg had said 'Goddammit, Chris, I'll break her fucking neck!'
Gabrielle had been given a sedative.

She was going to tell him then that she was going to meet Rodney and Cy in the morning, but it didn't seem the right moment.
'It's so fucking hot,' he said.
'Never mind, honey,' she said. 'You'll be back in London next week — lovely cold, wet London...'
'It would have been a lot easier if you had been there with me,' he said.

29

'You never said anything about me going back to the States with you,' she said.

'Do I have to spell it out, Goddammit?' His voice rose. 'I need you with me. I don't function properly when you're not around. I worry what you're doing — seems I was fucking right to be worried — didn't take long for you to go sneaking off with that bastard Rodney.'

'I didn't go sneaking off with Rodney,' said Lara. 'I have no desire to have anything to do with Rodney, except on a strictly professional basis. I didn't like him even when I was with him…'

'So why did you screw the bastard?' He was almost shouting — the intense face white and dark at the same time.

Lara shrugged. 'Look!' she said. 'I don't have to account to you for everything I've done in my life. What about your ex wife — the strings of beautiful girls? Are you going to tell me why you screwed all of them? You never said anything about me going to the States with you. As far as I am concerned, it's just another "Nice knowing you" situation. I'm not going to give up my career just so that you can have me around for a while, until you go off with someone else.'

'It's not like that,' he said.
'Oh yes it is,' said Lara. 'You'll soon get tired of having me around. You'll want someone new to stimulate and excite you.'

Distance clanged between them.

Christian sat up half the night, drinking tumblers of whisky, flicking the remote control on the TV — incomprehensible fragments of programmes interchanging — and made lengthy phone calls to New York and LA.

Lara removed her few things and returned to her flat. She thought he was being childish.
He should be pleased that she had been offered such a good part.
He had never intimated that he was expecting her to go back to the States with him. She was just an interlude in a long series of interludes.

On the set his temper flared and crackled. Bernard bearing the brunt of his displeasure. Cassandra was still searching for a suitable lake.

The weather improved, and they were able to shoot the rest of the outdoor scenes.

Christian was not happy with Lara's stand-in.

She was the right height and build, but lanky and listless, seemingly unable to grasp the simplest instructions.

Cassandra said it had been difficult finding someone tall enough, who was also a good rider. Sandra was an excellent rider.

Tabitha was supposed to make sure she knew what she had to do. She was not very successful.

'I did tell her to stop,' she said, tearfully, as Christian swore and shouted.

'She's supposed to stop at the clump of trees — then we cut to Lara dismounting, and leading the horse into the shade. And what does this fucking girl do? Gallops off into the fucking distance. We've tried it three times…'

'I have told her to stop at the trees,' said Tabitha, sniffing, wiping her nose with a crumpled tissue.

Christian wanted her hair streaming behind her as she galloped. Tabitha said it wasn't wise — she should wear a hard hat — if she fell she could get serious brain injuries.

Christian said she didn't have much fucking brain to injure.

'Don't be such a bully, honey,' said Lara. 'It's not Tabbie's fault if Sandra keeps getting it wrong. And it's safer if she wears the hat. I can take it off when I get off the horse, shake my hair free…'

Christian pretended not to hear. He turned his back and told Tabitha Sandra had to do it without her hat, and not to ride further than the fucking clump of trees. 'She'll need a wig,' he said. 'Get wardrobe to get on with it — thick and curly like Lara's.'

Sandra had long hair — mousy and thin. 'And get a bloody move on, before it starts raining again.'

30

Mercedes arrived in her newly-acquired Bugatti convertible — the colour of a lightly baked ratafia biscuit — wearing a leather flying suit complete with wide-cuffed gauntlets, helmet and goggles.

She slid down the bank towards them, waving her arms like a prehistoric bird.

They were waiting for Sandra to appear over the brow of the hill, cantering towards the trees, hair streaming behind her.

The tracking camera had got bogged down, tipping sideways in an unseen ditch.

'Hey, darlings!' she cried. 'What an absolutely super day! I've brought a picnic…'

'Jesus!' said Christian. 'This is all we need! Bernard! For Chrissake where's Bernard? Do something with her. Anything. Show her the gardens — take her to the canteen…'

Mercedes came to a stop, enfolding Christian in a creaking embrace, kissing him on both cheeks in French fashion.
She had just come back from Cannes — her face a polished bronze.
'Jonathan is bringing up the rear,' she said. 'He's got the food. I think I lost him at the crossroads. It's most frightfully hot. This get up is frightfully hot. Is there somewhere I can change…?'

'Swell, honey!' said Christian. 'Swell. Great to see you. Why don't you go with Bernard — you can change in the caravan.'
'Oh wonderful, darling!' said Mercedes. 'Hi, Bernard! Hi, Lara!'

Bernard guided her back up the slope in the direction of the caravan — a couple of stick insects with their long skinny arms and legs.

Sandra appeared on the horizon. She was wearing her hard hat, tresses of the blonde wig bunched untidily on her shoulders.

There was an expectant stillness.

Nobody looked at Christian.
Sandra dismounted and slouched against the horse, holding the reins loosely.

Christian spoke very slowly and very quietly.

'I want that fucking girl off this fucking set now. We will re-shoot the scene with Lara riding. It should be alright if she trots up to the trees. I presume she can trot...'

'Oh yes, Mr Zimmerman,' said Tabitha, who was standing rigid, hands clasped, waiting for the explosion. 'Miss Burns has really mastered the trot...'

'Get that fucking girl out of my sight now. Make sure I never fucking well see her again. And then get Lara ready. Don't just stand there for Chrissake! Move!'

Lara was to trot to the trees, dismount, and lead her horse among the leafy branches, coming upon Greg coincidentally riding his horse in the same place. There ensued a love scene on a mossy bank carefully planted with appropriate flowers.

I know a bank whereon the wild thyme blows
Where oxlips and the nodding violet grows —

She had done *A Midsummer Night's Dream* for GCSE.

Cooper, her orange makeup streaked and patchy, facing the class, trying to quell the hubbub sufficiently to explain the significance of Midsummer Night.

'It's just a stupid fairy story...'
'Do we have to do a stupid fairy story?'

'Who believes in fairies?'
'Can't we do something else?'
'It's so boring...'
'Do we have to read it at all?'
'I don't understand any of it. They talk all funny.'
Overriding the sniggers and incomprehension that blanketed the classroom like uncooked dough, she made everyone take turns reading a part.

Carmen objected to reading Bottom — making obscene gestures to compensate. Hetty a reluctant Titania.

St Agnes put on three performances at the Town Hall. All the English GCSE class were invited.

'Oh God!'
'Do we have to?'

Hardly anyone turned up.

Lara didn't go. She couldn't sit through the snooty girls of St Agnes poncing about spouting Shakespeare.
Dressed to kill, she went with Myra to a new wine bar in the High Street, where they sat in a corner, rattling with cheap jewellery, and smoked and drank half a bottle of sour red wine.

Cooper had given the whole class a detention.

'It was useful,' she said. 'Not very good of course, but useful.'

*   *   *

Greg was nowhere to be found.

'Try the caravan,' said Lara. 'He's probably with Mercedes.'
'What do you mean, he's with Mercedes?' said Christian, white round the mouth.
'You know — they're having a "thing",' said Lara.

'No,' said Christian. 'No, I didn't fucking know they were having a "thing".'

He didn't speak to her now, unless he had to — turning away when she approached.
'OK,' she thought, 'if that's the way you want it...'

31

There was no progress on the lake.

'Aren't there any Goddam lakes in this Goddam country?' said Christian.

Lara wanted to take his hand and tell him to calm down, but she couldn't.

Bernard said 'I'm really sorry about you and Christian. I —er — didn't know there was anything wrong.'
'Thanks,' she said. 'It's pretty silly really, Chris doesn't like me working for Cy...'

They sat in the hotel bedroom watching videos of lakes. Lara lay on the wide bed she no longer shared with Christian — smoking.

The room was foggy with smoke and cluttered with sloppy remnants of tea and coffee — messy saucers and torn biscuit packets, a half empty bottle of whisky and overflowing ashtrays.

Cassandra was apologetic. She had seen masses of lakes — she just couldn't find one that was absolutely right.

They spent a miserable wet day inspecting a possible one in Kent. A dubious stretch of thick brown water, with pines growing so close to the edge their lower branches floated rotting in the water. Thin drizzle plucked the surface, the reeds bedraggled and drooping.

'"The grey green greasy Limpopo",' murmured Bernard vaguely, wiping the mud off his handmade brogues with a clean white handkerchief.

Cassandra said it was really quite nice when the sun was shining.
'We are not making a horror movie,' said Christian, 'we are making a love story.'

'It is a bit grim,' said Bernard. 'Too dark, really.'

'Too dark!' said Christian. 'Too fucking dark! It's morbid! Goddam morbid!'

'A good picnic site for the Addams family,' said Lara.

They had picnicked by a lake when she was a kid.
Her father loved picnics.
Her mother hated them. She insisted on getting herself and Lara dressed up as if they were going to a party, and made dreadful sandwiches of tinned salmon, the bones crushed into the bread, cut very small to fit into the Tupperware box she had bought at a Tupperware party, with a salad bowl in which she kept plastic fruit, a collection of dusty apples and bananas.

Her father borrowed Sandy's old van — the back full of newspapers — frayed ropes, odd bits of machinery and fierce-looking tools.
It was dirty and uncomfortable.
Her mother wore a white dress with a full skirt and heart-shaped neckline, and white shoes with stiletto heels. She made Lara wear a pink dress and white socks with her new black school plimsolls.

'Really, Lionel,' said her mother. 'Do we have to go in this clapped out old heap?'

Her father had said they could hardly use his lorry, and it was good of Sandy to lend them his van.

'What's the matter with it?' he said.

By the time they reached the lake it had begun to rain, so they sat in the van and ate the sandwiches.

Afterwards her father had taken her to the edge of the water to see if they could see any fish jumping.

'Don't be so stupid, Lionel,' said her mother. 'Of course there aren't any fish.'

But her father had helped her climb onto some rocks to have a closer look. Lara had so wanted there to be some fish, just to spite her mother, but they didn't see anything except an old broken boot and a rusty bicycle trapped in the weeds.

32

Zack Muller was not pleased at having to change the end of his score. The soaring crescendo that would have accompanied the flight of white birds up into the azure sky was hardly appropriate for a scene of silvery moonlight.
'Perhaps you could have a few owls…' he said.

The telephone lines between London and LA sizzled.

'OK, OK,' he said, tired from arguing with Chris that if he brought it down an octave and put in some minor sixths it would do fine. 'OK — I'll rewrite the Goddam thing!'
'He should be grateful he hasn't got to do "Sailing Away With Swans",' said Lara.

Bernard said he would be glad when it was over.

Christian wanted the terrace cleared. There were several statues and an ornate stone bird bath, all in various stages of decay — likely to fall into a heap of dust if any attempt was made to move them.

Christian said they would replace them — get copies.

'That just isn't possible,' said Bernard. 'You can't replace old things like these — look at the carving on the bird bath.'
'I don't care a fuck about the carving on the bird bath,' said Christian. 'I want it off the terrace...'

Lara clashed with Annie Kovacs over her clothes. Annie had produced an off-the-shoulder white evening dress and a diamond necklace for the encounter with Greg on the terrace, and a blue satin affair with sequins for the final scene.
Lara refused to wear them.

'Nobody would be watching TV and drinking cocoa dressed like that,' she said. 'I'm supposed to be impoverished — huddled in a couple of icy rooms in my draughty mansion. I'd be wearing something sensible like a skirt and jumper...'
'Are you telling me how to do my fucking job?' said Annie.

Her assistant Denzil stood beside her, nervously clutching the sequinned satin to his bony chest.
He wore an overwashed T-shirt, worn jeans and white deck shoes.
He had cropped strawberry blonde hair and false eyelashes, giving him the appearance of a cartoon ostrich poised for flight. He had a dark red velvet pincushion attached to his wrist.

'You just don't understand the English upper class,' said Lara. 'They dress abominably. They are just not interested in clothes. They like wearing ancient skirts and jumpers. They would never wear things like these...'
'So you propose to do the last fucking moment of passion wearing an old skirt and jumper?' said Annie. 'This is a scene of ROMANCE in the Moonlight — romance in capital letters...'
'I wasn't expecting him,' said Lara. 'I wouldn't have had time to rush off and change into my best ballgown.'

Annie told Denzil to take the fucking dresses away, and stormed off to look for Christian.

He was being even more stand-offish than usual, having discovered

that morning that Lara's new leading man was to be Eugune Cassidy, another dizzy-making heart-throb.
He was on the terrace working out camera angles.

Bernard had offered the Duchess substantial compensation for any damage caused to her statues and bird bath when they were removed. She said she didn't like them much anyway, and had always thought the bird bath rather vulgar.
'Ostentatious,' she said. The compensation money would do very nicely for the repair to the conservatory roof.

Christian said they could all wear what they fucking liked.
Cassandra was called in to give her opinion.
She said Lara was absolutely right, and that the dresses were completely unsuitable and really rather ridiculous.

'She could wear a nice woollen dress,' she said.
'Jesus Christ!' said Annie. 'A *nice woollen dress*? I give up. I think I'll pack my fucking bags and get the Hell out of this Godawful place…'
They compromised.

Lara embraced a hatless Greg in a soft creamy blue blouse and long dark skirt. Greg tripped on the uneven crazy paving, and they got the giggles — rocking together in silent mirth as the camera moved in for the final close-up.

They had to shoot the scene five times.

Christian was coldly angry.

As soon as they were finished, he walked away without speaking.

33

She had been to Vanessa Carr's birthday party in the village. Vanessa had a small part as a nosy neighbour. She had the slick shallow smartness of a predatory female.

'Make them pay,' she said to Lara during a break in shooting. 'They want to use your body — you make them pay for it.'
She had been a dancer in a strip club gyrating automatically as she divested herself of her clothing.

'Some silly dame from Women's Rights, or something, asked what I thought about. I said usually what I was going to eat afterwards — I'm always hungry,' and she slurped the last of her milk shake through a straw, leaving a pink foam round her mouth.

The restaurant overlooked the wooded valley.
The lights of Florence sparkled below, as if the sky had been turned upside down.
The terrace was hung with coloured lights, and thick white candles guttered on the rough wooden tables — the moon an orange suspended ball.

Every evening groups of cast and crew congregated here to gossip and drink Valpolicella. This evening there had been wheels of pizza, thick with black olives and anchovies.

* * *

Cassandra had always given her anchovies to Chris. She found them much too salty, and Chris was very fond of anchovies.

Mercedes had given a dinner party for Cy whilst he was in London.

'Christian says he won't come if I invite Rodney Clarke,' she told Lara on the phone, 'and I said "Darling, I have to invite Rodney, it would look dreadfully peculiar if I didn't". He was very ratty. Perhaps you could speak to him…?'
'I don't think he'll listen to me,' said Lara.
'I hope it's not true that you two have split up,' said Mercedes. 'Jennifer Tredmont said you'd broken up, and I said nonsense, and not to spread malicious rumours.'

How the Hell did that bitch Jennifer know about her and Chris?

She hadn't seen her for months. How would anybody know? Just their behaviour on set, with Chris refusing to talk to her or come anywhere near her.

It was a small dinner party.

Mercedes and Cy, herself and Chris, Cassandra and Bernard, Lavinia and Tim, Rodney and Pia — a top-heavy blonde in revealing red velvet — Marcus Villiers of the hooded eyes and turkey neck bent drooling over her generously exposed flesh.

'So you want to be a Film Star, my dear,' he said. 'We shall have to see what we can do, won't we?'

His wife Jasmine, her face obscured by the customary veil of upper class hair was talking to Cy about filming in Italy.

'Very excitable people — they have inordinately long lunch breaks and are very argumentative...'
Jasmine had been married several times. She was rich. They were both rich. Mercedes had invited them hoping they might be encouraged to invest in the film world.

'Betrayal,' said Christian, staring straight at Lara. 'My next film will be about betrayal...'
'Great!' said Tim. 'I love war films — spies and plots and all that sort of stuff... Great!'
'Fab!' said Lavinia.
'It's not going to be a war film,' said Christian. 'It will be about personal betrayal...' His eyes didn't leave her face — his food untouched.
'Idiot,' thought Lara. 'Stupid bloody idiot...'

She pretended not to notice, taking a mouthful of the decorative vegetable dish that had been especially prepared for her. He had never indicated that he was expecting her to go back to America with him — that he wanted her to go back to America with him — was she supposed to be telepathic or something? She felt like telling him to shut up and stop being a complete fool.

'That should be interesting,' she said.

Rodney said, 'Not quite up your street old man — intrigue?'

Christian ignored him, continuing to look at Lara. He drained his glass of wine and turned to Mercedes.

'I'd like to borrow the Bentley for the weekend,' he said. 'Bernard is going to show me some sights before I leave. I want to go to Cambridge and York — might get as far as Scotland.'

'Sod him!' thought Lara. 'Sodding bastard!'
She couldn't eat the rest of her food.

He hadn't rung her to say goodbye.

Two days later she had left for Italy.

34

Vanessa's favourite waiter Guiseppe brought in the birthday cake — holding it shoulder high, fizzing with sparklers — 'Beuno Compleanno Vanessa' scrawled in runny chocolate on the sprinkled icing sugar.

Everybody sang Happy Birthday and Vanessa gave Guiseppe an extravagantly lengthy kiss. Everybody cheered. One of the lighting engineers got up on the table and sang 'Arrivederci Roma' in a strangled tenor.

The party became increasingly rowdy.

Lara had a nasty feeling that Rodney was about to come over and pester her. She had sat as far away from him as possible, but he kept leering at her.

He kept pestering her despite her having made it very clear that she didn't want anything to do with him.

Cy and Eugene had gone to Florence to meet some American friends. Cy's wife, Lou, had taken the twins to Sienna.
'We'll do Assissi and Spoleto as well,' she said. 'It seems a shame not to make the best of it whilst we're here…'
She spoke fluent Italian — the girls weren't bad at it either.
'You can't get the best from a country unless you speak the language,' she said.

Lou had known Chris's ex wife Bernice.
'They were always fighting,' she told Lara.

She had ordered coffee on the little terrace. It was overgrown with creepers. Lara didn't know what they were. Her knowledge of things horticultural was strictly limited. She had never managed to grow anything except marigolds, and they had not been a great success. These creepers with tiny flowers and spiky grey-green leaves smelt delicious.

Beneath them the twins played an energetic and noisy game of tennis. Soon they would have an Italian lesson, and then take their bikes and ride with Lou up into the hills for a picnic lunch.

Lou was knitting a mauve garment covered with bobbles. She kept pausing to wind the wool round the needle.

'I remember at one party she threw her drink — and the glass of course, at Chris, and he pushed her backwards into the pool — which gave her an excuse to take her clothes off — not that she ever needed an excuse. She just didn't understand the word faithful. She was always coming out of someone else's bedroom. Poor Chris! He got so worked up…'

Lara saw Rodney get up. He was coming over.

'So you've split up with that little shit Zimmerman,' he had said.

'I knew it wouldn't last — these little chaps are all embryonic Napoleons...'

He was tall. A tall thin Englishman with shoulders too narrow for his height.

'Creep,' thought Lara. 'Bloody creep...'

She must get out of here before he could get round the crowded table. Vanessa had waylaid him, leaning against him, laughing, holding the lapels of his jacket.

She left as quickly and unobtrusively as possible, and walked back up the hill to the hotel, cushioned by the sweet summer air.

She was on the balcony of her bedroom when the phone rang.

It was Christian. Pleasure and surprise took her breath away. She had steadfastly shut him out of her thoughts.

'Sorry, luv,' Eve had said, passing a formal message from Chris's office. 'That's the way the cookie crumbles.'

It was wonderful to hear his voice.

'I tried earlier,' he said.
'I was at a birthday party,' she said.
'Have fun?' he said. She could see him pretending he didn't care.
'It was OK,' she said. 'Everybody was getting rather drunk, so I left...'

There was a pause. Unasked questions crackled and spat.

'How're things?' he said.
'Fine,' she said. 'Just fine. How are things with you?'
'Fine,' he said. 'The film's looking really good...'

There was another pause. Tenuously joined by a rippling jerking telephone cable coiled deep under the ocean they could hear one another breathe.

'I want you to come to the Premiere with me,' he said.
'Oh,' she said. 'Well, I don't know. I don't know what the schedule here will be...'
'You can fly in and fly out — do it in a day. It's important. Cy would think it was important for you to be there...'

Desperately she didn't want him to hang up. She had so missed the phone calls whenever they had been apart. The nightly run down of the day's events — how he was feeling — what he was doing — what everybody else was doing...

'It's going to be a hit,' he said.
'How do you know?' she said.
'Because I do,' he said.
She wanted to tell him how much she had missed him. Filming with Cy was great. He was courteous and helpful, smoothing frayed tempers — always calm and unruffled. But she missed Chris — impatient, volatile, moody. Nobody remained uninvolved with Chris. The smallest detail was important — disputed — re-shot. He expected and received total commitment.

She really thought he had cared about her. He had made her feel he cared about her.

That was all over now. He probably had another girl. There were enough beautiful girls to choose from.

It was just great to hear his voice.

'How's the film coming?' he said.
'Oh fine!' she said. 'Just fine...'
'I'll be staying at the Dorchester,' he said. 'I'll speak to Eve...'

35

When she arrived at his suite there was no one else there.
She was wearing black — high at the front, low at the back, a dramatic creation designed by Xavier especially for the occasion. She had a black cloak fastened with a huge crystal brooch.

Cy had thought it most important that she should be at the Premiere.

He said they'd take a break from filming for a couple of days — they were well up to schedule. He wanted to go with Lou and the girls to Naples and Capri. Everybody could do with a rest...

Chris came out of the bathroom fiddling with his tie. It was wonderful to see him — she just stopped herself from going over to straighten his tie, as she had always used to.

'You look great,' he said. 'A real star. It's great to see you...'
He offered her a drink which she refused.
There would be too much drink at the party afterwards.

'Where's everybody?' she said.
'I wanted to see you alone,' he said.

They didn't look at each other.

'How's the film going?'
'Oh fine,' she said. 'It's quite fun. Eugene fools about a lot...'
'And Rodney?'
'Rodney's just Rodney. Look, Chris — don't start that again. Rodney is the producer. He is a good producer, and that's all...'
'Nothing between you then?'
'I'm not going to answer that Chris, it's none of your business.'
'And Cy?'
'Cy's a happily married man, with a wife who knits and recites Italian poetry, and twin daughters who want to be airline pilots.'

36

Chris took her arm to steer her through the crowds waiting outside the cinema.

Greg and Mercedes arrived just behind them — Greg superbly handsome in his dinner jacket, and Mercedes glittering from head to foot like the Snow Queen in the Hans Anderson fairy story.

Greg kissed her for the cameras.

Christian kissed her for the cameras.

'Can we have that again, Miss Burns? Mr Zimmerman? Greg? Just once more —'

The lights flashed and whizzed.

Chris kissed her again. 'Your hair smells wonderful,' he said. She stood between Greg and Chris.

'Over here, Miss Burns — Lara — lovely smile — that's great — once more over here.'

They both kissed her for the cameras.

37

She left the party at about 1.30.
She was tired.

It was loud and bright — splattered with shrieks of 'darling' and 'divine, sweetie' — the sincere and malicious pressing round to congratulate her.

She was disturbed by Christian's presence.

He held her to his side. The crush made it impossible for her to distance herself.

The band was playing 'Moon' tunes — 'Moonlight Serenade', 'Moonlight Becomes You', 'Blue Moon', 'Moonglow'. That was what the band had been playing the night they had met. They had danced together for the first time. There was no room to dance here, although Christian was holding her close enough.

'I have an early flight,' she said.
'I'll come with you, honey,' he said.
'That will not be necessary,' she said.

But he followed her into the lobby, and asked the doorman to tell his chauffeur to bring the car round.

'Where are you staying?' he said. 'Why don't you come back with me to the Dorchester?'
'I'm staying at my flat,' she said.
'I'll go with you,' he said. 'I'll drop you off.'

It was no use arguing.

In the car he tried to take her hand, but she avoided it.

'I've got used to being without you,' she said.
'Well I haven't got used to being without you,' he said. 'Let me come up...'
'No,' said Lara. 'I have an early flight. I'm tired. I want to go to bed...'

She left him standing by the car. She didn't look back.

As she took off her cloak and dropped it on the bed, the phone rang.

It was Chris.

'Now what, for God's sake?' she said.
'I have to speak to you,' he said.

'Where on earth are you,' she said wearily.

'I'm outside in a phone booth,' he said. 'I have to ask you something important. I want you to marry me.'

'Stop playing games, Chris,' she said. 'I'm tired.'

'I'm not playing games. I want you to marry me. I'm sick of missing you all the time. I just want you around. Please honey, say you'll marry me...'

'OK,' she said. 'OK. Now go away and let me get some sleep...'

Lightning Source UK Ltd.
Milton Keynes UK
UKHW041036050120
356372UK00001B/22/P